# All Change

ALSO BY PIPPA NIXON

*All Mine*

# All Change

# Pippa Nixon

First published in Great Britain in 2026 by Quercus
Part of John Murray Group

1

Copyright © 2026 Pippa Nixon

The moral right of Pippa Nixon to be
identified as the author of this work has been
asserted in accordance with the Copyright,
Designs and Patents Act, 1988.

All rights reserved. No part of this publication
may be reproduced or transmitted in any form
or by any means, electronic or mechanical,
including photocopy, recording, or any
information storage and retrieval system,
without permission in writing from the publisher.

This book is a work of fiction. Names, characters,
businesses, organizations, places and events are
either the product of the author's imagination
or used fictitiously. Any resemblance to
actual persons, living or dead, events or
locales is entirely coincidental.

A CIP catalogue record for this book is available
from the British Library

PB ISBN 978 1 52944 609 8
EBOOK ISBN 978 1 52944 610 4

Typeset in Swift by CC Book Production

Printed and bound in Great Britain by Clays Ltd, Elcograf S.p.A.

Papers used by Quercus are from well-managed forests and other responsible sources.

Quercus
Carmelite House
50 Victoria Embankment
London EC4Y 0DZ

John Murray Group
Part of Hodder & Stoughton Limited
An Hachette UK company

The authorised representative in the EEA is Hachette Ireland,
8 Castlecourt Centre, Dublin 15, D15 XTP3, Ireland (email: info@hbgi.ie)

For the next generation of amazing women in my life –
Erin, Emily, Lily and Sophia

# Chapter One

## Gabi

Gabi's right leg was heavy as hell in its ugly protective boot and the tops of her crutches dug uncomfortably into the soft hollow of her underarms. But at least she was on her own two feet. That in itself was a win after two months, flat on her back, in hospital. She eyed the two suitcases being unloaded from the back of the taxi and only then began to think maybe she should have phoned first. But her cousin was expecting her, and she was only a day ahead of schedule after all. Surely Isabella would love the surprise?

'In there, is it, miss?' The taxi driver nodded towards the doorway of Tutto Mio, Isabella's Italian restaurant. Gabi nodded and he lifted a large, leather, monogrammed case in each hand with a grunt.

'You don't need to . . .' Gabi started to say but then she sighed in defeat and thanked him instead. He did need to, apparently. Or *someone* needed to help her for approximately the next three months and Isabella had insisted that person would be her.

Isabella was the first person Gabi rang after the accident on the film set where she was working as a stuntwoman. It had been a great gig, the highlight of her career to date, a modern-day Western with plenty of action. She'd phoned from the hospital bed with her leg in traction, and described the shot that had gone wrong in detail gruesome enough to make Isabella groan. A horse-riding scene where the horse had spooked and bolted, throwing Gabi from the saddle and dragging her by her foot in the stirrup until everything went black. She woke in hospital the following day after surgery and with her leg suspended in the air by a series of pulleys.

Isabella had instructed her to come home as soon as she was allowed to fly and told her that she could move in with her for as long as was necessary. Gabi had been only too happy to accept. But the recovery was slow, and she'd spent all of February and most of March confined to bed, unable to move and all alone in Australia, counting down the days until she was released. She'd been so keen to get to Isabella and to Honeybridge that when she was discharged a day earlier than planned, she didn't hesitate in booking a last-minute ticket, and here she was.

Gabi hadn't seen Isabella in the five months since she had opened Tutto Mio and fallen head over heels in love with Etienne, the guy who owned the restaurant across the square, and she didn't want to wait any longer. It had already been too long, and she knew Isabella would understand. She swung along behind the driver on her crutches, glad of all the upper-body strength she had through training for her job in the past. Using crutches was certainly not for the weak.

The taxi driver opened the door and heaved the cases across the threshold and onto the restaurant floor. He straightened his back with a moan. She didn't think they'd been that heavy. But they were pretty full. She needed to have every base covered when she went on location for a shoot. Although this one of course had been cut short. Her contract had been 'broken' along with her leg. Naturally she had a very nice pay-off – being a stuntwoman had some perks. The fact that her leg was pinned in two places was not one of them.

She surveyed the room. The restaurant was almost empty, a couple lingering over coffees in a corner, a lone diner reading as he ate. All the other tables were already made up for the evening sitting. It was homely, wooden floors and rugs, hand-painted pictures on the walls, bright ceramic pots filled with herbs on the windowsills. A waitress, tidying the condiments tray, looked up and spotted her.

'Hi,' she said, taking a step towards her. 'I'm afraid the kitchen's closed . . .'

'I'm looking for Isabella actually,' Gabi said. 'I'm her cousin, Gabi.'

'Oh, wow! I heard you were coming!' The waitress smiled. 'I think she's in the kitchen . . .' She moved towards the door and Gabi gestured to stop her.

'Can I go in?' she whispered. 'I wanted to surprise her.'

The waitress shrugged and nodded, and Gabi grinned her thanks. The taxi driver coughed behind her to remind her of his presence. Gabi propped her crutch under her arm, freed her hand and pulled her phone from her pocket to tap and pay.

'Thanks again,' she said, adding a tip as he rubbed his back once more for emphasis. He saluted her and left, past the waitress who was now busy updating the specials board. Gabi felt excitement building as she quietly opened the kitchen door. Isabella was going to be blown away. She couldn't wait to see the look on her cousin's face.

It wasn't quite the greeting Gabi was expecting when she caught Isabella straddling Etienne's thigh as he leaned back against the stainless-steel draining board. Fully clothed they might be, but not for long by the looks of it. Isabella's eyes were shut and her mouth open as Etienne's arms pulled her closer and his lips ravished her neck. Gabi stopped dead. The couple were oblivious, locked in a moment so intense that Gabi felt her own cheeks blush. This was most definitely not the entrance she had planned. She tried to back up, desperate to get out, but forgetting her crutches and boot, she stumbled. She reached out a hand to save herself and knocked a pan from the counter with a clang that echoed around the walls.

Isabella and Etienne sprang apart, dazed and pink-cheeked. Isabella's hair had escaped its messy bun and tendrils hung around her face. Etienne had a smear of lip gloss across his mouth.

'Surprise . . .' Gabi said awkwardly. It took a full second for Isabella to focus properly on her cousin. Then, finally, she sprang into action.

'Gabi!' She flew across the room, arms outstretched. 'I thought you were coming tomorrow?' She wrapped gentle arms around Gabi and smothered her cheeks with kisses. All the things Gabi didn't know she had been hoping for. She closed her eyes for a second and leaned in, surprised to feel tears pricking her eyes. It had been a long, lonely few months, and it was so good to see her cousin.

Etienne stepped in next and kissed her on both cheeks.

'Sorry to interrupt,' Gabi stammered, still embarrassed, but Isabella and Etienne just flashed each other an appreciative look and laughed.

'Come, sit,' Isabella said, leading her back into the restaurant and pulling a chair out at one of the tables.

'Easier said than done,' Gabi said. 'I'll need two chairs; I have to keep my foot elevated as much as possible.' She sat on the nearest and lifted her leg with her hands to rest straight out in front of her, foot propped on the facing chair. Isabella pulled out the one next to her.

'Drinks?' Etienne asked. 'Wine? Or . . .'

'Coffee,' the women said simultaneously, which made them both smile. Etienne changed direction from bar to kitchen and Gabi watched Isabella drop her eyes to his bum as he left.

'Sorry about that,' Gabi whispered.

'No worries.' Isabella laughed. 'It's our fault. I just can't keep my hands off him!'

'Looked like the feeling was mutual,' Gabi said, marvelling at the soft glow of Isabella's face. She'd never seen her like this before. Isabella shook herself and turned her attention back to Gabi.

'What did the studio say?' Isabella asked. 'How's it all been left?'

'They were great. Gave me a reference, paid me some danger

money and brought in a new stuntwoman.' Gabi shrugged. 'The good news is that I will make a full recovery.'

'And the bad?' Isabella leaned forward in concern, her blue eyes wide.

'Is that it's going to take about three months and a lot of physio to get back to normal.' Gabi suddenly felt something she'd been feeling a lot recently. Vulnerable. And she didn't like it one bit.

She was used to living, travelling and managing independently. She was world renowned in her job. She got her pick of the biggest feature films and advertisements. She had always been fine on her own. Until now.

Etienne reappeared with a coffee pot and poured them each a cup. Gabi blew at the steaming drink, anticipating the first sip. It had been a long journey from the other side of the world. 'I don't want to get in your way obviously,' she said. 'And I think I can get through the physio quicker than they think . . .' she said.

'You can't rush these things, Gabi,' Isabella said, concerned. 'Just take your time.'

'I don't really need anything, apart from the odd lift to the doctors.'

'What about bathing?'

'I've got this waterproof cover. It's fine, I just have to stick my leg out of the shower.'

'And will you be able to manage the stairs?' Isabella nodded overhead to her apartment above the restaurant.

'I can go up and down on my bum,' Gabi reassured her. Etienne laughed.

'Well, the spare bedroom is yours,' Isabella said. 'For as long as you need it. You're family.' Isabella reached over and caught Gabi's hand in her own.

'Thanks, Isabella,' she said, squeezing back, 'I really mean it.'

'Welcome home,' Isabella said. 'Everything will be all right now. You'll see.'

# Chapter Two

*Walker*

Walker rubbed at his stubble, looking at himself in the mirror under the bright white of the bathroom lights, and sighed. He looked tired. He patted his cheeks and ran his hands through his hair, before shaking himself, physically. Time to throw off the night and get on with his day. He had shit to do.

He turned on the shower, dropped the towel wrapped around his waist and stepped under the jet. This would help. It always did.

As he soaped and lathered, he remembered the dream that had woken him in the night. It had been enough to make him sit bolt upright and cry out loud, his eyes searching the dark of the room. It was the same as always. The images that had haunted him since he was young. The sting of the ice on his skin. His scream coming out as a white plume of air. He plunged his head under the shower, trying to clear his dark thoughts.

As he dried himself, he wondered whether he'd woken Alex in his bedroom next door with the nightmare. He pressed his eyes shut and hoped fervently that Alex had slept through without hearing a thing. Walker had lived alone since he'd bought his first flat and had only recently started sharing when Alex moved to Honeybridge in the autumn. And anyway, it wasn't like these dreams happened every night. Already it was fading.

He rubbed himself roughly with the towel, pleased to see more colour in his face, more spark in his eyes. Appearances were important. He had to look organised, controlled. It was important so that people could rely on him. He knew what people expected of firefighters.

Physically and mentally, they had to be fit and strong. He had no problems there. But more importantly, they had to want to help people – which was what he tried to do every day. It was the only thing that helped keep the nightmares at bay. He towelled off his broad shoulders and checked his watch. Time for the gym before his shift.

In his bedroom, his duvet was crumpled and creased, as though he'd clutched at it, and he tugged it over the bed and smoothed it out, ready to come back to after his shift. He'd be exhausted, he knew that already. He caught himself smiling. What thirtysomething, fit, single man was making their bed on a Saturday morning with a desire to get back into it later – alone? To sleep? He laughed.

It wasn't that the bed didn't see action. It did, often. But it didn't see regular action with the same girl – or hadn't for a while. His last girlfriend, Mia, had taken a transfer with the brigade for a promotion and the long-distance thing, when coupled with two different shift patterns, just didn't work. Weekends together got less frequent, date nights became impossible and eventually the relationship was non-existent. Since then, the last few years had been casual and fun and nothing serious. Pick-ups at the local nightclub, The Bolthole, the odd date with someone through work. Which was all fine, Walker thought, as it meant that tonight, he'd be getting his bed to himself. He plumped the pillow in anticipation.

His phone rang. Etienne. He pressed green.

'Morning, buddy—' he said but he was immediately cut off.

'Isabella's got a leak in her apartment. Looks like the old sprinkler system for the restaurant in the attic.'

'On my way.' Walker pulled his T-shirt over his head and sprinted from the room. In an emergency, speed was everything. And he wouldn't be the one to let his friends down.

# Chapter Three

*Gabi*

It was not the lazy morning Gabi had anticipated. She'd fallen into bed the night before around nine, exhausted by the flight, and also enveloped in a warm, happy feeling now that she was back with Isabella. She'd no sooner closed her eyes than fallen asleep. Which must have been around the same time the leak had started in the loft.

Overnight the ceiling above her bed had bowed with the weight of water, until it could no longer support itself. A chunk of ceiling came down with a crash, showering Gabi's bed with plaster, old woodwork and about fifty litres of cold water. The noise had woken Isabella and Etienne too, and they'd come running in. Etienne carefully picked her up from the bed and carried her out of the room to safety, plonking her on her feet in the corridor and thrusting her crutches at her. After a quick check that her leg hadn't got wet, Isabella and Gabi huddled in the doorway, watching the water pour through the metre-wide hole in the ceiling, before another collapse drove them further into the hall.

Isabella helped Gabi into a fluffy white dressing gown to at least keep her warm. Etienne climbed through the loft hatch, now wearing a head torch and pyjama bottoms, which in any other circumstances, Gabi knew, would have made Isabella laugh. But Gabi could see her cousin was stricken.

'If it carries on, it will go through the floor to the restaurant!' Isabella gasped and started trying to position buckets and saucepans under the leak, rushing in and out of the damaged bedroom.

'Be careful,' Gabi said, one eye on the remaining half of the ceiling.

'I've not even been open for six months, I can't shut now.' Isabella threw a bunch of towels onto the carpet to sop up the water. Gabi tried to help but couldn't carry anything while using her crutches and, frustrated, realised the best thing she could do was get out of the way. She retreated to the sofa, from where she could see everything.

'There are two tanks up here!' Etienne shouted down and Isabella clasped her hands under her chin to think.

'One is the cold-water tank for the flat,' she said. 'The other is the old sprinkler system for the restaurant.'

Etienne appeared back down the ladder and grabbed his phone. 'Sprinklers – only one person to call . . .' he said, pressing dial already. He lifted his gaze to Isabella and nodded. They both said, together, 'Walker.'

Another chunk of plaster hit the floor, and Gabi crossed her fingers that Walker was the hero they all needed.

\*

He certainly seemed to fit the bill when he turned up although there was no time for introductions. From her seat in the sitting room, Gabi couldn't help but notice the breadth of his chest in his T-shirt as he jogged purposefully through the apartment. He disappeared immediately into the loft hatch and his feet hardly seemed to touch the rungs as he climbed the ladder on his way to investigate. Etienne and Isabella waited at the bottom, both anxious looking, dreading what a few weeks of closure could do to a new business if the restaurant ceiling collapsed too. Isabella was only just getting established. This could be catastrophic.

Walker called down for some tools which Etienne passed up, and then there was clanging and banging overhead. Suddenly, the steady gush of water stopped.

'I think that's got it!' Etienne shouted and Isabella put her hands to her cheeks in relief. The dripping water slowed. There was the sound of more banging and some grunts of effort before Walker's boots appeared, followed by a rather nice bum as he descended the ladder back into the bedroom.

Gabi watched Isabella and Etienne hover in the doorway behind him to survey the damage. She manoeuvred herself behind them and they all listened to the steady *drip, drip,* observed the sodden walls and peered up into the rafters through the large hole in the middle of the ceiling. Walker stepped carefully into the debris and began moving plasterboard sheets off the bed.

'Lucky it was just the spare bedroom!' he said in a soft Scottish accent. 'It could have been really nasty if someone was in it.'

'My cousin *was* in it, actually,' Isabella said. 'Thank God she wasn't hurt. Well, not any more than she already is!'

Walker frowned in confusion and bent to retrieve something wrapped around the toe of his boot.

'Who's your cousin?' he asked, turning something small and black in his hands.

'That'd be me,' Gabi said, shuffling forward. 'Gabriella. Everyone calls me Gabi.'

He lifted his face to her and sandy hair fell over the most vividly hazel eyes she'd ever seen. 'And that' – she pointed to the lacy black G-string he held in his fingers – 'would be mine.'

# Chapter Four

## Walker

He was holding a pair of pants in his hands. Walker realised that fact at the very last second when an elfin woman on crutches appeared in the doorway, almost engulfed in a fluffy white dressing gown, who he recognised as the cousin, Gabi – and the owner of the pants. She had the most mischievous smile he'd ever seen.

He mumbled an apology and handed the scrap of fabric over. She laughed and thanked him. For a moment he forgot what he was doing, until another clod of plasterboard hit the floor and then he took command.

'Isabella, strip the bed,' he said and she sprang into action.

'Now, Etienne, help me with the mattress.' Between them, they carried it to the back courtyard and then the bed frame was moved to the front room.

'Isabella, can you move the suitcases?' he asked. 'And anything else that's adding weight to the wet floor and risking the ceiling below.'

Gabi's suitcases were pulled out and stood in the hall.

'I feel so useless!' Gabi moaned as the three of them then worked together to rip up the sodden carpet and carried it downstairs to take to the dump later. It was as much as could be done – for now.

Walker exhaled slowly as he took it in. It was good he'd got here as quickly as he had but the room was wrecked. The ceiling was a write-off. The walls were streaming. The floor was down to bare floorboards. The bedroom was uninhabitable. But at least the restaurant was not impacted. He knew it was a win, but it was still a problem.

Walker suggested Gabi made coffee and everyone took a breather. Gabi looked relieved to be finally able to do something to help. Walker scrolled his phone for dehumidifiers and sent links to Isabella, to point her in the right direction.

'These will speed up the drying process,' he said, and she nodded her thanks, a worried frown on her face.

Over coffee, Isabella voiced the problem out loud.

'That room will take days to dry out and weeks to get repaired. So, for the time being, the spare room is out of action.' Walker watched Gabi bite her lip, waiting.

'We'll just have to keep the bed in here for you, Gabi,' Isabella said, motioning to the space in the front room where they'd positioned the bed frame, between the sofa and the television. They all looked at it. Walker watched Gabi shake her head, big brown eyes dark and serious.

'I can't do that to you,' she said decisively. 'I'll get a hotel.'

'No way! You're not supposed to live alone until you're fully recovered. You said that yourself. You need help.'

Gabi looked like she wanted the ground to swallow her up.

'Me living in your front room like Grandpa Joe in *Charlie and the Chocolate Factory* is never going to happen, Isabella. I know you mean well, but it wouldn't work. I'll get a hotel.'

The silence deepened as neither woman backed down. Walker cleared his throat.

'What about one of the girls?' he suggested. 'Rosie and Wren have a spare room. And there's Amber?'

He saw the quick lift of Gabi's chin. The hope on her face.

'I've met them all – briefly – last year,' she said.

'That could work ... I could certainly ask,' Isabella said thoughtfully. 'Give me a minute. I'll put it on the group chat.' Walker saw Gabi cross her fingers and tuck them in the oversized pocket of her dressing gown.

A second later the phone rang, and Isabella answered with a hopeful 'hello'. She listened intensely for a few seconds, then broke into a grin and put the phone on speaker.

'It's Amber,' she said, sinking on the sofa beside Gabi and holding the phone between them. 'And she'd love to have you.'

Gabi clapped her hands in delight. Leaning into the phone, she said, 'Hi, Amber, thanks so much!'

Amber's voice came through sing-song happy, as though she were already smiling.

'Gabi, girl, I've got a spare room on my ground floor with your name on it. And I've got a downstairs bathroom – what with it being an old house – so you won't need to worry about stairs.'

'Which is a much safer scenario,' Etienne chipped in, pointing at Gabi's boot.

'I'd pay rent,' Gabi said.

'No, you would not,' Amber replied.

'I'd stock the fridge,' Gabi suggested.

'You haven't seen how much Jayden eats yet,' Amber chuckled, reminding Gabi about her ten-year-old son.

'I'd pay the bills then,' Gabi tried again.

'You could do something more valuable than that, actually,' Amber said. 'You could do a bit of childcare for me?'

Gabi's face fell. 'I haven't got any experience ...' she said with a grimace.

'Oh, don't worry, Jayden is ten. I'd just need you to be there when he gets home from school. I'm normally at the restaurant until about five.'

Gabi's face lit up and she clasped Isabella's hand in hers.

'I could definitely do that,' Gabi said. 'I'll time my physio and gym around him.'

'Then it sounds perfect. In fact, you'd be doing me a favour. What time shall I expect you?'

Walker saw an opportunity to help and stood up.

'I can bring her over now, Amber, if that works for you?' he said.

'I'll put the kettle on,' Amber said, before hanging up the phone.

Walker found himself in the beam of a second dazzling smile from Gabi. He grinned back. He'd done good.

# Chapter Five

## Gabi

The knight in shining armour drove well. Gabi couldn't help but like that he drove a manual, and his gear changing was smooth and swift. Just as she liked it. One of her pleasures in life was driving. And if she couldn't do it herself at the moment, it was curiously satisfying to ride passenger to someone who obviously enjoyed it too.

'Do you think the restaurant will be okay?' she asked and was reassured by a firm nod as he kept his eyes on the road.

'I'd say so,' he replied, in his soft Scottish burr. 'I'll pop back later and take another look in the roof space, just to make sure.'

'Nice car,' she said, watching his hands expertly turning the wheel. 'On set, they always ferry us around in the smoothest, quietest electric cars. Sometimes, even driverless ones. But nothing feels like a revving engine.'

'I know exactly what you mean,' he said, flashing her a grin. 'I tried electric. But it wasn't for me.'

'Have you known Etienne for long?' she asked, remembering

the easy way they communicated and the hug they exchanged as Walker left.

'A good few years now,' he said. 'I met him when he took over The Bistro. He's a really good guy, and a changed man since he's fallen in love with your cousin.'

'They say love changes everything!' Gabi laughed. 'Although I'm probably not best qualified to confirm or deny.'

'I'm happy to be optimistic,' Walker said. 'You never know what's round the corner.'

Walker was relaxed as he drove, one hand on the wheel, which put her at ease and they chatted freely. Him telling her about his role as a firefighter and how he'd always wanted to be able to help people. Gabi reciprocating, explaining how she'd always been drawn to adrenaline and a job in stunts had seemed a great fit. It felt like only a minute or two before they pulled up outside Amber's old English cottage.

Walker carried her cases up the garden path as though they were empty. Gabi swung along behind him on her crutches as the front door opened and Amber appeared, just as gorgeous as Gabi remembered her.

'You're here!' Amber said. 'We're going to have such a good time.' She opened the door wide, beckoning them inside. 'It will be nice for me to have some grown-up conversation in the house.'

Jayden sat at the kitchen table watching something on an iPad. He raised his head when they entered and waved in Walker's direction before immediately returning his attention to the screen.

The kitchen was wide, and Gabi could navigate easily around

the wooden table with her crutches. Walker carried the cases down to the snug that Amber had turned into a spare bedroom, and Gabi sank into a chair.

'Tea or coffee?' Amber said and she got busy with the request for coffee, opening kitchen cupboards and picking out what she needed from the assorted jumble that Gabi could see inside. It was so different to her own kitchen in her London penthouse apartment. Her shelves were sparse. She wasn't there that much, so everything in there was long life: jars of sun-dried tomatoes, packets of pasta, coffee and bottles of sparkling water. Amber's pantry was stuffed with crisps, nuts, and sticky jars of jam and spreads. In the fridge, as Amber fetched the milk, Gabi spied jars of half-used pasta sauces. Chocolate biscuits and bars sat on the countertop in a box marked TREATS. On the table, a fruit bowl full of apples and grapes and bananas. Gabi never had fruit in the flat. It went off before she got a chance to eat it.

Walker stuck his head back in the door.

'Tea, Walker?' Amber waved a ceramic mug at him with 'world's best mum' painted on the side. He pushed the hair back off his forehead.

'No thanks, going to run. If I go now, I can still get to the gym before shift.'

'Thanks again,' Gabi said, thinking she should get up but suddenly unsure whether to give him a hug or shake his hand. The hand that had held her knickers.

'Happy to help.' He grinned, turned and was gone. The two women waited until they heard the front door click shut.

'That was lucky – Walker to the rescue!' Amber said, slopping milk into Gabi's coffee and passing it over.

'I don't normally need saving,' Gabi protested.

'I've no doubt about that. But everyone should have a Walker in their lives.' Gabi was impressed by the reputation he held with his friends. But then also slightly dubious. Nobody was that perfect. Not in her experience. She blew her coffee and changed the subject.

'So, last time I saw you,' Gabi said, 'was when Tutto Mio opened with such a bang.'

The two women eyed each other. 'Bang' was the right word. A gun had gone off, the restaurant trashed by a criminal gang the day before it was due to open. Etienne, the then town Romeo, had saved the day and professed his undying love for Isabella – all extraordinary events for Honeybridge. A day that changed life for Isabella and Etienne for the better and introduced Alex to the gang. Alex, the twin brother not many people knew that Etienne even had. Amber was one of those few who knew him from a past life. Isabella had told Gabi that Alex and Amber recognised each other on sight, and not in a good way, Amber giving him a resounding slap around the face, nobody quite sure why.

'That was quite a day,' Amber laughed. 'And now, look. The restaurant is booming. Isabella has done such a good job.' She ruffled Jayden's short afro and Gabi spotted his electric-blue hearing aids. He shook his head at his mum without looking up and Amber rolled her eyes. She poked him. Jayden glanced up and signed something to her. She signed back and he glanced shyly at Gabi.

'I've told Jayden you're coming to stay with us,' Amber said. Gabi smiled nervously and lifted a hand. She didn't know any sign language, apart from 'thank you' that she'd seen one year on *Strictly Come Dancing* when a clip of the winning dance went viral. She faced him directly.

'Is that okay with you, Jayden?' Gabi asked. Jayden shrugged. Amber nudged him in the ribs, and he changed the shrug to a nod.

Gabi lifted her four fingers flat to her chin and then extended them towards him, showing off her only move.

He shrugged, rose from the table and took his iPad into the other room.

'Don't worry. He doesn't bite. You'll be fine,' Amber said. Gabi nodded and hoped that was true. She had no experience of children. They weren't high on her wish list.

An hour later, the two women had worked out a plan. Amber would be home in the mornings to get Jayden out of the door to school on time and then she'd drop Gabi to the gym on her way to work mid-morning. Gabi assured her she'd be able to make her own way back, ensuring she was home in time for Jayden's return after three. Even better, Amber told her the gym was the one near Tutto Mio, so Gabi already had plans to pop in for coffee with her cousin after each session. Maybe this recuperation lark wouldn't be too bad after all.

The first week went faster than she'd expected. They found a routine, and everyone settled into it. Gabi joined the gym and loved beginning to test her body out again. She found a physio and started her exercises. The spring sunshine was gaining warmth, and she sat in Amber's small back garden to tan. She loved being able to drop in on Isabella and realised just how much she'd missed her. She made hot chocolates or ice cream floats for Jayden when he got home from school and then they'd choose an action movie to watch together, her on the sofa, him on the floor. Childcare was easier than she'd thought. They didn't even have to talk! She'd never had a week like it and maybe it was the novelty, but she was enjoying herself. This was so much better than being stuck on her own in an Australian hospital. This was homely to the millionth degree.

On Friday evening, Amber collapsed on the sofa beside her, the working week over.

'Chill day tomorrow. And then Sunday is going to be fun! You coming?' she said.

'Coming where?' Gabi asked, flicking channels to find Amber's favourite show.

'Fundraiser at the fire station,' Amber said. 'It's a pole-a-thon. Most distance covered on a fireman's pole in an hour. They want to beat the world record. It's for a good cause – but never mind the cause, hot men climbing ladders and sliding down poles? Interested?'

'Count me in,' Gabi said. 'Sounds like the perfect spectator sport.'

# Chapter Six

*Walker*

The crew had already tied the bunting to the fire station and the truck was gleaming in the spring sun. Walker felt a rush of pride, as he always did, to see it there in the car park. The local kids loved the chance to touch a real-life fire engine, climb up and into it. And he loved to see the excitement on their faces – you never knew who might end up wanting to be a firefighter themselves one day. He could remember the thrill of it – the first time he rode in the truck gave him butterflies; the first time with lights and sirens took his breath away. It still gave him a buzz every time they were called out on a job. The difference was that now he was Crew Manager and wore a yellow helmet, with two bars on his epaulettes. Along with the fancy fashion, he had the responsibility for the local incidents, as well as the training and safety of his crew. Something that, if he didn't already have nightmares, might give him them. But he tried not to think about that.

'Morning, Walker.' His Watch Commander, Dean Appleby,

was there, in full dress uniform. He would be in charge of timing the pole-a-thon and making sure that it was official.

'Morning, sir,' Walker said with a dip of his head. He liked the formality, the manners of the service.

'Good luck,' Appleby said and then, nodding at a couple arriving with a clipboard and an iPad, 'looks like the world record officiators have arrived. Excuse me.' He set off across the forecourt, raising his arm to get their attention. Walker's phone beeped.

The Brothers from Another Mother WhatsApp group was live. Originally it had just been him, Etienne who owned The Bistro, and silver-haired Fox, the games designer. But now that Etienne's twin brother had moved to the town – and in with Walker – he was part of the group.

**Etienne**: Good luck today, bro.
**Fox**: Hope your pole holds out.
**Walker**: Never had a problem before.
**Alex**: Thought I heard someone shout out in the night actually . . . Did you have company?

Walker cringed. He must have called out during his nightmare again.

**Walker**: Nope. You must have been dreaming! See you later.

He tucked his phone in his backpack with a sigh and set off to round up his crew.

An hour later, the fire station was heaving. All members of the Brothers from Another Mother were present and correct.

Fox came first, dragged along by Dingbat the dog, with human dynamos in the shape of his sons, seven-year-old Reggie and four-year-old George, streaking along beside him. They hit Walker at speed, grabbing a leg each, and Walker reached down to tickle them both.

Alex arrived second, and Walker was again struck by just how similar he was to Etienne. Their colouring was different, Alex was blond to Etienne's brown, but their features were remarkably alike. Alex had his guitar on his back – must be off to rehearsal afterwards, Walker thought. Alex had taught himself how to play, one of his fixations since he quit poker. Once an addict, always an addict, he jokingly said, but today instead of being addicted to gambling, it was guitar playing or running cross country.

Walker had spotted them all as they arrived but still found himself scanning the crowd.

He laid out some gym mats beneath the pole, knowing it was usually totally unnecessary. But because today they were going to be acting at such speed, and with repetition and competition thrown in, he'd opted for safety first.

He spotted Wren and Rosie who ran the Lit Lounge bookshop, with Riley their daughter swinging between them by their hands. Rosie raised her hand in a hello. Wren grinned and raised her takeaway coffee in a cheers. He watched as Riley ran ahead to see a friend and Wren took the opportunity to wrap her arm around Rosie and pull her in for a kiss.

Funny to think that he'd done the same to Rosie, when they were both sixteen – kissed and hugged and held her to his chest. Before she realised she preferred women, and he decided she was the best friend he'd ever had. He waved at her now and cast his eyes over the crowd for a final check.

At the last minute he saw Etienne and Isabella as they turned the corner to join the fun, entwined as they had been for the past five months. And behind them, Amber, Jayden and finally Gabi, swinging along on her crutches. It was only when he spotted her that he realised he'd been hoping she'd come.

He swung the bell. Time to get started.

# Chapter Seven

## Gabi

'Are you all right standing?' Isabella asked, a frown creasing her nose.

'I'm fine,' Gabi said, shrugging off the concern, ignoring the fact that her back was starting to ache. Her boot put her off balance and her back paid the price.

'Do you want a sip of this?' Rosie suggested, pulling a small silver flask from her oversized handbag and offering it around. 'Must have left it in here after the last night out at The Bolthole.'

'Do you think you should?' Isabella asked. Gabi reached for the flask and tipped it back without bothering to reply. It hit with a burn she wasn't expecting. She coughed. She'd been thinking wine, not whisky. Rosie laughed.

'Are you on medication? Taking any pills?' Isabella asked, that damn frown between her eyes again.

'Yep!' Gabi grinned. 'But only little ones!' She took another hit and passed the drink back to Rosie, who smiled and said, with a glance at Wren, 'Keep it, we're no good at day drinking.'

Gabi held the flask up in glee. Isabella rolled her eyes and turned back to Etienne. Good. Maybe she'd stop clucking around her like a mother hen.

Truth be told, Gabi *was* still taking painkillers. The pain had been excruciating before the operation, and not much better afterwards, when she'd been told the pins were in the right position and she just had to give things time to settle and heal. It wasn't just the pain of the break itself, it was the constant backache, the sore skin under her arms where she took her weight on the crutch pads. It was the muscles in her shoulders that were doing all the work. The painkillers definitely took the edge off.

She breathed out slowly. The hip flask was the first alcohol she'd had in months. She never drank on set when she was working, and she'd gone straight from one film set at the end of last year to Australia for the Western in January. She had to have a clear head for the stunt work. She literally couldn't even remember having had a toast to bring in the new year or celebrate Christmas. She took another nice, long swallow. The heat of it seemed to go directly to the ache in her back and soothe it, like a hot water bottle. Bliss.

'What's new then, Gabi?' Fox appeared beside her, in his signature silver grey quiff and checked shirt. He had that wholesome, lumberjack, outdoorsy thing going on and she'd forgotten how good-looking he was.

'You mean, apart from the obvious . . .' Gabi pointed to her leg with a smile which Fox returned. His eyes twinkled.

'I thought it was rule number one for stuntwomen. Don't fall off.' She laughed outright.

'No, the first rule is don't be scared of falling.'

He grinned and reached for the flask she still held. She swigged again before handing it over. As if by magic, his two sons, Reggie and George, appeared beside him just as he tipped the drink to his lips, and she watched his Adam's apple bob as he rushed his swallow. Too late. He was caught in the act.

'Can we have some?' Reggie's hands were already on the flask.

'No, it's not mine. It's Gabi's,' Fox said quickly, passing it back and swinging George up onto his shoulders.

And just like that Gabi remembered why, however gorgeous Fox might be, he was a hot dad and that was a big enough reason to stay away even if they did seem to enjoy a bit of harmless flirtation. She glanced up at George with his sticky hands in Fox's quiff, and then down at Reggie who was threading through the crowd to get to the front. However cute they were, she didn't want them, or any others like them, in her life. Children were not a part of her future. Having been one herself, she thought children were totally overrated.

Gabi held the drink out towards Amber, who eyed it wishfully but then pushed it back. 'I need to be able to drive you home!'

Gabi put the flask back to her own lips but was surprised to find it empty. She shook it. Fox must have had a right old mouthful. Rosie appeared at her shoulder.

'Oops,' Gabi said. 'Really sorry! We finished your drink!'

'No worries.' Rosie smiled and Rosie pointed at the fire crew, who were warming up with bleep tests, running between two points at ever increasing speed. Gabi spotted Walker, who made it look easy. Head down, shoulders wide as an ox, he powered up his lane before lifting his head to check where his crew were at. Gabi considered the strength he must have in those legs. Now that was a thought. In fact, thinking about it, firefighters probably had all the right characteristics to be stunt workers if they ever fancied a change of career. They were strong, brave, athletic. She wondered idly if Walker could ride a horse.

She grinned to herself. Her back had not felt this relaxed since she'd been using the crutches.

She watched Walker flick his sandy hair off his face, then turn at the end and run with his back to her. She took in the width of his shoulders. *He'd* have no problem giving her a fireman's lift, that was for certain. Although saying that, with Gabi being only five foot three, Jayden could probably give her a fireman's lift if he put his mind to it. She smiled to herself. Maybe even Reggie. She snorted.

'Having a good time?' Isabella was beside her, arm around her shoulders.

'Yup,' said Gabi decisively. She really was. Her leg didn't hurt. Her back didn't ache. She was back in Honeybridge, and she was getting to know the gang better. Maybe a broken leg wasn't so bad.

Alex edged his way into the circle next to his twin. Gabi noticed Amber roll her eyes and angle her shoulder away from him. A definite rebuff.

'Hmm,' Gabi whispered to herself, making a note to get the gossip later when she and Amber were alone.

'Pardon?' Isabella said.

'Nothing,' Gabi replied.

'Shall I try to find you a chair?' Isabella said, but Gabi waved her away.

'Really, I'm fine. I'm literally feeling no pain.' Never a truer word. In fact, she was starting to feel quite good.

The beep test finished, the spectators were shepherded into the fire station to a cordoned off area in view of the bottom of the pole. The officiates gathered: the big moment had arrived.

'Come on, team! You can do it!' Walker shouted to his crew as they lined up at the bottom of the ladder. 'And you lot,' Walker called to the crowd. 'Dig deep! It's for a great cause. The Honeybridge Fire Service Hardship Fund. Get your wallets out!'

The klaxon sounded and the record attempt began. Walker was first up the ladder, disappearing up into the hatch to the platform and appearing a few seconds later on the pole. His legs wrapped around it gently and he slid down silently, landing on and bouncing off the landing pad in one balletic movement. Gabi made a small sound of appreciation in her throat as the rest of the gang cheered.

The next firefighter was on his heels as he ascended the ladder again. The race was on. To beat the world record they had to cover the most metres down the pole in an hour and by the look on Walker's face, he wasn't going to let anything stand in his way. Gabi was suddenly glad she had a front-row view.

'Go on, Walker! You can do it!' Gabi found herself shouting, a little too closely to Isabella's ear, who nearly jumped out of her skin.

'Are you sure you don't want to sit down?' Isabella asked again. 'How much of that flask did you drink?' Gabi hit her cousin on the ankle with her crutch.

'Please don't worry. I'm fine. Just happy to be here.' Although to be fair, she did feel a bit fuzzy inside. She hadn't drunk alcohol for so long, it certainly seemed to be having an impact.

The hour sped past. In fact, it could be said it passed in a bit of a blur. Gabi started off counting how many times she saw Walker slide down the pole, but after twenty minutes or so, she lost count. Instead, she tried to watch him go up the ladder, thinking it might be slightly slower ... plus she got a nice view of his bum. But she lost track of that too, about the same time she wished there was another flask to be found somewhere. Someone was hogging the booze at this party. She glanced round the gang to see who it might be, but everyone looked remarkably sober.

'Last big push,' Walker said over the microphone. 'According to my count, we need another twelve descents in the next minute ...'

The crowd roared its encouragement. Gabi waved a crutch in the air, much to Fox's surprise who luckily ducked at the right moment. His kids were jumping up and down on the spot. Jayden had Riley on his shoulders so that she could see better.

Walker took to the steps again with a fresh burst of energy. She could see the set of his jaw as he dropped down the pole and took his place again in the queue. As it turned out, he was the last drop. He was the number twelve that took their meterage over the current world record and as he hit the landing pad, he dropped forward into a deep bend and then, as the klaxon sounded again, he bowed.

The crowd went wild, and Gabi found herself cheering along.

The officiates had their heads together, comparing their notes. Both having counted separately, it was now a case of waiting to make sure that everyone agreed with the result. It had to be unanimous, or it would be disallowed. The audience quieted as one of them approached the microphone.

'Congratulations to Honeybridge Fire and Rescue on a valiant attempt,' the man said, before allowing a broad smile to break through. 'You're the new world record holders!'

Walker and his crew threw themselves at each other in massive bear hugs, clapping each other's backs. Gabi felt surprisingly emotional but then saw that everyone else was the same. Isabella and Etienne were taking the opportunity to kiss. Wren and Rosie rubbed noses with each other and grinned. Fox and Amber hugged. Gabi watched Alex look on and then glance away.

'Hmmm,' she whispered again.

'Pardon?' Isabella said, still hanging off Etienne.

'Pardon?' Gabi said back.

Fox waved to Walker and shouted, 'Coming over?'

Walker signalled he'd be there in five and turned back to debrief his team. The cordon was lifted, and kids were allowed into the performance area. They swarmed to the soft bounciness of the landing pad, squealing in delight.

The gang all turned inwards to talk, reminiscing about a night out they'd had recently. Although it sounded like it had been fun, it made Gabi feel strangely left out and she turned back to look at the crew.

Walker was shaking everyone by the hand, saying a few words to each of his team individually. His muscles filled his T-shirt out nicely under those braces. Gabi smirked to herself. There weren't many people in the world that could make wearing braces sexy, but Walker was one of them.

The ladder gleamed in the sunlight. Twelve rungs. She wondered how fast she personally could climb the ladder, cross the top and drop the other side down the pole. The crew had made it look easy, but surely she'd have no problem, even with this blasted boot on? She was a stuntwoman, after all. She was used to looking danger in the face and laughing at it. A small giggle escaped her. She glanced at the gang, but they were all deep in conversation.

She eyed the ladder again. It did look like fun.

# Chapter Eight

*Walker*

Walker was pumped. His chest heaved as he debriefed the team, shook hands and clapped backs. The hour had sped by, and he'd loved every minute of it. Not just the activity itself, but taking time to encourage the team, urge them onwards, rally the crowds and encourage them to drop an extra donation in the bucket. Every penny would help a family in need after a fire. It felt good to do good.

Fox beckoned to him, but he just needed to make sure everything was safe and sorted before he joined them. He spotted kids jumping around on the landing pad and he made his way over to check, but they were being supervised by parents or grandparents, and all seemed fine. He moved over to the fire truck to find some of the crew already there, managing the flow of children that wanted to see the inside of the vehicle. Reggie was currently sitting in the driving seat, wildly sweeping his hands around the steering wheel as if driving at high speed.

It looked like everything was exactly as it should be, everything in order. Until, that was, he saw a small boy put his foot on the first rung of the ladder. The hair prickled on the back of Walker's neck. Nobody should be going up the ladder. They might miss their footing, slip and hurt themselves.

He crossed the landing pad in four strides, before the boy had time to place his foot on the second rung. Putting his hands on the boy's middle, he detached him from the ladder and lifted him high into the air, trying to make a game of the change of direction.

'Not up there, I'm afraid, little guy,' he said to the boy who kicked his legs wildly as Walker lowered him back on the ground.

'But . . .' He stamped his tiny foot, outraged. 'That's not fair.'

'It's out of bounds up there, fella,' Walker said, trying to ruffle the boy's hair to soften the blow, but the boy yanked his head out of reach.

'Not fair!' he said again, louder this time, his face red with rage. Walker backed up a step. This kid looked like he was likely to kick him in the balls at any given moment.

A woman approached and the boy immediately burst into tears and threw himself, face first, into her thighs. She cradled the back of his head before looking accusingly at Walker.

'Is there a problem?' she asked, looking like there better not be one.

'Not at all,' Walker said calmly. 'I just had to tell him the ladder is out of bounds.' The boy's crying heightened a notch, and the mother smoothed his hair.

'He couldn't even have a tiny go?' the woman said, with a strange, coy smile. She lifted her hand towards Walker, with her finger and thumb held just an inch apart. 'I'd be really grateful ...' The boy lifted his head from her skirt and gave him a similar, creepy smile which he thought would seal the deal. Walker took another step back. Normally he liked kids. Scratch that, normally he loved kids. He was godparent to Fox's Reg and Rosie's Riley, and hoped to have his own one day. As long as they didn't act like this one.

'Sorry, not even a tiny go. Because he might still get a tiny bit broken if he falls off.'

The boy shook his fists in frustration and groaned and Walker fought the urge to laugh.

'Well, you shouldn't have set the expectation the kids could go on the ladder ...' the woman said and Walker decided enough was enough.

'Exactly,' he nodded in agreement. 'You're exactly right. Which is why I'm just going to put the chain across it and a notice on it to make it absolutely clear that it's not safe.'

He turned to do exactly that when the boy pointed to the top of the launch pad, shouting, 'Why didn't you tell her to come down then?'

Walker and the mum both looked up. There was nobody to be seen. But Walker was suddenly very conscious of the fact he'd had his eye off the ladder for a good minute while trying to sort out the devil child and his mother. Had someone managed to sneak past and climb up through the hatch to the platform?

'Who was it?' he asked, stepping closer to the kid. 'Did a little girl go up there?' The kid clamped his mouth shut and Walker crouched down to his level.

'A woman,' the kid said suddenly, taking his chance and

landing a kick at Walker's shins, which caught him painfully on the bone. Walker swallowed a swear word and limped to the bottom of the ladder, looking up through the hole. Nothing.

A commotion sounded behind him. Lots of gasping, a few 'ooh's and 'ah's. His stomach dropped with the immediate knowledge that something was wrong. He was looking in the wrong place. He swivelled.

A group of kids and parents were all gathered round the base of the pole, looking upwards. He was there in a second.

He put a hand on the pole to act as a safety net before he even saw what was coming towards him. A woman, tiny as she might be, but definitely a fully grown adult, threw herself at the top of the pole with a 'woohoo'.

She did it with such abandon that she was leaning back, facing skywards. It was only when he saw the black boot sticking straight out in front of her that he recognised Gabi. But he didn't have a second to admire the view as she slid down the gleaming pole towards him – and the pile of onlookers who were just about to have a boot hit them on the head.

He reached his hands out, only thinking of landing her safely, and protecting those people whose heads she could crack. He caught her with a grunt in his arms and stepped away from the pole. There was a collective sigh and then a spontaneous round of applause.

Walker breathed out. Crisis averted. Everyone clear of danger. Thank goodness. He realised he was still holding Gabi, legs in one arm, shoulders in the other. She lay against his chest, laughing.

'Walker!' Gabi grinned up into his face.

'Gabi,' he acknowledged her in return, gobsmacked.

'That was amazing,' Gabi said.

'That was dangerous,' Walker corrected.

'Ah, come on,' Gabi said, and he caught the slight slur in her voice. 'I laugh in the face of danger. I'm a stuntwoman.'

'Not a very good one at the moment by the look of it.' Walker nodded at her leg.

'Why did you stop me?'

'I didn't want you to fall.'

'I wasn't going to fall,' she said incredulously. 'I wasn't even afraid of falling. That's the first rule of being a stunt person.' She wriggled against him, and he realised again he was still holding her. He lowered her legs to the ground gently and she straightened herself against his arm and wiggled a finger in his face to make her point. 'Don't be afraid of falling.'

'I just wanted to keep everyone safe,' Walker said.

'Don't worry about me, Walker. I can look after myself.' Gabi glanced about her and grinned as Isabella dashed through the crowd carrying the crutches she'd left at the edge of the landing pad.

'What the hell?' Isabella asked but Gabi just laughed.

'He's already read me the riot act, you don't need to say anything.' Gabi indicated Walker with her head as she positioned a crutch under each arm. Isabella glanced at Walker and rolled her eyes in solidarity. Gabi started her three-legged walk with crutches towards the gang and they both watched her go.

'What was she thinking?' Isabella asked quietly.

'What was she drinking?' Walker replied. Isabella sighed and squeezed his arm before following her cousin.

'Thanks for saving me, Walker!' Gabi called over her shoulder, smiling without a care in the world, making it abundantly clear he shouldn't have bothered.

'That's okay,' he called after her. Then quietly to himself he said, 'That's just what I do.'

### Brothers from Another Mother WhatsApp group

**Fox**: Brilliant day, Walker. Boys both knackered and straight to sleep. I owe you a beer.

**Etienne**: Bet Gabi's asleep already too. Remind me never to drink on painkillers.

**Alex**: She was quite a handful, wasn't she?

**Walker**: More of an armful, actually.

# Chapter Nine

*Gabi*

Amber was already at the table in the morning sipping a steaming coffee when Gabi hobbled in. Jayden glanced up and then returned his attention to his huge bowl of cereal. Amber pushed a chair out for Gabi with her bare feet and Gabi sank into it thankfully.

'How's the head?' Amber asked, raising one eyebrow. Gabi shook it to say it wasn't good but then realised that wasn't the best idea.

'Not great,' she said instead. How much whisky had she drunk?

'We keep supplies for these occasions up here.' Amber pulled open a top cupboard, one too tall for Jayden to reach, and rummaged until she found a packet of painkillers. She passed them, and a glass of cold water, across to Gabi and sat down again.

'Thanks,' Gabi said, swallowing two immediately and groaning.

Jayden lifted the bowl to his mouth and began slurping the

milky bits from the bottom. When he lowered it again, he had a perfect white moustache. Amber laughed and reached over to thumb it away, but he rubbed it roughly with the back of his own hand before she could reach him. His chair screeched as he stood up. He was dressed for school, the local primary badge on the breast of his polo shirt.

'Grab your book bag then, love,' Amber said to him, and he dragged his feet out of the room. Amber turned back to Gabi.

'Not a bad way to end your day,' Amber said. 'In the arms of the local hero . . .'

'Bit of an overreaction on his part, I think,' Gabi said.

'Doesn't matter,' Amber replied. 'There's plenty of girls who wouldn't mind being carried home by him.'

'Not me. I can limp along quite nicely on my own,' Gabi said automatically. But for a second, she remembered the way Walker had caught her and the solidity of his arms around her.

Amber blew her coffee as Jayden appeared in the doorway, backpack now in place. Amber reached a hand out to straighten his collar, but he ducked and waved, signing instead.

'See you later,' Amber replied. 'Walk straight home tonight and don't forget Gabi will be here when you get here.' Gabi managed a weak wave. Thank God she had all day to recover before she was on Jayden duty. She put her head in her hands, only lifting it when Amber placed a frothy coffee in front of her. The tablets were at last kicking in as she remembered she wanted to ask Amber something.

'I saw you and Alex together yesterday. Or rather, I saw that you were never together. In fact, you were obviously avoiding him. And I realised, I never did hear about how you knew

Alex, or what he did to deserve that slap when he arrived in Honeybridge.'

Amber snorted. 'Don't get me started on what that man did!' But Gabi leaned forward on her elbows, settling in for the story. Amber rolled her eyes, before nodding gently.

'Okaaaaaaay.' She pulled her chair into the table. 'Buckle up.' Gabi sipped and the hot coffee was deliciously creamy. She licked the froth from her lips and waited for Amber to begin.

'We were both working for a hotel. I was on front desk, he was bar. We had an instant sort of . . .' – Amber rubbed her hands together and then popped them apart – '*connection*. You know?' Gabi nodded, at the same time thinking she hadn't felt a connection of any kind recently. Even the last guy she'd had a thing with on set had been no more than a tingle, come to think of it.

'We used to find opportunities to see each other, flirt outrageously . . .' Amber fanned her face with her hand. 'It all started off as a bit of fun, and God was it good fun!' She laughed outright now, leaning back in her chair.

'Soon we were seeing each other all the time – whenever Jayden was at school or staying at a friend's house. I couldn't get enough of Alex, and he certainly seemed to be hungry for me.' She closed her eyes momentarily and sighed. 'The things that man could do with his hands. It's no wonder he's good at guitar.'

Gabi choked on her coffee and laughed. 'Sounds promising.'

'I thought so too. We'd been seeing each other for a few months, and I thought it was time to introduce him to Jayden.' Her turquoise eyes were suddenly clear and direct. 'It felt like we were getting serious – and we come as a package.'

Gabi nodded. From the little she'd seen of Amber and Jayden

together, she knew there was nothing Amber wouldn't do for her son.

'I'd never been that serious about anyone before that I wanted to introduce them to Jayden. After Jayden's dad took off when he heard about the hearing loss, I just thought I'd do family my way, myself. That way I could look after him and protect him. We didn't need anyone else.'

'I understand that completely,' Gabi acknowledged.

'Anyway, it felt right so I did it. For the first time *ever* I introduced my boy to my boyfriend.' She leaned back in the chair and her shoulders deflated. She seemed to shrink.

'Did it not go well?' Gabi asked. Amber let out a long breath.

'Actually, it went brilliantly,' she said with a rueful smile. 'They got on so well. I didn't realise how much Jayden was missing a man in his life until I saw him with Alex.'

'So, what happened?' Gabi sipped her coffee, but didn't take her eyes from Amber, who blinked sadly and bit her lip.

'I fell in love,' Amber said. Gabi raised her eyebrow. She hadn't known it was anything as serious as this. She let out a long, low whistle.

'Did you tell him how you felt?' Gabi asked and the women locked eyes.

'No, *I* didn't tell him that I loved him,' she said, emphasising the I. She pressed her lips together tightly as if in pain. 'But Jayden told him that *he* loved *him*.'

Gabi's eyes widened as Amber continued.

'I had no idea he felt that way. But he did.' Amber rubbed her face with both hands. 'In fact, I only found out after the event when Alex did a runner.'

'What?' Gabi gasped. 'Arsehole.' Amber nodded.

'I turned up at work one day and he just wasn't there. The manager told me he'd quit. I messaged him and he ghosted me. I knew then that something was very, very wrong. I went home that night and kept it a secret from Jayden. I still thought there must be a misunderstanding. Told myself all the usual bullshit we tell ourselves. Maybe Alex had suffered an accident. Maybe he'd lost his phone. Maybe he'd lost his memory!' She slapped herself on the forehead. 'But he hadn't. He'd left.'

'I can't believe it.' Gabi could see the impact of it in Amber's eyes as she told the story. The complete and utter disbelief. The hurt.

'I couldn't either. Especially when I finally told Jayden that Alex had left and Jayden confessed that he had told him he loved him. And when I put him to bed that night, he asked me, in all seriousness, if I thought he had scared Alex off. If he shouldn't have said anything. That nobody wanted him because he was deaf. Honestly, Gabi, my heart hurt for him.' Gabi reached over the wooden kitchen table and grasped her hand. Amber squeezed it back, so hard it grated Gabi's knuckles against each other.

'I'm a big girl, you know, Gabs. I can handle being hurt.' Pain flashed over Amber's face like an echo, showing it was still there. It wasn't over, despite her bravado. She straightened in the chair. 'But nobody breaks Jayden's heart and gets away with it.'

Gabi nodded. She might not have children of her own, but she had family, and she understood the ferocity of that sort of love. She'd do anything for Isabella. God save Etienne if he ever did the dirty on her.

Amber shook herself.

'So, we moved here. Fresh start and all that. And until that day in Tutto Mio, I hadn't seen him for almost two years. And if he was surprised by the slap, all I can say is he got away lightly.' Amber allowed herself a laugh, but she didn't sound amused.

'Do the others know?' Gabi asked quietly.

'Not all of it, no. It's tricky, what with him and Etienne being twins. I didn't want to cause any friction in the group.' Gabi nodded. Amber worked for Isabella at Tutto Mio and now that Isabella and Etienne were so loved up, she could see how it could cause problems.

'But he's still here!' Gabi said. 'How's that working out? Have you actually had a conversation with him since?'

'What on earth could he say that would mean anything to me?' Amber challenged and Gabi thought for a moment.

'Don't you even want to know why he left? Hear it from his side?'

Amber snorted. 'Nope.'

'Maybe he wants to apologise.' Gabi downed the rest of her coffee and turned the warm cup around in her hands.

'I just need to keep my distance. Better that way.' Amber sighed and rolled her blue eyes across the table. 'Especially because I still feel that connection.' Gabi's mouth fell open. She hadn't been expecting that.

'Still?' she said.

'Yup. The magnetism is strong in that one,' Amber admitted. 'Even though there is no future for us.' Amber stood and stretched her arms above her head, circling her shoulders.

'I'd better get ready for the restaurant,' she said, moving to put her mug in the dishwasher, picking up Jayden's cereal bowl as she went. 'Shall I make you some toast or any more coffee before I go?'

Gabi shook her head. 'Thanks, but I'll be fine.'

'What are you going to do with your day?' Amber said, nodding at Gabi's leg propped on the chair.

'I scheduled in a long snooze this morning.' Amber groaned with jealousy. 'And then I'm off to physio.'

'Will you be okay on your own?'

'Always am,' Gabi said, and Amber dropped a kiss on her cropped black hair as she left.

The physio session cleared any residual hangover that might have been clinging on and by the time Gabi hit the pavement afterwards, she felt the best she had all day. That was, until her phone pinged with a text. Her heart sank when she saw his name and realised it must be the first of April. Shame his text wasn't an April Fool.

**Papà**: How are you, Gabriella? Do you need anything?

Ha. As if he really wanted to know. She frowned and tapped out a reply.

**Gabi**: Actually, I had an accident, broke my leg, had surgery to pin it back together and have had to move in with a friend of Isabella's for six weeks minimum. So not great, no.

Her fingers hovered for just a second before she shook her head and deleted it. There was no point. Instead, she typed a few words and pressed send.

**Gabi**: I'm fine, thanks. And no, nothing at all.

She shoved the phone into her pocket before swinging determinedly down the street towards home. Her phone beeped again, and she stopped mid-stride. He never replied usually. Never. Something bubbled through her. Anxiety.

But the text, when she opened it, was from Walker. Which was a much nicer surprise and she happily pushed all thoughts of Papà to the back of her mind. A glimmer of guilt flashed through her, as she remembered Walker's face yesterday. He'd only been trying to do the right thing, to make sure she didn't hurt herself – or anyone else. He couldn't help it, she supposed. He didn't know her well enough to see that she'd be fine.

She clicked the message.

**Walker**: I found an earring. It was under the pole. Is it yours?

An image downloaded, and there was her gold stud. She never normally wore anything fancier – she couldn't when she was performing anyway; they got in the way of wigs or safety or equipment. She touched her earlobes, and the left one was empty. How had she not noticed this morning? Maybe she had been more hungover than she thought.

She typed back.

**Gabi**: Yes! Thanks. Can I pop by and pick it up?

She watched the ticks turn blue and then he sent a reply, saying that he was at the fire station and to swing by any time. She grinned again and swung straight around. No time like the present.

\*

Walker was inspecting the fire truck in the forecourt as she crossed the yard. She paused for a moment to catch her breath from the walk and admire the view. His braces hung around his waist, and his chest was snug in a fitted T-shirt. He looked like he could have walked out of a Diet Coke advert. Maybe he felt the weight of her stare because he turned around. She waved.

'That was quick!' he said, walking over and hitching his braces over his shoulders. As he approached, he put his hand in his trouser pocket and pulled out the earring. It glinted gold between his fingers as he passed it over.

'Thanks so much,' Gabi said. 'I didn't even realise I'd lost it.' She pulled the stud from its back and held it towards her ear.

'Don't you want to clean that first?' Walker said, a frown pinching between his eyebrows. 'It was on the floor.'

Gabi peered at the jewellery, and then popped it into her mouth, sucked it clean and stuck it into her ear.

'That's one way to do it, I suppose,' Walker said, 'but you don't know where that's been!'

She poked her tongue out at him briefly. 'I'm sure I've had worse in my mouth,' she said and grinned as he choked on a laugh.

'How does it feel to be a world record holder then, Walker?' Gabi asked when the stud was safely in place.

'Pretty good.' Walker nodded. His hazel eyes glinted suddenly, and he grinned. 'Who would have thought going up and down on a pole could be so much fun?'

Gabi snorted in surprise. So, there was a funny side to the hero too?

'The good thing is, we raised a lot of money for the fund.'

His eyes were serious again. Gabi had a sudden urge to bring back his playful side.

'It all went really well, I thought,' said Gabi. 'You seemed to have planned for all contingencies...' She flashed her own eyes at him, bit her lip. 'Apart from maybe a drunk woman with a broken leg deciding anything you can do, she can do better.'

'I think I did have that scenario in my risk-planning document actually,' smiled Walker. 'It was number one thousand and twenty-two.'

Gabi giggled. Her day was definitely on the up.

'And what about your lifting and carrying procedures? Were they all met when you caught me?' Gabi poked Walker in the chest and was surprised again by the solidity of his muscle.

'Funny, I would normally tip you over my shoulder in a proper fireman's lift...' he said, and he looked her up and down, as though considering it. 'But I think I managed okay.'

Gabi looked up at his face, remembering the angle of it yesterday as she was nestled against his chest, the jut of his jaw. The straight line of his nose.

'Walker!' someone called from the operations building. He turned and acknowledged them with a hand in the air.

'Better go,' he said, and she felt a rush of disappointment.

'Of course, me too,' she said with a shrug. 'I've got a pressing appointment too... with the sofa and a film.' He put his head on one side, eyes holding hers.

'You okay? Coping all right?'

She pulled herself upright, not wanting him to get the wrong impression. 'Oh yes, all fine,' she said with a shake of her head. 'It's just frustrating more than anything. I have to remember to put my phone in my pocket every time I move. Or carry a little bag around with me. But I can't carry anything because of the crutches, and you can't put a plate of sandwiches or a cup of coffee in your bag.' She shrugged too and then laughed. 'It's only for a short time.'

'Walker!' came the shout again.

He nodded towards the caller and she straightened, bracing herself for her first step home. Her underarms felt tender, her back ached. And she was now feeling the exertions of her physio. The sofa suddenly seemed quite appealing. She reached the crutches out and put her weight into the movement, when all of a sudden, her right stick slipped on something on the tarmac, a loose stone, which sent her tumbling forward into Walker's chest as her crutch skidded wildly to the right. Walker's arms caught her in an instant. His hold was like a metal band, strong and secure, and she gasped out loud, partly with the shock of the slip and partly with the jolt of his proximity.

She pushed herself upright, both hands on his torso.

'I'm all right,' she reassured him, even though he hadn't asked. 'I wouldn't have fallen.'

He shook his head, but didn't argue. Instead, he checked his watch.

'Do you want me to give you a lift home?' he asked. 'I'm off shift in ten.' Tempting. But no. She didn't need any help.

He was still holding her elbows, and her hands still spanned his chest. She picked up his braces between thumbs and forefingers and stretched them playfully towards her, looking straight into those hazel eyes, before letting them go with a snap onto his chest. He laughed, shocked.

'I told you, I can manage,' she grinned. 'But thanks.'

'Little Miss Independent . . .' he said.

'Less of the little,' she said with a wink as she transferred her weight away from him. Carefully manoeuvring now so as to prove herself, she turned slowly and hobbled away.

'See you soon, Gabi,' he called after her and she had the distinct feeling he was watching her go.

# Chapter Ten

*Walker*

It was little more than ten minutes later when Walker actually left the fire station, and by then he had plenty to think about. He'd been called in to talk to his boss, Appleby, who'd arrived unannounced at the station, wanting to talk about his future with the fire service. As he eased his car out of the forecourt, he felt the urge to drive and keep driving. It might ease his mind. He could do with the distraction.

Halfway up the big hill to town, he spotted a familiar sight. Gabi. Leaning against a wall for support, taking a breather. She obviously hadn't made it home yet. It couldn't be more perfect. He needed a distraction and there she was. He didn't think twice before flicking on an indicator and pulling in beside her. He lowered his window.

'Fancy a ride?' he asked, noticing her pink cheeks. No matter how fit she was, this hill must be a killer on crutches.

'I'm fine,' she insisted.

'I know you are,' he reassured her. 'I just fancied a drive.

Wondered if you wanted the scenic tour of Honeybridge?' She grinned and he watched her move towards the car. He rubbed his chest where the braces had pinged against him earlier. It hadn't hurt as much as shocked him. He could still feel her hands there on his chest. She was petite, Gabi. He guessed maybe five foot four in her trainers. And she looked smaller now that she was settled in his passenger seat, smiling expectantly. He waited for her to click her seat belt in before checking his mirror and easing out. Within minutes he was leaving the town and driving along country roads bordered by fields and farms. She gazed out of the window, and he heard her long, slow exhale.

'This is so different from where I live,' she said after a while, turning to face him. 'My apartment is on the top floor – the twelfth – of a complex. We have a doorman and a gym on site. And from my window, I can see the Thames and the London skyline. Which is stunning, but hardly any green at all.'

'Sounds fancy,' he said, two hands lightly turning the wheel. She laughed and it made him smile.

'And expensive,' he pushed and she laughed again.

'I bought it about five years ago after one of my films that year.' He remembered the monogrammed luggage sets that he'd carried for her. She was obviously well paid for what she did.

'You looking forward to getting back to work?' he asked, taking a turn to follow the wide, meandering river.

'Can't wait. Rang my agent a couple of days ago to update her on my recovery schedule. She'll start looking for appropriate roles for me. I'm always wanting the next one to be bigger. Better.'

'My boss wants me to take on a bigger role too,' he found

himself saying, but without the same excitement as she had in her voice. 'He literally just told me after you left.'

'A promotion?' Gabi asked, clapping her hands. 'Congratulations!'

Walker focused on his driving, remembering his Commander's praise. 'Seems they want me to consider taking the job as Station Commander for this area,' he said. Gabi clapped again.

'When do you start?'

He blinked. She made it sound so easy whereas just saying it out loud made his stomach drop. It was a lot of responsibility. What if he wasn't up to it?

'I asked if I could think about it,' he said, keeping his eyes on the road.

Gabi made a small noise of surprise. 'What's to think about?' she asked, sounding genuinely interested. He considered for a moment before replying.

'The existing Station Commander is a guy called Perkins. I've worked with him since I joined the brigade. And I've never seen him out of breath, or panicked, or flustered. Not at major car crashes on the motorway, or house fires where we've rescued sleeping babies, or even when we found an unexploded bomb on the old army site. He always takes everything in his stride, gives clear and concise orders and seems to have planned ahead for every eventuality.'

'So?' Gabi challenged

He slowed into a turn, expertly keeping his line on the road as he turned back into town.

'What if I can't do that?' He pressed his lips together to prevent himself saying anything else. He could sense Gabi watching him and he could feel the colour rising in his cheeks. When she spoke, she was unusually serious.

'They wouldn't ask you if they didn't think they could depend on you.'

He pulled up outside Amber's house, suddenly sorry he hadn't taken a longer route home. He ran round the car to open her door for her. She steadied her hand momentarily against his chest as she arranged her crutches.

'You should do it, Walker,' she said, looking up into his face, and then, over her shoulder as she swung up the path, she said, 'Honestly, what's stopping you?'

The words hung in the air between them as Walker watched her navigate the path and let herself in. What was stopping him? Good question. He climbed back into the car and reversed easily out of the drive, turning towards home, thinking. It was only as he pulled up outside that he acknowledged his fear to himself.

The truth was, everyone knew that when the time came, Perkins would always do exactly what he needed to do to save the day. But Walker couldn't say the same. He gripped the steering wheel, tight, and closed his eyes, trying to block out images that he only normally saw in his nightmares. He shook his head to clear them, not letting them in. Not letting fear win. But the doubt remained. His stomach tumbled away inside. What if, when it all came down to him, he froze in front of everyone, and they saw him for who he really was?

Later, Walker stood at the open fridge in his kitchen, staring blankly at the contents inside until the fridge alarm beeped. 'You all right, bud?' Alex pulled the braces away from Walker's back and let them snap. Walker yelped and bolted upright. Alex had used full force, as opposed to Gabi's playful little ping earlier. Alex laughed.

'Second person to do that today!' Walker said, turning back to the shelves. 'You in for dinner?' he asked without looking.

'Where else am I going to be?' Alex said. He had a point. Unless it was Tuesday or Thursday when he went out for band practice, Alex was usually home in the evenings. Depending on Walker's shifts, they sometimes met up with the Brothers from Another Mother for a couple of beers if Fox could get a babysitter or if Etienne could disentangle himself from Isabella. Both seemed quite hard to do lately. So, Walker and Alex had spent a lot of time together since Alex moved in. In fact, they'd become a bit of a double act around mealtimes.

'Right,' Walker said. 'Let's eat.' He rummaged inside the refrigerator, pulling out a tray of chicken thighs and grabbing a bag of fresh pasta which he tossed over his shoulder without warning. Alex caught it deftly and set it on the table, spinning on the spot immediately to catch the next items, tomatoes – which came flying one, two, three over Walker's shoulder – followed by a solitary onion. He placed them all next to the pasta, neat in a row, and got chopping. Walker turned on the music.

They moved around each other in the kitchen as though choreographed. Walker sidestepped when Alex passed him to get a saucepan. Alex ducked down to choose a saucepan from the bottom drawer as Walker swung open the cupboard door above his head to find the salt. The chicken was chopped and fried, Alex reaching over to sprinkle paprika in the pan as Walker stirred. The pasta was boiled and Walker threw in the salt. By the time the meal was ready to serve up, Walker had chopped feta cheese and Alex had opened them both a beer.

It might not have been restaurant standard – Etienne and Isabella would have made something much fancier – but it was good, healthy and protein rich, which both of them needed for their gym schedules.

'Table or lap?' Alex asked as they plated up the food.

Walker laughed. 'Lap. I'm knackered.'

Alex grabbed two trays and passed one over. A minute later they were side by side on the sofa, Walker's ginger rescue cat, Fatboy Jim, squished in between them, TV on and tucking in.

'You're like my wife,' Walker said, over a mouthful.

'Get out of it, mate,' Alex said. 'You're like my wife.'

Walker coughed and swallowed his mouthful.

'We need to get out more.'

'True, that.'

They ate in silence for a moment or two, watching a car show on TV.

'But it's also nice just to have some company at home, you know?' Walker said, thinking how his mood had improved once he'd got home from work. Having Alex there was good for him. It stopped him spiralling or his thoughts crowding into his head. It distracted him.

'I know, mate. And it's good not having to worry that every time I enter a room, I might catch my brother or his girlfriend in various stages of undress.' Walker laughed. He'd seen for himself the lovestruck look on Etienne's face that had been pretty much permanent since last autumn. The guy just couldn't get enough of Isabella. And by the way Isabella wrapped herself around her man, the feeling was mutual. Walker couldn't remember feeling that intensity with his ex-girlfriend Mia. It had felt more like a warmth, rather than a fire.

'Have you ever lived with a girlfriend?' Walker asked as he speared his last bit of chicken.

Alex shook his head, chewing.

'Been close?'

'Yup.'

This was news.

'When?'

'Few years ago.' Alex contorted his face at the memory. 'Well, I hoped it was heading that way anyway. With Amber.' He put his knife and fork down and sighed. 'I thought I'd end up living with her and Jayden.'

Walker choked on his chicken. Alex slammed him on the back. Fatboy Jim opened one eye to check he wasn't going to die and then closed it again.

'I didn't realise it had been that serious,' he said when he could talk.

'Ancient history now, mate.' Alex settled back into the sofa.

'What happened?' Walker asked, far more interested in this story than the prattling presenter on television. Alex took a pull of his own beer and then began.

'I fucked up, mate. That's what happened. I did what I always did when things got tough. I ran away rather than stay and sort things out.'

Walker knew Alex's history. He'd heard from Etienne how Alex had become addicted to gambling in his late teens. How it started with arcade games and fruit machines. After their parents died in a car crash, Alex had sought to escape his grief in backroom poker games run by the local gangsters with impossibly high stakes. He'd run up a massive gambling debt and had to run away for his own safety when he couldn't repay it. He'd lived almost on the run like that for four long years. It was when he contacted Etienne again after all that time, asking for help to repay the debt and regain his life, that Etienne had enlisted the help of Walker and Fox, and they'd made a plan to bring him back. Which didn't quite go to plan and ended up with an attack at Tutto Mio and the first gunshot injury in Honeybridge in a decade. None of them had known of the romance between Alex and Amber, who had moved to the town a year or so before Alex arrived. When they found out there had been a relationship, everyone had presumed a one-night wonder, or perhaps a brief fling, because neither party seemed to want to go into detail. In fact, if he was honest about it, Walker had presumed Alex had cheated on Amber because she seemed to want nothing to do with him. 'Why did you run?'

'Long story, Walks. Let's just say I made the wrong call. I thought I was making the right move, but I made the wrong bet.'

Walker sipped his beer thoughtfully.

'Anything still there?' he asked.

Alex shrugged. 'Wouldn't matter if there was,' he said. 'She hates me. She moves away if I get anywhere near her.' He screwed his eyes closed. 'I really fucked it up.'

'So, you don't think she feels anything?'

Alex exhaled slowly through his nose.

'I *hope* she still feels the connection,' he said. 'But she's definitely not letting herself act on it.' He half laughed and Fatboy snapped out a paw in surprise and caught Alex's hand in his claws.

'Steady there, boy,' Alex said, holding very still until the cat relaxed again and went back to purring. 'Anyway, enough about that. Who else snapped your braces today then?' Alex abruptly changed the subject. Gabi's face flashed into Walker's mind – her smile as she looked up at him, leaning against his chest.

'Gabi,' he said.

'Feisty,' Alex said.

Walker snorted. It was a good word for Gabi. Feisty. Funny. Feminine. Flirty? He caught himself with the last one. He saw the flash of her eyes under her dark lashes as she laughed. They had been flirting earlier. Just a little, but there had definitely been something there. And the way she'd listened in the car had been surprising. Her encouragement of him to take the promotion. He'd add another F. Fearless. She was all the Fs.

'She came by for her earring. She was saying she finds it hard in the day when she's on her own to move about, to carry things.'

'I can imagine,' Alex said, standing and lifting his tray from his lap at the same time. 'I'll sort the kitchen.'

'Thanks, darling,' Walker smiled.

'Fuck off.' Alex laughed.

Walker watched him go but his mind was lingering on Gabi's face.

# Chapter Eleven

## Gabi

Isabella waved Gabi towards what had already, in the few weeks she'd been in town, become their usual table in Tutto Mio. Cosy in the corner next to the window, it was set up for two, complete with a vase of fresh white tulips. Gabi sat and positioned her foot, leaning her crutches against the wall, and waited for Isabella with the coffee.

Funny how quickly she'd settled in to Honeybridge. She knew her way around the kitchen at Amber's, and Jayden's favourite snacks after school. She was fast becoming her physio's favourite client for all the work she was putting in. She could see her cousin every day if she wanted to, and she got to give Nonna a hug whenever she liked.

Isabella brought a tray with her, laden with frothy coffees and biscuits. Gabi groaned at the sight of them, knowing they were homemade by Nonna, and therefore impossible to resist.

'How do you stay so slim?' she asked, reaching for one already. 'With these to tempt you all the time?'

'Let's just say, I do a lot of a certain exercise . . .' Isabella's eyes twinkled, and Gabi shook her head with a laugh. There was no denying that Isabella and Etienne were mad about each other. Gabi saw the way they looked at each other, the way they could almost tell what the other was thinking. The little touches, reassurances, smiles. It was as though they were in their own little bubble, dependent only on each other. It might look idyllic, but Gabi didn't ever want to depend on someone like that. They'd only let you down eventually.

Isabella was excited, telling her she was hoping to book a holiday in the summer with Etienne.

'Just a week,' she said. 'It's so difficult for us to both leave the restaurants.'

'Where will you go?' Gabi asked, blowing her steaming coffee.

'Italy!' Isabella said, as if there really was no other answer. 'Nonna said we can use the house and that way I can show Etienne all of the old places. The lakes, the mountains – a real trip down memory lane.'

Gabi took a big gulp, and the coffee scorched her throat. She coughed.

'Mamma and Papà might meet us there too for a few days, now that they are home from their travels.'

'Amazing,' Gabi managed, feeling a stab of jealousy which she tried to swallow alongside her coffee. She coughed again. Isabella reached a hand across the table suddenly and held hers.

'You could come?' Isabella said hopefully.

'And crash your sex fest?' Gabi tried to laugh it off. 'No thanks!' Isabella held on.

'Have you heard anything from your papà?' she asked quietly.

'Just the usual,' she said. Gabi forced a smile to make Isabella stop frowning. 'You know he's not much of a talker.' Gabi shrugged.

She remembered the dip on her bed as a child as Papà sat, the weight of him being there dragging her down inside too. Knowing that he wanted to talk to her about her day – only to find out what her mamma had done. The furrow on his brow, the way he twisted his fingers together when she told him that Mamma had gone out in a new dress. She knew that what she told him was hurting him, but she couldn't tell a lie. That was bad too, she knew that. He'd sigh and ruffle her hair or bend to kiss her cheek before he left, and she'd wish with all her might he would pull her to him and hold her tight. To stop the feeling that something was wrong. To show her she wasn't alone.

'Ancient history,' she said now with a shrug. 'I'm fine on my own, you know that.'

'You're not on your own, Gabi. You know that too.' Gabi squeezed Isabella's hand back. Isabella relaxed and then said, 'The other thing I meant to ask you was whether you'd help out Rosie and Wren on Thursday evening?'

'If I can . . .' Gabi said, interested.

'They need a reader for Story Stars – it's an event where they have a different person reading the bedtime story for the kids each week. But this week was meant to be that famous actor who lives up the river – I forget his name – but he's cancelled last minute. And they've sold tickets for charity – because it's a special, celebrity one-off. So, they asked if you could do it instead?'

Gabi laughed. 'Me? Why me?'

'You've been in films!' Isabella said.

'But nobody knows who I am!' Gabi laughed.

'Doesn't matter.' Isabella flapped a hand, dismissing Gabi's concerns. 'Rosie said she'd put up movie posters and images showing you in action.'

Gabi hesitated.

'It's just a bit of fun, honestly. The kids love the books. The adults only come for the wine. All the yummy mummies turn out when Fox or Walker read.'

'They do it too?' Gabi said. Isabella nodded.

'And let's face it, you're the closest thing to a famous person we've got,' she said, serious again. 'We need you.'

Gabi smiled at the unexpected surge of pleasure she felt.

'Okay,' she said with a rush of confidence. 'I'll do it.'

She noticed the clock on the wall behind Isabella's head and downed the rest of her coffee.

'Got to run. I've got my induction at the gym.'

She dropped a kiss on her cousin's cheek and blew one more to Nonna in the kitchen as she left Tutto Mio.

# Chapter Twelve

*Walker*

Walker stared hard at himself in the mirror at the gym as he worked his way through his weight reps. He was almost at the end of his set and yet he wasn't feeling the normal satisfaction, or release, that came with exhaustion. Instead, he was jangled.

It had been a long week since the pole-a-thon. Earlier that day Appleby had visited the station. He'd called together a team briefing and announced that the results had finally been officially verified and the accounts signed off. They'd raised over ten thousand pounds. It was an even better fundraiser than the annual open day. Appleby had congratulated everyone, but made a point of thanking Walker in particular for his organisation and execution of the day, saying it was commitment like this that made the difference in the service. That creating opportunities like this took you on to bigger and brighter things. Walker had felt the weight of the comment. He hadn't responded yet to the conversation about the promotion and Appleby's searching eyes as he shook his hand told him he was getting impatient to hear his decision. Walker had just looked away, his stomach dropping.

Now, he swapped his hand weights for a heavier pair. His biceps bulged as he started his curls, welcoming the pain that went with them, lifting until his arms shook.

The anxiety sitting in his gut about the promotion had only got worse when he got home from shift and opened his post. Aside from the usual circulars and promos there was a formal-looking white envelope and when he opened it, the first thing he spotted was the mayoral badge at the top of the paper. Then the signature at the bottom – in actual ink. Laurence Higginbottom. He scanned the page quickly and then forced himself to read it again, trying to make sense of the words. He, Walker McBride, was being nominated for a new award, the Everyday Hero Award, in the Honeybridge Annual Community Awards in May. The words punched him hard in the gut. There must be some mistake. He read on. He was to be invited to the awards ceremony evening where the winners would be announced. It was to be attended by all nominees and their guests, as well as local media and dignitaries. The mayor wanted to congratulate him on the nomination, which was testament to the bravery he showed every day, and wished him well for the evening. He looked at the words again. *For the bravery he shows every day.* He'd thrown the letter in the bin. For fuck's sake. If only they knew.

He moved over to the punching bag and pulled on his gloves, wanting to hit something, hurt something, obliterate his memories. He was the last person he knew that deserved a promotion. The worst choice for a bravery award. He threw frantic punches until the sweat ran into his eyes and he collapsed against the bag, his breath rasping. It was only as he hung there, panting, that he spotted Gabi watching him in the mirror. He was surprised by the easy smile that sprang to her face when he looked her way. She began to hobble over the short space in her boot, leaving her crutches propped against the wall. She looked good in her kit. But he was not in the mood for small talk.

'Hi!' she said, pink-cheeked with exertion.

'I didn't know you'd joined?' he said, keeping his eyes above the neck, very aware of her toned abs showing between her bra top and leggings.

'I need to stay fit,' she said, fanning her face. 'And I'm determined to beat my physio schedule.'

He nodded, unable to think of the next thing to say. Wishing he could have the same determination to rise to a challenge, but his gut still churning at the thought of the letter. The responsibility.

'You looked like you were really in the zone,' Gabi continued.

He pawed at his glove, trying to free the strap to remove it. But it was impossible without use of his fingers. His gloves knocked together pointlessly. Gabi laughed lightly and pulled his hand towards her, resting the glove against her taut stomach to undo the tie at the wrist. He could see the gentle rise and fall of her chest as she concentrated. He looked away.

'There,' she said, holding the glove for him to remove his right hand.

'Thanks,' he said, turning his attention to the left. Still, he couldn't think of anything to add. There was only one award he should be nominated for. Loser of the year. In fact, decade. He sighed and dropped the gloves to the mat.

'Sorry, I'm probably interrupting . . .' He watched Gabi bite her lip and start to turn. 'I'll leave you to it.'

'No,' he said in a rush of guilt. 'Honestly. I'm finished actually.' It was true, his whole body was heavy with fatigue. She tilted her head to check his expression. 'My head was just somewhere else,' he said. 'Sorry.'

'Thought it might be. You looked like you were working off some serious frustration.' She mimed a little jab, an upper cut, and grinned. He exhaled slowly.

'That bad, huh?' she said.

'Worse,' he said, surprising himself.

'Want to talk about it?' she asked, and then, when the pause grew too long, 'Of course you don't. Sorry, I wasn't trying to be nosy.'

He could tell she was going to leave.

'I've been nominated for an award by the council – Everyday Hero of Honeybridge.' The words fell out of him, and he realised just how much he did want to talk about it.

She paused and perched instead on the edge of the nearest bench to take the weight from her foot, and her lips curled into the biggest smile.

'That's amazing, Walker!' she said and then, taking in the look on his face, she frowned. 'But you obviously don't think so?'

'It's such a big deal, you know?' he said. 'It feels . . . heavy on me. Like people expect a lot of me.'

Gabi paused, her eyes holding his while she considered her response.

'But isn't this to recognise things you've already done?' she asked. 'To thank you for something in the past?'

Walker screwed up his nose. 'I think it's to do with the fire last year at Hearts of Honeybridge.'

'Sounds like a good reason.'

'But people are expecting more of me now because of it. The promotion. The award. They're all relying on me. It makes me feel a bit . . . panicked.'

'I can understand that,' Gabi said. 'You're in a responsible position. But you've coped well so far.'

'Not always,' Walker said, pushing his damp hair from his forehead and sinking to the bench beside her.

The image of his breath pluming in front of his face made Walker close his eyes, but the blackness behind his eyelids made him remember a million nightmares. He'd wake to crumpled sheets and crying out. He'd slept with a nightlight until he'd almost left secondary school. This was the part of his life he kept hidden. The fear. He opened them again and she was still watching him, an open, curious look on her face.

'I used to suffer with anxiety,' he said in the understatement of the year. 'And now, it feels like people's expectations of me are getting higher. Like I have more riding on me. What if I make a wrong decision and someone gets hurt? Worse still, what if I make the right decision – *but too slowly* – and someone dies?'

He exhaled deeply and met Gabi's eyes again.

'It's a lot of pressure, I can see that.' Gabi was listening. Really listening. Walker suddenly wanted to tell her everything, the whole story. It had been inside him for so long. He'd never even told Rosie. But where to start?

'You're obviously bloody good at your job, Walker,' Gabi said. 'If they want you to take the lead at work, it's because they all trust you to do the right thing. You are an everyday hero. Just keep doing what you're doing. One day at a time. It's absolutely the right award for you to be nominated for.'

Walker exhaled. He was feeling calmer. One day at a time was good advice. Gabi's reassurances had helped.

'And you haven't even won it yet, you've only been nominated! So don't be worrying about that.' She laughed outright. 'You might be up against a doctor who has been working on a new cancer cure, or a nurse who gave her own blood in an operation.'

Walker chuckled.

'Or someone who gave mouth-to-mouth to a guide dog to keep it alive for his blind neighbour!' Walker let go and laughed.

'True,' he agreed. 'There's nothing to say I'm going to win.'

'Exactly, so even if I think you easily deserve the award, try to stop worrying about winning it. Have a bit of fun.' She grinned encouragingly. 'Right, now. I'd better get back to it.' She turned and began to hobble back to her bench. 'See you around.'

'Thanks, Gabi,' Walker said, finally allowing his eyes to drop to admire her bum.

# Chapter Thirteen

*Gabi*

The Lit Lounge was laid out and ready for Story Stars. A long wooden table bulged with crisps, biscuits, vegetables and hummus at one end, and an array of wine glasses and bottles at the other. The walls were adorned with children's drawings of Easter eggs and bright yellow chicks, and the place was packed with people on Easter holidays looking for entertainment.

Wren was on the door, checking tickets and greeting people. Rosie was organising tiny children's wooden chairs in a semi-circle, leaving a good amount of space at the front for Gabi's leg on the carpet when she sat in the reading chair. The resident bookshop cats were draped over shelves, curled up in reading corners or stretched out in the window.

Gabi was strangely nervous. This was right out of her comfort zone. Tell her to swing on a trapeze thirty feet above the ground? Fine. Jump from a second-floor window as though catapulted by an explosion inside? No problem. Face a group of chattering children and read them a book? Terrifying. But she was determined to think of it as a new stunt to be conquered. She was ready for it.

'Got your book ready?' Rosie asked, appearing beside her. Gabi swallowed and waved the book in her hand. Rosie squeezed her shoulder and turned to help a family find what they were looking for. Children seemed to be everywhere. More than Gabi had ever seen in one place at one time before. On chairs and under them, behind curtains, running around bookshelves, rolling on the mat. The excitement levels were deafening.

She'd never had the maternal urge. Hardly surprising, given the family example she'd been set by her mamma and papà. But she had thought that desire to have a baby might kick in as she worked her way through her twenties and turned thirty. That biological clock she heard people talk about. But her feelings hadn't changed. And as she observed the chaos in the bookshop around her, she wasn't unhappy about that.

Looking at the book in her hands, she wracked her brains to see if she could remember books being a part of her life when she was a child. Had her mamma read to her in bed? Had her papà ever taken her to the bookshop and let her choose a new book? She snorted. The woman next to her jumped and she waved apologetically and pretended to blow her nose. The only thing she could remember her mother buying her was a video recorder, so that Gabriella could watch more action movies and stay out of her way. And as for her papà? The biggest thing he'd ever bought her was a one-way ticket to stay with her zio, zia and Isabella.

She sighed. These children were already winning at life, she decided. They had someone who cared about them enough to bring them to a bookshop.

'Ready for action?' Fox said, strolling towards her, wearing his signature checked shirt and a twinkling smile.

'As I'll ever be . . .' Gabi said. 'Although I'm not really sure what I've let myself in for.'

Fox slung an arm around her shoulder and she leaned against him momentarily. 'Nothing a daring stuntwoman can't handle,' he joked and she nudged him in the ribs.

'Can I shout cut at the end?' Alex grinned, appearing beside him, guitar on his back.

'Don't worry, they don't bite,' said Etienne, bringing up the rear.

'Ha ha.' Gabi grimaced.

'Actually, that's not strictly true . . .' said Fox. 'Little Tommy Malone bit my leg when I was reading. Luckily, he only had baby teeth, so it didn't really hurt.'

Gabi spluttered.

'You'll be all right, though.' Fox nodded at her boot. 'He can't get to yours.'

'What am I doing?' Gabi groaned, banging the book on her forehead.

Isabella and Amber joined the group, both with large glasses of white wine in their hands. Isabella lowered the book from Gabi's face to kiss her, and Gabi smelled the lemon scent of her shampoo, felt the reassuring touch of her free hand on her arm.

Isabella smelled like family, like home, or the closest thing she had to it. Gabi had tried using that shampoo herself, but it wasn't the same. She squeezed Isabella's hand in return.

'I need one of those.' She nodded at the wine.

'Afterwards!' Isabella said, moving the bottle out of the way.

'Spoilsport,' hissed Gabi.

'You can't be drunk as the reader,' Isabella chided.

'There's a first time for everything,' Gabi said.

Someone moved in next to her. She turned, directly into Walker's chest as he joined the group. Her eyes were yet again level with his pecs. The pecs that she knew were rock hard under that T-shirt. She'd felt them at the fire station and eyed them at the gym when he wasn't looking. She forced her gaze upwards, and he was smiling down at her.

'Looking forward to your performance,' he said. 'Hope they let you finish and don't cut you off like the last guy.'

Gabi felt her mouth fall open.

'What! They heckle too?'

He laughed.

'I wouldn't call it heckling. They just get bored or restless and lose their concentration.'

'Shit, shit, shit,' Gabi muttered with feeling.

Isabella nudged her sharply and nodded at the toddler watching them from her vantage point on her father's shoulders. 'Language,' she whispered quietly. The girl had big brown eyes. She fixed them on Gabi.

'Shit,' the little girl said quite clearly.

Walker laughed. 'Now look what you've done!' He steered her away, tucking them into the book corner with her back to the child.

'What are you reading?' Walker asked. Gabi held up her book.

'It's about a girl who isn't great at school, but she's brilliant in the circus,' she said.

'Why did you choose that?' he asked, flipping the pages.

Gabi's voice dropped now with urgency. 'To show the kids that they can do whatever they want to do. They can be whatever they want to be, they just need to be brave and give things a go.'

His mouth curled upwards, and she felt a small glow of pleasure that she'd made him smile. He'd looked so worried the other day at the gym. 'You're going to be just fine,' he said. 'They're going to love it.' She didn't have time to thank him as Rosie called for attention at the front and began her introduction.

'Here she is, our guest reader for the night: Gabriella Tucci. The best stuntwoman in the business. She works in Hollywood and all around the world doing death-defying action shots for the movies.'

The children gasped while Isabella cheered.

'Over to you, Gabi!' Rosie started clapping, and the children followed on. Gabi shifted slightly in her seat and took a deep breath. Time to take to the high board and jump. She dropped her eyes to the book, and then leaned forward to bring her face to the children's height.

'Today's story will make you gasp,' she said, with a loud intake of breath which the children copied. 'It will make you cheer!' She raised her fists in the air and the children whooped. 'And it might even make you scream!' The children shrieked and several parents put their hands over their ears, while the cats all scarpered. Grinning, Gabi opened the book and cleared her throat. She was off.

# Chapter Fourteen

## Walker

'Well, well. Gabi is a woman of many talents,' said Alex, placing his empty beer bottle on the nearest table. 'The kids loved it.'

'I quite enjoyed it too,' said Walker truthfully.

He was impressed. Gabi had them in the palm of her hand for every page. They couldn't help but be swept along with the story, when Gabi read it as she did, acting out the words and using a French accent that made Alex and Etienne nod in appreciation when she read the words of the circus master.

Alex laughed and then cut it off abruptly as Amber bumped into him. She was head down, looking for something on the floor, and didn't realise who she was standing in front of until she raised her head.

'Hi . . .' Alex stammered.

'Oh. Hi,' said Amber, a flash of something passing over her face. Walker didn't bother saying hello as nobody was interested in him anyway.

He saw a tiny smile on Alex's mouth.

'How have you been?' Alex asked.

'Oh, you know. Busy. Working mum. No time to waste on stuff that doesn't count.'

Alex flinched but then reached out to touch her wrist. She looked at the contact; they both did. Walker took a half-step back. He felt like he was right in the middle of something.

'Do you fancy a coffee sometime?' Alex pressed. 'We could talk.'

Amber raised her ocean-coloured eyes and Walker almost whistled out loud. She was going to say yes, he could see it. Her face was full of emotion. She wanted to meet him; he'd put money on that. And it wasn't even him that was the reformed gambler.

'There's nothing to say, Alex . . .' Her halo of curls shimmered with a minute shake of her head, but her voice was soft.

'I know you still feel it, Amber,' Alex said. 'I do too.' Walker edged another half-step away and tried to give them some space. Jayden unfortunately had different ideas and when he spied them together, ran up and skidded to a halt between them. He looked first at his mum's face and then Alex's, ready to read their lips.

Amber snapped her hand away and her face changed. She glanced at Jayden and then back at Alex. Her eyes were now shooting bullets and Walker was glad he was out of the firing line.

'No time, as I said, for things that don't mean anything.' This time, her voice was sharp. 'Come on, Jayden.' Amber tugged the boy by the hand and headed for the exit. Walker saw Jayden turn and put a hand up to Alex in goodbye and watched Alex wave sadly back.

'Wow, I thought you were getting somewhere there. But she's still really angry at you,' Walker said.

Alex shrugged. 'Told you, man.' He heaved his guitar onto his back. 'Anyway, gotta go to practice. See you later at home.'

Gabi arrived back in the circle as Alex left, her cheeks pink and her eyes bright.

'I just got asked for my autograph!' She laughed.

The guests were leaving around them and the gang followed suit. Fox had to take the boys home to bed. Isabella kissed Gabi goodbye and left, wrapped up in Etienne. The shop emptied in five minutes, leaving it strewn with glasses and snack bowls and napkins.

'Stay, Gabi,' Wren said from the counter, opening a bottle of wine. 'We owe you a drink to say thank you. That was a five-star performance.' She poured her a glass of wine and brought it over.

'And Walker – you stay too,' Rosie added, passing him a beer and leaning against his chest briefly. 'I haven't seen you for ages.'

'I can help you clear up,' he offered.

'In a bit,' Rosie said, pouring herself and Wren a large glass of water.

They all collapsed into the comfy chairs, discussing the evening and laughing about the kids' questions at the end. Gabi had surprised them all, admitting to diving through windows, doing the high trapeze and getting shot out of a cannon.

Gabi was just telling them about a stunt involving an umbrella when Rosie's phone rang. 'It's the babysitter,' she said, answering with a frown on her face. She listened, agreed, then hung up the phone and stood in one movement.

'Riley's thrown up,' she said to Wren. 'And has a fever.'

Wren stood too, immediately, then looked around the bookshop at the debris that remained. Walker spoke without hesitation.

'You two go, I'll clear up.'

The two women glanced at each other and then Wren threw the bookshop keys through the air in a high arc. Walker caught them in one hand.

'Walker to the rescue,' Rosie said, already pulling on her coat.

'We owe you,' she said, as she hurried out the door.

'I'll drop the keys through your letter box,' he said. 'Text me later how she is.' Wren turned off the main lights as she went, leaving Walker and Gabi in the lamplight in their reading corner.

The bell jangled as the door shut and then it was just the two of them. And about four hundred cats. One of them butted against his shins and he bent to stroke it.

'Do you like cats?' Gabi asked. She looked more relaxed now, snuggled into the corner of the chair.

'Love them,' he said. 'I've got one of my own. Fatboy Jim. He's the biggest ginger cat you've ever seen. More like a small dog.'

Gabi laughed and sipped her wine.

'Not that you would have believed it when I first rescued him. Someone dumped him by the bins at the fire station. He was the most pathetic little thing I'd ever seen. Hardly more than a few weeks old.'

He gave the cat at his feet a final stroke and sat back in his chair, taking a pull of his beer.

'Have you got pets?' he asked.

Gabi shook her head, thinking of her penthouse, all glass and stainless steel and white walls. Hardly cat territory.

'What about when you were a kid?' he asked. She shook her head again and looked away.

'We weren't a very cosy kind of family,' she said eventually. 'Which is probably why tonight felt right out of my comfort zone. My parents never read to me.'

Walker felt his eyes widen.

'Never?' he asked.

'Mamma only liked fashion magazines and there's not much to read to your daughter in *Vogue* . . .'

'And your dad?'

'He was away on business a lot,' Gabi said. She rolled her shoulders against the back of the sofa and groaned.

'You okay?' Walker asked.

'It's just these crutches. They're such a pain. I can't carry anything with them. I already owe Amber three mugs that I've broken. And they're agony on your shoulders after a while.' She closed her eyes momentarily and rocked her head side to side to relieve her neck. 'Maybe I need a good massage.' The words hung in the air between them as he watched her, remembering the feel of her body in his arms when he caught her. The shape of her body at the gym.

'I can do that,' he said, suddenly wanting to, very much indeed.

She glanced at him and there was that challenge in her eyes again. That glint of mischief.

'Are you any good?' she asked, one eyebrow raised. He stood, smiling.

'I'll let you be the judge of that,' he said.

Walker moved to the back of her chair, looking down on the crown of her head. He rubbed his palms together briskly to warm them before taking gentle hold of her cardigan and sliding it from each shoulder, leaving her shoulders bare apart from the straps of her vest top. He heard her take a deep breath of anticipation and he saw the rise of her breast.

For a few seconds he just rested his palms on her shoulders, feeling the heat of her skin. She made the tiniest sound, almost inaudible, at the contact. Moving slowly, he ran his thumbs up either side of her spine and then began a gentle, rolling massage movement over her shoulders which drew out an inadvertent, louder moan. Walker laughed low in his throat.

'Your muscles are so tight,' he said softly. 'I can feel how much you need this.'

He felt Gabi relax under his fingers as he concentrated his energy, his focus, his feeling into his palms. He saw the tic of a pulse at the side of her neck, letting his fingers move over her collarbones, her throat. He wasn't aware of the bookshop around him. He was just lost in the rhythm, the pressure, the rub and press of his fingers on her skin. Her body seemed to spark under his hands, and it was lighting something within him.

'Good?' Walker asked, his mouth bent close to her ear. Her head dropped backwards towards him; her lips fell apart. God, he hoped it was good. Her body was like fire. He couldn't help but imagine moving down from her shoulders, exploring her body with his hands, his mouth.

The jangle of the doorbell jolted them out of the spell. Rosie stood in the shop doorway, wide-eyed, open-mouthed.

'Oops,' Rosie said with a little giggle. 'I came back to help sort the shop out. Maybe I should have stayed home.'

Gabi recovered quicker than he did. She coughed and straightened, shrugging herself back into her cardigan.

'Not at all!' Gabi said. 'Walker was just relieving my tension.'

'I bet he was.' Rosie laughed. Walker found he'd lost the ability to speak. His fingers still tingled with the energy that had forged between them.

'So that I can help with the clearing up!' Gabi said.

'I can't let you do that!' Rosie said. 'You're our star performer. And you can't carry anything either. So, I'll drop you home and then come back and help Walker.'

It was decided. Gabi threw him a look, playful, naughty even, and Walker watched her as she swung through the door. The feel of her under his fingers had started a fire burning.

It was Gabi herself that had told him to enjoy life. To have fun. So, maybe a little distraction with Gabi for the next couple of months was exactly what he needed.

# Chapter Fifteen

## Gabi

Gabi was feeling good the day after Story Stars. She'd had a surprisingly sexy dream about a masseur with wandering hands and woken up with a huge grin on her face. Walker certainly had a magic touch. She'd been sliding down that chair under his fingers, and God knows what would have happened if Rosie hadn't come back, but she had a pretty good idea.

For the rest of the week, Gabi found herself chatting to people who had been in the audience at the Lit Lounge. When she took Jayden to the park after school, children ran to her at the park bench to ask questions about stunts. People called her name in the street and waved across the road when they spotted her. She made an effort to remember names and faces, committing them to memory as soon as she heard them. She'd even had an invitation from the local secondary school to go in and give a talk on being a stuntwoman and a call from the local radio station to do an interview on air about her career. It was amazing how quickly her name had got around. She wasn't used to being known. Not as a local. It was strange.

Gabi's job usually took her away so much, she didn't really feel like she belonged where she lived. The only person she knew in her entire building was the doorman, and he wasn't exactly chatty. He only glanced up from his newspaper long enough to check you were a resident in the building and in the three years she'd lived there, he hadn't once called her by name.

It was the same when she was away on a shoot. People knew who she was, but she had a part to be played. It was a job. She came in when necessary and performed whatever death-defying stunt she was employed to do, and then she left again. She was on nodding acquaintance with some of the directors as they moved between different jobs. She recognised some of the make-up artists or set builders, but it was a transient community. Nobody stayed still. Everyone was always looking for the next gig. It didn't lend itself to lasting relationships. Not even deep friendships.

The local coffee shop didn't know Gabi's order. In fact, some of the baristas were new every time she went in there. She didn't have a 'table' at the local pub. She didn't even have a local pub, come to think of it. The last few weeks were beginning to feel like a familiar, pleasant holiday destination she could come back to sometime, although as soon as this boot was off, so was she. Back to reality. Back to her life.

The front door slammed so hard it literally shook the house. She started. Jayden rounded the corner and shot his bag at the hook without looking. His face was thunderous.

'What is it?' Gabi asked, throwing her hands up in question.

He shook his head, looking so much like Amber when she was fierce.

He threw himself down in the chair, almost knocking over her coffee. He grabbed a pen and leaned over the page. A few seconds later, he held it up. A sentence in spiky writing, almost joined up but not quite.

*We have to do a family tree.*

He folded his arms, bottom lip protruding. Gabi breathed out, feeling the frustration coming off him in waves.

'For a project?' she asked.

He banged the table with his hand and signed something furiously at her. She frowned and pointed at the pen again. He sighed, wrote just two words and held the pad up for her.

It had the word *Mum* at the top. Then an arrow to the word *Me* at the bottom.

He threw his hands up.

She reached over for his chair, surprising herself – and Jayden. She pulled his chair closer until she could put an arm around his shoulder. His ten-year-old body trembled with emotion, and she was struck by the intensity of it. Because she recognised it. She had felt the same. She still did sometimes.

Taking the paper from him, she drew her own family tree. She put the word *Mamma* in the top left-hand corner. The word *Papà* in the top right-hand corner. Then the word *Me* at the bottom in the middle. She purposefully didn't draw arrows linking any of them together.

Jayden raised his eyes to her and then flicked his finger between them, as though demonstrating he and she were the same, but Gabi shook her head.

'Not the same,' she said, 'because you have a mum who loves you very much.'

Gabi leaned forwards, determined to make Jayden feel better.

'We can ask your mum tonight about her family in Jamaica,' Gabi said, pulling his page towards her. She chose a bright red pen and wrote aunts, uncles, cousins, Grandma, Grandpa on his sheet around the word *Me*. His face brightened.

'And we could put on all the people that love you as family here in Honeybridge. They're just as good as family.' She wrote Rosie, Wren, Riley and added exclamation marks. Round the edges of the paper, she added Fox and his boys, Walker, Etienne, Isabella.

Suddenly the page looked full to bursting. She glanced back at her sheet beside it on the table. The word *Me* sat in splendid isolation at the bottom in the middle of the page. Who could she add apart from Isabella, Zio and Zia? Nobody.

Jayden picked up both pages and compared them in his hands. His full one. Her empty one. Picking up the pen again, he bent his head and circled one word on her page. Dad. The moment sat heavy between them. Gabi was so far out of her depth she needed a life belt. She knew Jayden's dad had left when Jayden's hearing loss was confirmed and had never shown his face again. She knew that since then, the only man Jayden had had a relationship with was Alex and it hadn't ended well. Her heart hammered.

Jayden took the pen.

*I wish I had a dad.*

There it was. A simple truth. She sighed and nodded, realising the only thing she could do was acknowledge his feelings. She'd had the latest text from her papà yesterday, on the first of May.

And even though she knew her papà, the same words rang true for her. She wished she had a dad.

'But your mum is a ten out of ten,' she said, nudging him. The mood needed changing, and Gabi knew just how to do it. Something physical which would shake him up and out of his gloom. Something that would make them both laugh.

'Let's do something different tonight,' she said. 'Go and get changed. I'm going to teach you how to fall – safely. You're going to be a stuntman.'

His eyes lit up and he surprised her with a hot, small-boy hug before racing from the room. Great, his worries were already forgotten. She wished she could forget her family worries as easily. She started looking around for something they could use as a crash pad when the doorbell rang.

She limped her way down the hall and opened the front door to a very unexpected pleasure. Walker.

'Hi,' he said, in his soft Scottish voice. He was in jeans and a Scottish rugby shirt, obviously not on shift. He looked so fine, holding a plain parcel wrapped in brown paper. 'I was hoping you'd be home.'

'Then it's your lucky day,' Gabi said, thinking the same and glad that she was in. She held the door open and sneaked a look at his denim-clad bum as he preceded her down the hall.

'How's your week been?' she asked, which immediately made her think of the last time she'd seen him. Or felt him, more like.

'Busy,' he said. 'A house fire, two school visits and one woman trapped in a toilet.' Gabi snorted. 'How about yours?'

'Busy too,' she said. 'Three physio sessions, four gym sessions and two trips to the shops to replace things I've dropped.'

'I might be able to help with that,' Walker said. 'I was thinking about what you said, about how you can't carry anything. So, I made you this.' He held the parcel out between them and Gabi bit her lip in surprise.

She couldn't remember the last time anyone apart from Isabella had bought her a present. She was quite often away working for her birthday, and usually celebrated quietly with a cake and a card signed by the crew, if she was lucky. If she was at home, she might meet Isabella for dinner or drinks. Her parents didn't send anything. Her dad always remembered the day at least and sent her his usual message. Her mum occasionally remembered – depending on how much fun she was having. So, presents were few and far between. At Christmas, if she joined Isabella and her parents, then there were always gifts. But her zia and zio had been travelling for the past couple of years and instead FaceTimed her on Christmas Day with a beach or a jungle in the background. Still, that was a present in itself.

Walker pressed the gift closer to her now, and she took it in her hands, lost for words.

The paper wasn't fancy. It was brown, thick, and sellotaped neatly along the edges. Gabi peeled the tape carefully and folded the paper back to reveal a wooden, rectangular tray which had been customised with the addition of a pair of elastic braces to the handles on the sides.

Gabi lifted it towards her, realising what it was designed to be, and made a small sound of amazement.

'You made this?' she asked and saw a slight colour in his cheeks as he nodded.

'Here, let me,' he said, taking the tray out of her hands. She held her breath as he moved behind her and she felt his fingers against her lower back, clipping the braces onto her jeans. Then he was in front of her, close enough for her to see the rise of his chest as he settled the straps over her shoulders and smoothed them down.

'Comfy?' he asked and waited for her nod before moving back. The tray was now balanced against her waist, perfectly level and steady.

She picked up her crutches and gave him the nod.

'Let's try this out,' she said and Walker grabbed her forgotten coffee cup from the table and placed it on the tray. She made her way one full circuit of the table. The coffee didn't spill.

'Walker, that's so thoughtful!' she said, turning back to where he was watching her progress anxiously. Unloading the tray again, she snapped off the braces and detangled herself. 'It's going to make life so much easier!'

He looked genuinely pleased.

'Thank you, really.' She took the couple of steps towards him in her boot, wanting to show him just how touched she was. She put both hands to his chest, which felt as though it had been carved from stone, and turned her face up to his. Close up, he smelled of peppery spice and his jaw was freshly shaven and firm against hers as she pressed her lips to his cheek. His hands found her elbows, holding her gently, and she had the sudden urge to twist her arms around his neck and taste his mouth. Get a grip, she thought. It was just a kiss on the cheek. But all of a sudden, she wanted to ravish the man in the middle of the afternoon.

Jayden's descent on the stairs sounded like a herd of elephants, but served to bring her back to reality. She stepped back slightly, her hand falling from Walker's chest. He was watching her carefully, and suddenly she thought that maybe he'd wanted the kiss too. She could see the amber in his hazel eyes, like small sparks of fire. Her breath caught.

'I didn't realise Jayden was here,' Walker said. Was that disappointment in his voice? Or was she imagining it?

'Yes, he gets home at three thirty every day,' Gabi said, wondering why the hell she was being so specific. Unless she wanted him to come by another time?

'Shame,' said Walker quietly, and his eyes burned into hers. 'I thought you might need a massage.'

Gabi felt a jolt of pure excitement. So, she wasn't mistaken. He did feel it too.

'That would have been nice,' she said just before Jayden raced into the kitchen, wearing jogging bottoms and ready for instruction. 'But we are doing fall guy training here today,' Gabi said, raising her voice.

'Another time then,' Walker said, turning to leave. He paused, then turned to face her. 'Are you coming to the hoedown at The Bolthole at the weekend? Fox texted the girls about it. Apparently he has a special announcement to make.'

Gabi grinned. He wanted her to go. Who knew what might happen?

'I'll be there,' she said, and he nodded. Pushing his hair off his face, he gave her one last scorching look before walking towards the front door.

Ten minutes later, as Jayden practised his forward rolls on the crash mat in the garden, Gabi sat in a nearby wicker chair and inspected her new tray. Not just a present, a *handmade* present. It had taken time and thought and patience. She ran her fingers down the elastic. They turned in her hands and she saw the name tag, Walker McBride. He'd used his own braces. And suddenly all her thoughts of Honeybridge as a holiday destination came flooding back – after all, a holiday wasn't a holiday without a holiday romance.

# Chapter Sixteen

*Walker*

Their usual high, round table at The Bolthole was already two deep with bottles of beer. Walker sat next to Fox who, he noticed, wore a brand-new checked shirt and a secretive smile, but he insisted he wasn't sharing his big news until everyone was there. Although they were chatting, Walker clocked Etienne eyeing the door for Isabella. He nudged him.

'Missing her already?'

Etienne shrugged and tilted the cowboy hat back on his head. 'What can I say, mate? I can't get enough of her.'

Walker shook his head in mock dismay. 'Who would have thought it? Etienne the one-night wonder practically living with his girlfriend.' They clinked bottles at the enormity of the change.

'Now that I've found her, I just want to be with her all the time.'

'Everything changed so quickly,' Walker said.

'From the very first time I touched her,' Etienne replied.

Walker had a sudden flash of memory, the feeling of Gabi's skin under his hands. He found himself following Etienne's lead and glancing towards the entrance.

'Same for me and Amber,' Alex joined in. 'Although obviously mine didn't end in a happy ever after.'

'There's still time, Al.' Etienne slung his free arm around his brother's shoulders.

'Did you not see her at Story Stars?' Alex snorted to dismiss the idea.

'What about you, Fox?' Walker asked. 'Anything to report?'

'Reggie lost another tooth,' Fox said happily. Walker laughed.

'How about your love life?'

'What love life?!'

'What about your sex life then?' Etienne asked.

'Nothing happening, man.'

'You're telling me you haven't been with a woman since that one-night stand last autumn at the games convention?' Etienne asked disbelievingly. Everyone leaned in for the answer.

'Nope,' Fox said.

'And nothing came of that?' Alex asked.

'Nothing at all,' Fox said. 'It couldn't really, after I snuck out in the morning. I don't even know her name. She was using a gamer tag – Red777.'

'Have you looked for her when you're playing online?' Walker asked.

Fox shook his head no, but Walker wasn't convinced. He opened his mouth to say something else, but Fox cut him off.

'No time, no energy.' He held a hand up.

Alex nodded his understanding, and they clinked bottles.

A whoop from the door told them that the girls had arrived, and all four men turned at once. Let the fun begin.

Isabella was across the room and entwined with Etienne in seconds, snatching his cowboy hat from his head and placing it firmly onto her own. Amber headed directly to the bar in skinny jeans and cowboy boots, and Walker watched Gabi swing herself across the dance floor on her crutches, breathing out only when she crossed safely and arrived at their table. Holy shit, he thought. She looked scorching, wearing a checked shirt tied above her midriff and a low-slung denim skirt. Her bare left leg was tucked into a brown cowboy boot, protective boot on the right. A tall guy with impeccable facial hair followed behind. Walker bristled at the hand he had on Gabi's back, until he recognised the amazingly sculpted face of Isabella's friend, Jesse.

'You all remember Jesse, don't you? My bestie from university?' Isabella said, grabbing the man's arm and bringing him into the inner circle. 'He's come to visit – and he has a date while he's here!'

'Anyone we know?' Etienne asked. Jesse theatrically looked around in case anyone was listening in, then beckoned everyone close.

'Toby!' he stage whispered.

'As in, Rosie and Wren's donor daddy?' Walker asked. They all knew Toby; he was at all of Riley's parties, nursery events and sports days.

'The very same. God, he's so good-looking . . .' Jesse fanned his face and looked as though he were fainting. Luckily Amber arrived with a tray of drinks at exactly the right time, and he drank to cool himself off. Walker flashed a glance at Gabi as she took a glass, spotting a glimpse of her toned stomach between shirt and skirt. Her skin gleamed as though she'd just put on body oil. She met his look full on, and his stomach dropped. She looked full of fire.

At exactly that moment, Fox decided the time was right to share his news. He tapped his glass with a pen and cleared his throat, waiting for everyone's attention.

'So, what's going on?' Walker asked. Fox took a deep breath.

'I sold my game,' he said simply, running his hand through his silver quiff, as though it were nothing special. As though he hadn't worked on this computer game design endlessly for the last couple of years, nights, weekends, every hour he could while the boys were at school. This was big news. Bigger than big. This was massive.

'Congratulations, bro,' Walker said, pulling him in tight for a hug.

'Thanks, Walker.' Fox grinned. The table broke into claps and cheers and people reached out, kissed him and squeezed his arm, clapped his back, wherever they could reach, knowing how much of himself he'd put into this game. Walker found himself next to Gabi and caught the scent of her soft, musky perfume as she reached to congratulate Fox.

'Not only sold it, though,' said Fox when he could speak again. 'But sold it to the biggest games corporation in the world. It's a multi-million-pound deal ... and we signed today.' Fox said the last few words in a rush and then clapped his hand over his mouth. Someone stammered. Everyone else went silent. Walker looked at his oldest male friend and felt the breath catch in his throat.

'Multi-million pound?' Walker repeated. Everyone looked at each other around the table. Fox nodded and a burst of laughter escaped his mouth.

'Multi-million pound,' Fox confirmed, before lifting his chin and howling spectacularly at the ceiling.

The table erupted. Walker and Fox jumped up and down, holding arms. Alex and Etienne jumped on in a tangle of man love.

'You know what this means, don't you?' asked Fox, when the table calmed.

'It means you're richer than your wildest dreams?' suggested Etienne.

'It means your whole life is about to change,' added Walker.

'It means . . .' Fox said, clearing his throat, 'Drinks are on me!'

# Chapter Seventeen

*Gabi*

Drinks were flowing, literally. Fox had organised champagne, and it just kept coming. Gabi had to put her hand over her glass to avoid being constantly topped up. She was a lightweight, and she knew it.

'Is this what we can get used to now, when we come out with you?' Gabi asked Fox as he popped the cork from the third – or was it the fourth? – bottle. Walker was the only one not drinking anything at all, as he was on call at the station.

'Yup,' said Fox. 'And limousines home afterwards.'

'I love a limo!' Gabi laughed. 'Count me in. What about a holiday house in the French Riviera?'

'On my list,' he said. 'I'll save a sunbed for you.'

Fox moved on to top up drinks and Gabi caught Walker watching her from across the table. Their eyes met and her breath hitched. He made his move and slid into the empty seat beside her, his knee pressing against hers under the table. Her stomach flipped. She glanced at his hands and shifted on her stool. Now that she'd felt them on her body, she couldn't seem to think of anything else. It was like she was obsessed.

'How's the rest of your week been?' he asked, bending his head towards her. His breath tickled her earlobe.

'Been quite boring since I last saw you actually,' she said with a tilt of her chin. 'All physio and no play makes Gabi a dull girl . . .'

'You need some light entertainment.' Walker's tone was serious, but his eyes were twinkling.

'I need a pick-me-up, that's for sure,' Gabi agreed, lifting her chin to him, meeting his mischief with a bite of her lip. His eyes widened and he was just beginning to smile when a fiddle began to play, and Walker broke the look to glance at the stage.

'You're in the right place,' he said, putting a cowboy hat on his head.

'It's *yeeha* time,' said Fox, reappearing beside him and securing his own Stetson. The spotlights illuminated the stage and a singer stepped out with a tambourine. A second later Fox, Etienne and Walker bowed to the girls and took to the dance floor, forming a line. Other men joined at each end until it stretched right the way across the room. They had their backs to the stage, facing the audience. A second fiddle began to play, and all the men tucked their thumbs in their belt loops.

The woman on stage started to sing and the tambourine kept time. Gabi nearly spat out her champagne as the men began to line dance, as one, in step. Right heel out and dip. Left heel out and dip. Grapevine right. Grapevine left. Turn ninety degrees. Clap. They didn't even need a caller, it seemed like they knew the dance by heart.

Women lined the edge of the dance floor now, clapping along, geeing them up. The men carried on doing their thing, getting into the rhythm, enjoying their moment. Now they were facing the stage, the women could appreciate the rear view, and the noise levels were rising.

'They're good, aren't they?' Amber said. 'Fox, Walker and Et have been coming for years.'

Gabi made an effort to close her mouth. They were so synchronised, so sure of themselves and so damned sexy. Amber laughed out loud.

'I know exactly how you feel, girl. Felt it the same first time I saw them,' she said. 'Tonight, though, I'm more interested in the band.' Gabi glanced at the group on stage and saw Alex there on guitar, playing chords with a half-smile and half-closed eyes. Amber was glued. 'He always was good with his hands,' she said.

The men turned and clapped again, facing to the left.

Isabella fanned her face. 'Every girl loves a cowboy,' she said reverently. 'I can't wait to get mine home.'

The line of men turned again and clapped and now they were facing the front and Gabi found her eyes locked with Walker. As if he had turned to her and she had been waiting for him. He dipped his head under his hat in greeting and held her gaze. She felt almost winded, like she had been holding her breath, that it had been him she had been watching all along. She knew there was a whole line of men, but she hadn't noticed any of them.

'Holy cow,' she said under her breath, watching the sway of his hips.

'You ain't seen nothing yet,' said Isabella, licking her lips in anticipation.

Suddenly, the music stopped dead. The crowd held its collective breath. The men simultaneously ripped their shirts apart, buttons flying like confetti at a wedding. They twirled their shirts above their heads like lassos. The men did a low hip roll on the spot, round and round, bare-chested and spotlit, before stopping dead.

'Yeeha!' they shouted as one. The Bolthole erupted. The waiting crowd surged the line, unable to hold back any more. Isabella cantered forward and jumped onto Etienne's waist. Amber muttered something under her breath and moseyed with intention towards the stage door.

Gabi felt like she'd lost the power of speech. Walker's shoulders were the stuff dreams were made of. He pushed his sandy hair back from his forehead and fist-bumped Fox.

The band started with the next song and new lines were formed, mixed men and women this time. Gabi saw Jesse and Toby take to the floor, the best-groomed cowboys in town. She watched Isabella stake her claim next to Etienne while Fox was swarmed by a handful of single mums from the boys' school. When they organised themselves into formation for the next dance, she realised she'd lost sight of Walker. She sagged against the table, wanting to be up there, but knowing her crutches would get in everyone's way. Walker was probably surrounded by women too. He deserved to be. Her mood dropped. She whacked the table leg with her crutch, and it made a satisfying thump.

'Howdy,' a Scottish voice said beside her, and she turned directly into his chest, clothed again in a shirt which hung open at the front. She could feel the heat from his body, and he smelled divine.

'That was quite a show, cowboy,' she managed. 'Who knew you had lasso in your box of tricks.'

'You'd be surprised how useful it is for getting cats out of trees.'

Gabi snorted. 'Thought you'd want to be out there,' she said, nodding at the crowd.

Walker leaned next to her, surveying the dance floor which was in full line dancing delight.

'Wanted to check you were okay—' he said.

'I can look after myself, you know,' Gabi interrupted automatically.

'And see if you wanted to dance,' he said, stopping her in her tracks. That was unexpected, but in a very good way.

'I'd love to,' she said. The band started again, a slow song, and he moved in.

'What about these?' Gabi asked, holding up her crutches.

'We don't need those . . .' Walker took them from her hands and leaned them against the table. She stood, balancing for a moment, and then hooked her fingers into his belt buckle, pulling him close. The spicy smell of him made her stomach flip.

'I'll need something to hang on to,' she said.

'Hold on to me.' His voice was against her ear, and it flashed her back to the bookshop, evoking the same urge, the desire to rest against him. He wrapped his arms around her back and took her weight, ensuring she wasn't putting pressure on her bad leg. She was cocooned against him, weightless as a trapeze swinger, her feet a few inches off the floor. Completely powerless. He walked them onto the edge of the dance floor and they began to move. She twisted her arms up and around Walker's neck, as she'd wanted to the other day. His hands tightened their hold, and she heard her own breath. Being held by Walker was like jumping off a building.

The tiniest stroke of his thumb against the bare skin of her lower back made her ache in the pit of her stomach. She rested her head against his shoulder and breathed in the scent of his chest. Every cell in her body felt alive, hyperaware of every point of contact between them. The flat, hard muscle of his stomach. The press of his thigh against hers as he moved.

The song ended and they paused. Gabi felt a lurch of disappointment when it was replaced by a DJ, a fast beat. Walker's arms relaxed and lowered her the half inch back down to the floor, supporting her while she took the weight again on her own feet. Her chest banged with excitement; her stomach was hollow with anticipation.

'Thank you,' she said, and it came out husky.

He looked down at her and, on impulse, she raised her face, tipping her mouth close to his. His surprise was momentary, she saw the flicker of his eyes as they widened, and then the softening of his jaw as his head inched tantalisingly slowly towards her. She felt her lips part in anticipation. She closed her eyes and felt the same anticipation as diving from a high board.

'Ahem.' Fox cleared his throat beside her. 'I'm off.' Walker straightened too quickly, and Gabi held on for dear life, unsure whether she could stand on her own. Fox lifted his cowboy hat and winked. 'Sorry.'

'Where are the others?' Walker asked, scanning the dance floor which had spiralled into country chaos. Women rode on men's backs, galloping across the dance floor. Toby and Jesse were do-si-do-ing, linking arms at the elbow and spinning in circles. People whooped, slapped their thighs, women lassoed men with their belts, and someone was shooting toy guns with the word 'bang' hanging out of them.

'Etienne said something about checking Isabella's coat into the cloakroom,' Fox said. Gabi snorted. Isabella hadn't been wearing a jacket. Obviously one cowgirl couldn't wait long enough to get her man home.

'And Amber said she had something to do.'

'Something?' Gabi snorted again. 'More like somebody.' She glanced at the stage and noticed the band was on its break. Alex was nowhere to be seen.

'Anyway, sorry to interrupt, just wanted to tell you the bar bill's paid,' Fox said. 'Enjoy the rest of your night.' Fox picked up the one remaining bottle of champagne from the bucket and carried it by its neck through the crowd. Gabi watched him go and realised she was still holding on to Walker. And more to the point, he was holding on to her.

'Shall we go?' Walker asked.

She looked into his face and took a risk. Of all the risks she was used to taking in her everyday life, this one felt like quite a big one.

'To mine?' Gabi asked.

'Definitely,' he said with a smile. They turned as one to the table to collect the crutches she'd left leaning in the corner, but they were gone.

'What the hell?' Gabi looked around her furiously. They hadn't slipped down underneath the table. They'd been pinched.

'Hmmm,' Walker said with a half-smile. 'Only one thing for

it.' He dipped in front of her. She felt his arm behind her legs, and he scooped her up as though she weighed nothing. She gasped.

'What are you doing?' Gabi asked, leaning against his chest and looking up into his chiselled face.

'Taking you home,' he said, starting the walk across the floor. As they went, she saw two women galloping across the dance floor, riding one of her crutches each like a horse. She slid her arms around Walker's neck again and said nothing at all.

# Chapter Eighteen

*Walker*

The five-minute walk to Amber's was too long. Walker lengthened his stride and did it in four. They didn't say a word to each other on the way, but there was an energy building, an anticipation of what was going to happen. He had her in his arms and he wasn't putting her down until it was on a bed. He used Gabi's keys to open the front door and carried her inside.

'Down there at the end,' Gabi whispered, and he needed no further encouragement. He could see the flush on her cheeks and recognised the same rush of blood he felt just from holding her.

He took the corridor still carrying her. Her lips trailed to his neck, and he felt the flutter of her eyelashes there on his skin as she traced kisses to his collar. He was hot and hard by the time they reached her bedroom door and he carried her inside. The room was softly illuminated by moonlight through the open curtains and neither of them reached for a light.

Walker kicked the door shut before lowering her slowly to

the bed, taking a moment to drink her in before their mouths crashed together in a kiss. Her lips parted for him, her chin lifted, and he tasted her with his tongue.

He paused above her, watching the rise and fall of her breast. The white of her throat, the dark of her eyes. Ever since the Lit Lounge, he'd wanted to touch her body again. When she'd kissed his cheek the other afternoon, he'd wanted to crush her against him. The energy inside her drew him like a magnet. Now, she tilted her face to him, half in invitation, half in defiance, and he couldn't wait any more.

He cupped her head in his hands and devoured her mouth. Gabi moaned in response and the sound was like a match to kindling. He kissed her again, deep and long and hungry. She pressed back, her tongue searching for his. His hands dropped to her back, and he found the gap between her shirt and her skirt, the bare skin as soft and smooth as velvet. He spanned her stomach with his fingers, feeling her arch against his body at his touch. She wrapped one hand around his neck and ran the other up and into his hair. She was matching him move for move and the fierceness of it, the rush of it was electrifying.

Catching her hands, Walker pushed them above her head, pinning them to the pillow easily in one of his own. Her chest heaved and he could hear his own ragged breathing. Again, they faced each other, and he saw the flash of excitement in her eyes, like a dare, a challenge. Walker dropped his free hand to the top button of her checked shirt and flicked it open. Gabi's eyes widened. He moved to the next one, feeling for the tiny pearl button and releasing it. The only thing holding her shirt together now was the knot she'd tied beneath her breasts.

'Don't move,' he growled, letting go of her hands and using both hands to untie the material in his way and pull each side apart, uncovering her body in the moonlight. Her breasts were pale against the black lacy bra, fuller than he'd expected with her tiny frame. He ran his hands up and over them, pushing the shirt clear on both sides. Gabi moaned softly and dropped her head back against the pillow, offering herself to him. Walker blazed. He rounded his hands over her breasts. His fingers were gentle, tracing the shape of her, but his palms were firm, squeezing her until she moaned.

Tugging the bra out of the way, he exposed her and watched the cool of the night air drag goosebumps over her skin as he brushed his thumb over her nipples.

'Walker,' Gabi moaned and the sound of his name on her breath set him alight. He dropped his mouth to her breast and nipped at her nipple, sucking it until she gasped. He moved to the other, biting lightly at the swell of her breast. Her hands dropped from their position and wrapped his head, pressing him to her, wanting more. He feasted on her, only aware of her body, of the heat in his own.

Something beeped somewhere at the edge of his consciousness. The sound was like an alarm going off when he was in deep sleep. It beeped again. It took him a moment to realise what it was, to drag himself up through his layers of desire to the surface. Walker lifted his head, blinked himself into awareness, and reached for his back pocket.

'What is that?' Gabi looked dazed as though just waking herself.

'My phone,' Walker murmured, pulling it out and glancing

at the screen. He groaned. 'It's the station.' He straightened and ran a hand through his hair.

'I have to go,' he said.

'You're joking?'

'I wish I was.' He let himself look at her one more time before gently pulling Gabi's shirt together. 'Looks like the current crew needs a helping hand.'

'I know how they feel,' Gabi groaned. Walker laughed.

'I'll try to come straight back,' Walker said. 'But I don't know when that might be.'

'Take my keys.' Gabi threw them and he caught them in one hand.

'Will you be all right? Without your crutches?'

'I'll be fine.' She rolled her eyes and he stopped her by dropping one last kiss on her mouth before turning away and striding down the corridor.

Fuck, fuck and fuck. Talk about timing.

# Chapter Nineteen

*Gabi*

The front door closed quietly, leaving Gabi listening to her own heavy breathing in the silence of her bedroom.

Shit, shit, shit.

She hobbled to the window and stared out at the moonlit garden, waiting for her pulse to return to normal. Wrapping her arms around herself, she felt the tug of desire still very much present and wished her arms were his.

She felt as though she'd just ridden a roller coaster. Once he'd touched her, she was gone and there was no going back. In terms of the light entertainment he'd suggested, it couldn't have been better. And although it hadn't been the kind of pick-me-up she had in mind when she said it earlier, she'd never had a pick-me-up-and-carry-me-home before and it surpassed all expectations.

Gabi breathed out, very long and very slow. Was he going to come back?

The front door opened, and Gabi's stomach felt hollow. She held her breath to hear. Noises in the corridor. Was it him returning straight away? Maybe it had been a false alarm. She hoped it was. Then voices in the kitchen, low and laughing, the clink of glasses and the slam of the fridge door. Footsteps on the stairs, then Amber's whoop from her bedroom, and the soft sound of a guitar. Hmm, who would have thought it? At least someone was getting some. She checked the time. 12.43 a.m.

She hobbled to her dressing table and sat, taking out wipes and lotions to remove her make-up. Her face was flushed and her eyes bright. Walker's face flashed into her mind, his eyes lowered to her chest. How long would it take him to sort out what was needed and come back? An hour? Two? What if it was a major incident? He could be gone all night and then feel too tired to even think about this, about her.

Stripping off her clothes, she let them fall where they landed and pulled on a T-shirt. Edging to the bed, she lifted her boot and got comfortable, pillow behind her head, iPad on her lap. She flicked through the film library, wanting to choose something to distract herself. Nothing with sex. Nothing starring handsome men with big shoulders. She bit her fist and chose a film about a woman explorer who single-handedly saved a jungle species. Halfway through, she became aware of some animalistic noises closer by, coming from upstairs, and then the bang of the bed, and she screamed silently into her pillow before turning up the volume on her iPad. Dear God, she was horny. 1.47 a.m.

The credits rolled at 2.30 a.m. and she threw her iPad aside in frustration. He obviously wasn't coming back, and she couldn't wait any longer. She was reaching under the bed for her vibrator, ready to satisfy herself instead, when her phone rang.

Walker.

She felt a rush of surprise, and then disappointment. It obviously meant he was stuck at the station. Dammit.

'Hello,' she murmured, her voice low in the quiet of the house.

'Hullo.' His accent sounded stronger over the phone. It felt strangely exciting and surprisingly intimate to have a late-night phone call, given how they'd just been naked with each other.

'Where are you?'

'At the station. I just came outside to call you.'

She lay back on the pillow, imagining him there in the dark.

'One of the crew has had to leave with a migraine,' he said. 'I have to stay and fill in.'

'Shame,' she said. 'But needs must, I suppose.'

'I'd rather be focused on your needs,' Walker said, and she heard it as though he'd whispered it directly into her ear. She smiled.

'Really?' she murmured.

'What have you been doing?' he asked, and his voice was urgent.

'Just lounging in bed,' she said, wiggling in her sheets, feeling the rise of anticipation again.

'What are you wearing?' he asked and she caught her breath.

'As little as possible, hoping you'd make it back,' she said.

'Tell me exactly, so that I can picture you.' His voice had lowered.

'Just a T-shirt,' she said. 'With nothing underneath.'

He groaned down the line.

'Now you're going to have to trust me, Gabi. I know what you need and you're going to do exactly what I say.' Gabi moistened her lips that suddenly felt dry with excitement. His voice was doing things to her.

'Put your hand on your throat,' he said. Her pulse felt fast beneath her touch as her heart beat faster for him. She waited.

'Open your fingers wide and move them down your body,' Walker said. 'Think about my hands there, my fingers covering your nipples. My palms cupping your breasts.'

Gabi's breath felt ragged. Her breasts pushed against her palm, desperate for his touch. She felt the peak of her nipples, the tightening that seemed to send signals between her legs.

'Remember how my mouth felt on yours . . .' Walker's voice was intense. She could imagine his lips against her neck.

'Keep moving down,' Walker said. 'Over your belly button piercing. Down to the bottom of your T-shirt.' Gabi could feel the tremble in her own hands, as she followed his command without thinking. For once happy to be told what to do. She held her hemline between her thumb and forefinger and awaited his instruction.

'Lift it,' he said simply, and she did, exposing herself as she did so.

'Are you naked there now?' he asked. She had to swallow before she could speak.

'Yes.'

'Spread your legs,' he said quietly.

She closed her eyes and opened her legs.

'And now?'

'Touch yourself,' he said. His voice was an order. She trailed her fingers up her thigh to her centre. She was soft and slick and wet and her whole body arched as her fingers began to stroke her core. She was so ready. She heard a noise, a low moan, and realised it had come from her.

'Be my hand,' Walker said into her ear. 'Use my fingers.' A gasp broke from her as her thumb brushed her clit.

'Yes.' Her voice broke.

'Let me make you come,' he breathed.

She felt the tension build inside her. Her hand moved as if it was under his control, her eyes fluttering as she increased the pace. She remembered the look on his face as he moved over her body. The concentration, the intensity, the absolute desire. Her clit was swollen with need. She rubbed it and thought of him and reached the edge of the precipice.

'Walker,' she gasped as she threw herself off.

# Chapter Twenty

*Walker*

It was a week later when the fire station alarm rang halfway through the Thursday afternoon shift.

'Let's go, team,' Walker shouted immediately, and his crew scrambled to don fire suits. The truck pulled out with everyone aboard one minute later. The lights were flashing, and pedestrians turned to look as they sped past.

Walker sat upfront on the phone with the dispatcher, plugging in the address and awaiting further information. Today was his first afternoon shift after a very quiet week of night shifts where the highlight had been catching a stray dog on the common. The team had all undertaken physical training together that morning and now he took a deep breath, feeling his adrenaline rise.

It hadn't been the only thing that had risen that morning. He'd woken after the deepest and most satisfying sleeps he'd had in a long time to a hard-on worthy of a flag. Since that almost-night with Gabriella, he'd only been thinking of when he might get to actually complete the night in person. The images in his head were certainly proving a good distraction, as he hadn't had a bad dream all week. He'd texted her the day after their late-night phone call, telling her he'd found her crutches abandoned at The Bolthole and had left them outside her door and posted her keys through the letter box. She'd texted back immediately asking him if she could thank him in person, adding a little devil emoji. But he'd had to postpone, as he'd been on his way to start night shifts for the week. Something he'd never minded, until then. Now that he was back on days, he fully intended to message her and ask for a repeat performance.

The dispatcher crackled back onto the line.

'Incident at Treetop Challenge,' she said and then the words that made his blood run cold. 'Involving children from the Honeybridge Tots.'

Walker's stomach clenched. That was Riley's nursery. He'd been there himself with Rosie to collect Riley on occasion. He'd stood outside and waited for her to appear on the doorstep. Riley, his red-headed goddaughter, usually paint-speckled, often wearing dungarees, always hungry.

'Are the children all safe?' he asked.

'Not all of them.'

John threw a glance at Walker and then sounded the siren. Walker set his jaw, all thoughts of Gabi forgotten for the time being.

Treetop Challenge was a series of high ropes between platforms in the trees, ending with a zipline back to the ground. All perfectly safe, with different levels for different age groups, strapped in and clipped on at all times. Walker couldn't imagine what the incident could be – and found it hard to believe even when he stood in front of it.

He dropped out of his door before the engine skidded to a stop. A woman beckoned him from the clearing in the woods and he jogged over. She wore the Honeybridge Tots sweatshirt, and she and another helper were surrounded by children, some crying, others sucking thumbs. A quick scan told him Riley was not among them.

'What's happened?' he asked without preamble.

'There was a massive crack.' The woman looked stricken. She wrung her hands and couldn't take her eyes from the trees ahead. Walker scanned the canopy but couldn't spot what she was staring at.

'A tree fell,' the woman continued. 'It crashed through one of the wired walkways. All the lines were broken.'

'Anyone hurt?' Walker asked.

'Luckily, no. Most of the children were off the bridge at the time. They carried on to the end of the course and we've got them down. But one girl had her foot trapped in the bridge as it fell. She's stuck.'

She pointed a shaking finger up at the canopy and Walker saw his worst fears confirmed. Riley's red hair dangled towards the ground as she hung upside down under the broken bridge.

'Is she still strapped in?' Walker demanded, motioning his crew to reverse the fire engine closer.

'We're not sure . . .' This came from the attendant from Treetop Challenge. 'The falling tree seems to have taken down most of the wiring.'

There was already a crowd forming. This kind of news spread like wildfire. The mums and dads would all be on social media, and he knew that meant Rosie would hear about it soon.

Riley could be hanging there by her shoe alone, tangled in the ropes, without any harness attached. Walker jogged back to his truck and gave a brief download, then jumped on the back of the truck and told his team to raise the ladder. The mechanism clicked into motion and the ladder began to ascend. Walker climbed onto it and held on with one hand.

'Riley, it's Walker,' he called calmly through the leaves as he rose towards her. 'How are you doing?'

'I'm stuck . . .'

Her voice was quiet and sounded like she was crying, but at least she was conscious. For how long, though, hanging upside down like that?

The ladder reached its full length and Walker's heart fell again. It was about six feet short. Even stretching to his full height on the very top rung he would not be able to reach her. 'Hang on in there, Riley,' he called. 'I'm coming for you.'

'I'm scared,' Riley sobbed. 'I'm going to fall.'

'I'll be right back.'

He descended at lightning speed, shouting his plan to his team at the bottom who grabbed his supplies. He armed himself with the equipment he needed, scaling the ladder again as if running up a flight of stairs. He chose a branch above where Riley was hanging and threw a perfect snake of rope over the top of the bough. Securing himself with knots and a makeshift pulley, he hoisted himself from the top of the ladder until he hung directly next to where Riley was suspended.

'Hello, kiddo,' he said quietly as she turned a tear-streaked, freckled face towards him. 'Ride time. Hold on tight.' He held her easily with one arm as he detangled her foot from the ropes. She clutched at him as he finally freed her and swung her against his body. Allowing himself one brief moment of relief, he began to lower himself again, one-handed, with his homemade pulley. By the time he got to the ladder, his teammate was waiting for him to pass Riley over so that they could all descend safely.

At the bottom of the ladder, Riley sprang out of his crewmate's arms and back into his. He hugged her back, fiercely.

The crew moved round him, past him, retracting the ladder and storing the supplies. He saw Rosie running through the crowd and a second later she crashed against his side. Walker caught her, pressing her and her daughter together.

'She's okay,' he said into her hair. 'She's okay.'

Rosie grasped at him, and he held her to keep her upright.

'Thank you,' Rosie said, and it came out as a sob. 'I thought she was going to fall . . .'

Walker shook his head, not wanting to go there. He couldn't have borne it. Once was enough. Everyone he saved now was just trying to make up for the one he hadn't been able to.

'Thank you,' Rosie said again, dropping to her knees to cover her daughter's chubby face with kisses.

# Chapter Twenty-One

*Gabi*

Spring had well and truly sprung. The trees were covered with blossom, the sun had some warmth in it and the park was busy again after school. Gabi made herself comfortable on the bench while Jayden hung off the climbing frame with his mates, back from a week-long residential with the school.

Gabi was surprisingly glad he was back. The days had been longer without Jayden there to break up the afternoons. And he'd surprised her, running to give her a hug after Amber had finished squeezing him. Amber had made the most of her time with Jayden away; Gabi knew she'd met up several times with Alex for some 'grown-up fun'. Although Amber swore it was nothing more than that when Gabi pressed her.

The opportunity for a little bit of adult activity of her own had been out of Gabi's reach all week, not that it stopped her thinking about it. That 'almost' night with Walker had certainly given her hope that her time in Honeybridge might have a few unexpected benefits to it. Every time her phone rang, it made her squeeze her thighs together at the memory of that phone call. His voice, that accent, his taking command. But Walker had been on nights all week and she'd had to make her own entertainment – which reminded her, she needed to pick up batteries on the way home.

She put her head back to feel the sun on her face. She hadn't felt any sort of heat since Australia on that film set, working beneath wide-open skies. She could feel the tension in her body easing with the warmth. The film would have wrapped now, everyone going their separate ways to their own corner of the globe for a break or moving on to the next project. The only person she'd heard from was the wardrobe manager who wanted to know where to mail the headphones she'd left there by mistake. Maybe she'd meet the rest of the crew again down the road, the next time she jumped out of a building or dived from the roof of a train. Maybe not.

The thought jogged her into action, and she dialled her agent.

'Gabi! You must have read my mind. I was going to call you today, there is something I think you'd be perfect for.'

Gabi listened as her agent described the opportunity, a film – big budget – which would start shooting in Los Angeles in late June, which was perfect timing. She'd be the primary stunt double for an A-list actress for all dangerous and fast-moving scenes. She felt the buzz of excitement. Los Angeles – she'd never shot there before. Box office hit. Everything she heard was exciting.

'So shall I put you forward?' her agent said.

'That would be great, thanks,' Gabi replied. 'Let me know the next steps when you hear.'

She hung up. God, she had so much energy stored inside. She needed a release. Walker flashed into her mind again, holding her hands above her head as he took in her body. Fuck, he was sexy. And he'd made sure she wasn't holding on to any tension when he rang her later that night. He was due to finish nights yesterday; maybe she could text him later. Might as well make the most of this holiday romance. But at this moment in time, Walker was nowhere to be seen, and she needed to distract herself.

She hobbled over to the swings in just her boot. Jayden skidded over and jumped on the one next to her, delighted. They grinned at each other and leaned back, legs pointed to the sky. Less than a minute later, Gabriella was in full swing, enjoying the rush. Jayden whooped and hollered next to her, sounding surprisingly like Amber. Eventually, they slowed until her one trainer scuffed the dirt, and finally swung to a stop.

'Wow, that looked like fun!' a mum called over from a nearby bench. She was feeding a baby and had another toddler at her feet. 'I remember that feeling – total freedom.' She laughed and shook her head. 'Two babies in two years kind of changes things. Not that I'd have it any other way.'

Gabi dismounted and Jayden hightailed it back to his friends. She resumed her place on her own bench, thinking about what the woman said.

Maybe that was what her own mamma missed when Gabi was little. That sense of freedom. The ability to do whatever, whenever. If Gabi had followed her mamma's example, she'd be living somewhere in Europe with a rich man who liked to show her off. She'd prioritise her looks and her figure, but not for fitness and health, more for arm-candy appeal. Gabi ran a hand through her crop and almost smiled at the thought of her mother's face if she saw it. How she'd always insisted on keeping Gabi's hair long as a child and got the au pair to brush it every night, while she'd gone out to a party or a club. After her mamma finally left for good with the most exciting new man she could find, Gabi took the scissors to her waist-length black hair, making her au pair scream when she came in to say goodnight. Gabi had been dragged to the hairdresser's to repair what damage they could before her mother saw it. But she never did. Because she never came home again.

Maybe she'd followed her papà's example more closely. He'd thrown himself into work after Mamma left, moving higher up at work until he spent all day yelling at his team in glass buildings and all night schmoozing clients at roof-top dinners. Maybe he couldn't face seeing Gabi waiting for him when he got home. Maybe he couldn't bear the silence left by his wife. But soon he 'thought it best' for her to go to a boarding school 'with an incredible reputation' on the other side of the country, and then, as if that wasn't enough, she would stay with her aunt and uncle, and her cousin Isabella, in the school holidays – as they were closer to the school. It sounded like a business recommendation that he might make to the board. Little did Gabi know that it had already been decided. The fees had already been paid. The ticket was already in his wallet. Zio and Zia were looking forward to having her. And just like that, she was on her own. At first, Mamma remembered her on her birthday every year, sending something exotic and useless from a far-off place. Papà had originally messaged her regularly, asking for the details of her school life, checking in after exams and results, but over time, it slowed. Nowadays, he made sure to message her every month to assuage his guilt and make sure she was at least still alive. Whenever he asked her if she needed anything, she made a point of replying 'nothing at all'. It was her small victory.

Her phone beeped. The Girl Gang WhatsApp group was popping off.

> **Wren**: Is everyone around tomorrow afternoon?
> **Rosie**: We need to celebrate . . . Walker saved Riley's life today.
> **Amber**: OMIGOD! What?
> **Isabella**: Is she okay?
> **Wren**: She's fine.
> **Rosie**: Thanks to Walker.
> **Isabella**: Come to Tutto Mio for a late lunch. I'll save a table.
> **Wren**: Perfect. We just want to thank him properly – and he can blow off steam after the week he's had.
> **Amber**: Fab. Jayden's on a sleepover so see you then.
> **Isabella**: Count us in.

Gabi shook her head in disbelief as she took it all in. Walker McBride was an actual saint as well as a horny devil. The phone beeped again.

> **Isabella**: Gabi, are you free?

Gabi typed a quick 'yes please' and added a smiley face before putting the phone in her lap. A chance to get out of the house, have some fun *and* see Walker again. Maybe she could mislay her crutches somewhere along the way. Shit, she might even snap a crutch in half herself if it meant he carried her home and finished what he started.

# Chapter Twenty-Two

## Walker

Walker was absolutely knackered. He'd had a terrible night's sleep after the high ropes stress yesterday, and on top of a week of night shifts, it meant the last thing he wanted was to go out for dinner. What he actually wanted was a nap. But he was very aware Gabi might be there, and that was enough to drag him off the sofa and into the shower before setting off.

He spotted her as soon as he opened the door at Tutto Mio. She was talking with Amber, in jeans and a fitted top. Her body was so hot, with curves in all the right places, but still so strong. It was that combination that made her so irresistible.

He was halfway across the restaurant towards her when Wren shouted, 'He's here!' and Rosie turned round and started singing 'For he's a jolly good fellow' at the top of her voice.

'The man himself!' Wren said, standing up from the table.

'Our hero!' Rosie added, and then they were both on top of him in a double hug. He hugged them both, so that he could hide his face from everyone else.

'Just doing my job,' he said quietly into Rosie's hair.

'Well, thank you for being so good at it then,' she whispered back, and her voice was choked.

'Really,' he said. 'You didn't need to do any of this . . .'

'Of course we did,' Wren said. 'It's not every day our daughter gets rescued!'

Yesterday he had been lucky. He knew he would have saved Riley or died trying, and they were both very fortunate it had worked out. Riley was okay. But it had taken it out of him. He kept imagining how it could have ended very differently. He'd pictured himself frozen by fear and her plunging past him. What if he'd hesitated too long and her shoe had worked itself free? He'd had to get up in the night, pacing his bedroom, trying to clear his mind of old images of times when things hadn't gone right. He was exhausted. And any thanks were unnecessary. In fact, he'd just like to turn his attention to something else entirely. Or someone. He glanced across at Gabi and found her watching him. Their eyes met.

'Riley made you this.' Rosie handed over a card and everyone gathered in to see. Hand-drawn and colourful, the card showed a stick man wearing a helmet, with something in his hands. Something long and thick. They all stared. Gabi giggled.

'What the hell is he holding between his legs?' Isabella asked. Rosie snorted.

'That's his *pole*, apparently.'

'Wow.' Amber cracked a smile. 'It's *massive*.'

Walker felt his mood lighten with relief as the girls pulled appreciative faces. He looked up at Gabi again and she raised an inquisitive eyebrow. He winked and her eyes widened. If she wanted to know, he'd be only too happy to oblige.

The waitress approached and the group went to sit at the table. Walker took his chance, moving closer to Gabi now that the focus was off him. She smelled of shampoo and soft, musky perfume. Delicious. He pulled up the chair next to her and trailed a finger down the side of her arm when nobody was watching. She shot him a look under her eyelashes, and he did it again. She bit her lip. The waitress appeared between them and he reluctantly let his hand drop.

Everyone ordered meatballs, as that was the only thing on the menu. Isabella's brainchild of a restaurant had been a resolute hit with the locals.

'We're booking a massive table for the Honeybridge Community Awards next weekend because Walker's been nominated for an award. Who's in?' Alex said as drinks were poured. Everyone shouted their acceptances.

'Let's hope you win,' Etienne said, raising his beer bottle in a salute.

'I'll do my very best,' Walker said, wishing that the mention didn't fill him with anxiety.

'You always do,' Wren added, saluting him with her wine glass.

'You certainly did your best by me the other day,' Gabi said quietly. 'Didn't leave a job half done.' He turned to her, glad to change the subject. And the subject of her body was probably his favourite topic right now. The only thing that didn't come with extra stress.

'What can I say? I like to please.' Walker shrugged, and she laughed, a throaty chuckle. He might be tired, but he decided to shoot his shot.

'What are you doing later?' he asked and her eyes caught his.

'You, hopefully,' she said mischievously, and the spark was lit.

By the time they managed to escape, it was early evening. All afternoon, she'd teased him. Letting her hand trail on his thigh under the table as they ate or rubbing her leg against his own. He gave as good as he got, accidentally on purpose knocking her shoulder so her top's strap slipped down her arm. She was in full force, telling stories about her co-stars, impersonating their accents, and he found her husky laugh as sexy as her body. As tired as he was, the energy between them was keeping him going.

'Can you do a Scottish accent?' he asked her, remembering the French accent she used at Story Stars.

She shook her head. 'Maybe I could do with a little one-on-one tuition?' She looked at him cheekily.

'I'd be happy to help.' He winked.

'Do you ever wear a kilt?' she asked.

He grinned. 'Yep.' She raised her eyebrow again.

'I'd be interested in seeing that,' she said. She dropped her voice and leaned in. 'And what's underneath it.'

He laughed outright.

Everyone watched them leave together but nobody said a word, apart from Isabella who laughingly warned her to watch out for his pole. It wasn't just them that were heading off for an after-party either. He'd seen the flirty looks between Amber and Alex flying all day.

As they'd each settled their share of the bill, Alex had whispered to him, 'Amber is coming back to ours for a while.'

Walker had nodded at his hopeful expression. 'You'll have the place to yourselves. I'm going back with Gabi.' They'd bumped fists discreetly, wishing each other well.

It started as soon as he closed the door. Gabi came at him this time, letting her crutches fall to the floor and winding her arms around his neck. He crushed her body against his and his mouth found hers, forcefully, unable to wait any longer. She kissed him back ferociously. Only when Walker heard her gasp did he pause for breath, before scooping her up in his arms. He kicked the bedroom door shut behind him before laying her in the middle of the bed. He clicked on the bedside lamp and peeled his T-shirt off in the orange glow. Her eyes were almost black as they roamed over his chest. Gabi wiggled expertly out of her vest top, and he licked his lips at seeing her breasts again, spilling out of a tiny bra, nipples almost escaping. She unclipped the clasp and the fabric fell away. He watched the nipples bud under his gaze. She reached a hand out for him. He didn't need asking twice. The bed dipped as he joined her, rolling her in close.

Gabi's fingers traced the tattoos on his shoulders, leaving tiny trails in their wake. She ran her palms over his pecs and circled his nipples. He clutched her against him, her breasts pressed to his chest, and then he kissed her deeper than before. She wound her fingers into his hair, and he was hard and straining for more. He thrust against her, and she moaned. Suddenly she stopped.

'Lie back,' she said, breath ragged. Walker hesitated, torn

between wanting to explore her body more and wanting her to take the lead. 'Lie back,' she repeated. 'It's your turn.'

He started to shake his head, but she pushed firmly on his shoulder, and he settled backwards onto the soft bed. Her hand skimmed down his chest again, caressed his abs, stopping only when she reached his fly. She tugged insistently at the buttons and they sprang open.

'Moment of truth,' Gabi said, and he could tell she was smiling even though he couldn't see her face. Her hand pressed downwards. He stilled as her fingers circled him – or tried to. She gasped.

'Wow, they weren't lying,' she murmured. His cock leapt as she stroked him slowly, taking in his whole length from root to tip and back again.

Gabi shifted position suddenly, curling herself down the bed, and he felt the heat of her breath against his stomach. Walker cupped the back of her head and felt the skin on the nape of her neck. She inched lower, pressing tiny hot kisses and trailing the tip of her tongue as she went. She hovered above him in the half-light and he held his breath, releasing it in a rush as her mouth encircled him. She sucked him, deeply, and made a low hum in her throat, which vibrated to his core. His head pushed back into the pillow as one of her hands pulled at his hip and she took more, sucked him deeper. He arched against her as she worked him. Her mouth was like hot ecstasy. Walker groaned and knew he was close.

He pulled Gabi back up the bed, held her tight against him, his cock hard and hot against her body. Her skin was the softest he'd ever felt as he stripped her and ran his hand between her legs, finally finding the heat of her. She groaned into his mouth, holding him tighter, and her breath was ragged on his lips. He thumbed her clit until she gasped and begged, so then he rolled her onto her back and knelt between her spread legs, looking down at her from above.

'Wait, I should get something.' Their eyes met, dark and wanting, asking questions of each other.

'I'm on the pill,' Gabi whispered.

'And I'm clean and tested,' he said. There was just the flicker of a smile between them as she pulled him closer until suddenly he was there at her entrance.

'Yes,' Gabi insisted, and she lifted against him as he pushed, gently, easing himself into her, feeling her body stretch to accommodate him. Gabi arched again, taking him deeper, inch by inch until Walker was fully inside the hot centre of her body, never taking his eyes from hers.

'Let's see how long you can last,' Walker challenged, and Gabi wrapped her arms around him as he began to move, slowly at first until they were crashing against each other, nothing else mattering apart from the feeling and friction between their bodies.

'Hold it there, baby,' he growled as he sensed she was close and she gasped, lip trembling, waiting for his command.

'Now come for me,' he said and she made a cry of complete release as she let go. And only when he felt her come against him, around him, did he let himself explode inside her.

# Chapter Twenty-Three

*Gabi*

Walker's chest was heaving as he collapsed beside her. His eyes were the darkest she'd ever seen. They searched hers, dazed as his hair flopped across his forehead. He kissed her, hard and long. She could feel his heart banging through his ribs. Hear his breath as it slowed. He groaned aloud and slumped further into the mattress. She needed a moment to gather herself.

'Bathroom . . .' she murmured and he loosened his hold on her. Gabi grabbed one crutch as an aid and hobbled out, wishing she could dash out sexily, flashing a glimpse of butt as she went.

She blinked, shell-shocked, at herself in the mirror, taking a moment to calm down. The way Walker had groaned her name as he came was a total turn-on. His hands on her head, so strong, but so gentle at the same time as she blew him. That eye contact as they fucked. The thing that was between them – this intensity, this energy – she'd never experienced it before.

She licked a finger and ran it under her eyelashes, catching the mascara where it had run. She tousled her hair and ran some toothpaste around her mouth, still aware of the rush of her blood, the ache between her legs.

The man had a body to die for. Or kill for. Or both. She gave herself a onceover, top to bottom. She blew herself a kiss in the mirror and couldn't help but smile as she turned off the light. She was ready for more fun.

He was on his side, facing towards her, when she made it back to the bedroom, although she couldn't make out his face in the semi-darkness of the room. She edged onto the bed and moved towards him.

'I'm back,' she whispered.

He made a noise of acknowledgement, a grunt of appreciation maybe? She inched closer. He threw a heavy arm over her and pulled her in, turning her back towards him. Her stomach dropped away in anticipation. Walker muttered something unintelligible at the back of her neck and then tucked her into his chest, fitting her butt to his groin, his thighs to the back of her legs. The perfect spoon. Wait? What? She listened to his breathing, slow and steady. The gentle hum of a snore on every exhale. There was no denying it. The man was asleep.

Gabi lay in disbelief for a full minute and then swallowed a bubble of laughter. She cleared her throat, thinking that might do the trick. But he only pulled her closer and sighed into her hair. He was dead to the world. There was nothing for it. Looked like she was having a sleepover until he woke up and wanted round two.

It took a few minutes to relax. Gabi didn't do sleepovers. She calmed her breathing, as much as she could with a six-foot-two sex god wrapped around her, and tried to think wholesome thoughts.

Walker nestled further into her hair with his nose and made a sound of contentment. Gabi gave in, allowing her limbs to get heavy, to sink against him and into the pillow. She couldn't even remember the last time she'd slept with someone in a bed.

She remembered the sleepovers with Isabella as a girl, when they'd share a bed and talk all night about dreams and dramas. That feeling of closeness when the lights were out. The sense that you could be honest and brave, be the real you in the dark. She'd loved that.

She turned to lean over Walker then, just enough to reach the lamp and switch it off. She snuggled back against him and wrapped her arms over his, holding him in place. She closed her eyes. She could wait.

A sudden shout ripped through the room as Gabi woke with a start. Something was on her, dragging her down the bed. She struggled to move, terrified. She thrashed, as much as she could with her leg heavy and immobile. She twisted to escape, but hands held her by the waist and tugged. The shout came again, and her brain recognised him. Walker. He cried out and it sounded like it came from the depths of his soul.

His hands grasped at her, and Gabi didn't know whether to hold on to them or push them away. Was he trying to hurt her or help her? She didn't know and she wasn't sure he did either.

'Walker!' she yelled but he didn't stop.

He was frantic now, scratching at the bed as though trying to get through the sheets themselves, looking for something, searching. He muttered under his breath, but she couldn't catch the words.

'Walker, what are you doing?' No response.

Gabi threw herself towards the light switch and brightness flooded the room. She dragged herself to sitting and reached her hands out to him. Walker's eyes were open but unseeing. His mouth moved constantly, a conversation with someone she couldn't see. He was dreaming. But by the look of fear on his face, it was a nightmare. Gabi held his shoulders in her hands.

'Walker, it's me.' Her voice was firmer this time. She shook him, gently at first, and then with force. His head snapped up; his eyes took focus. He sat bolt upright. First, he saw her, really recognised her, then his gaze danced around the room, into the shadows of the corners, out towards the door, before finding her face again.

'You were having a nightmare,' Gabi said, keeping her voice soft, soothing. She'd heard you shouldn't wake people if they were sleepwalking. Was it the same with people having nightmares?

Walker dropped his face into his hands. Gabi rubbed his arms, suddenly realising how cold he looked in the spring night. She moved to pull a blanket around his stiff, tense shoulders.

'It's okay now,' she murmured, leaning her forehead on his. 'It's okay,' she repeated. He rested there for a second, then stood abruptly, making the bed rock.

'It's not okay, though.' Walker's voice was broken, flat. He ran his hand through his hair. 'It never will be.'

Before she could answer or even think of what to say, he pulled his jeans on and slipped his T-shirt over his head. Gabi pulled the covers up to her front, unsure as to what was happening, suddenly feeling naked and exposed. The light no longer felt like a warm glow, more like the aftermath of a bonfire when it's nothing but ash and ember. It threw dark shadows beneath Walker's eyes.

'Walker,' she said again, to avert whatever was about to happen. 'Don't go.'

Their gaze met and held. His eyes flashed with some pain she didn't understand, and his jaw was set hard. She reached her hand out to him in an effort to make some kind of connection, to bring him back from wherever he'd gone. But he shook his head, picked his boots up from the floor and turned away.

# Chapter Twenty-Four

*Walker*

Walker ran. His arms pumped, his chest heaved, and still he couldn't get the images out of his head. His boots echoed on the pavement as he pounded towards home. The streets were deserted, the houses were dark.

He eased through his own front door and took the stairs two at a time, glad that it was silent and still inside. He couldn't face small talk with Alex and Amber. When he saw that Alex's door was closed, Walker breathed a sigh of relief and slipped into his own room.

A wave of anxiety overtook him. The fear from his nightmare still lay there, dark and slick like oil at the bottom of his belly. But it was morphing into something else, into desperation that he'd never escape from his past.

He threw himself onto his bed and slammed the mattress with his fists. Why had he fallen asleep? How the hell could he have let that happen? It had been such a good day, and he'd thought he'd be having a night of fun with Gabi. He never should have closed his eyes.

The images rose again in his mind's eye like an old black and white movie. He saw the plume of his breath in the winter air. He heard his own voice calling out, and felt the burn of his fingertips against the ice. He shook his head violently, rubbing at his own face with his hands. If he could claw those memories out, he would. But he could never forget. And he could never forgive himself.

His phone rang. Gabi's name on the screen. He pressed red. How could he talk to her again after that? She must think he was a real coward. Scared of a dream. And then overreacting to the point of running away. He punched the wall, hard, and the sharp pain in his knuckles felt almost good.

His phone rang again. Gabi. He stared at the handset, wanting it to stop. He let it go to voicemail but it rang immediately again. There was nothing for it. He should just apologise and get it over with. Then at least he'd have done the right thing. Even if she didn't want to ever see him again. Why would she? He accepted her call.

'Walker?' Her voice was low, urgent. 'Are you okay?'

He opened his mouth to reply but, to his horror, nothing came out apart from a strangled type of sob.

'Oh, Walker.' Gabi's voice dropped even lower, and he pressed the phone against his head and closed his eyes. The darkness engulfed him and all he wanted was to fall into it, with no dreams, no images, no ghosts.

'I want you to listen to me,' Gabi said. He swallowed and nodded, wordlessly, holding the phone like a lifeline.

'Trust me, Walker, because I know what you need right now, and I want you to do exactly what I say.' He recognised her choice of words. They came from a time when he was in control, not the pathetic mess of a man he'd turned into. If she wanted a strong man, then she'd come to the wrong place.

'Are you still wearing your boots, Walker?' Gabi asked softly and he cleared his throat and managed to say yes.

'Take them off now.'

He did as she instructed. Pushing them off by the heels, he let them drop with a clunk to the bedroom floor.

'Now, get into bed.' Gabi's voice was caring but firm. He obeyed. He slipped between the covers, still in his jeans and T-shirt, and pulled the duvet up to his neck. Despite his clothes, his bed was cold, and he shivered.

'You need to rest,' Gabi was saying. 'So, get comfortable. Turn on your side, on your right. Curl your legs up.' She waited a moment, and he did as he was told, wondering how she'd remembered his favourite position to sleep.

'There. Now put the phone on the pillow,' she said, and he felt a rush of heat as tears gathered behind his eyes. He didn't want her to go. He wished she was right beside him, someone whole and warm and solid to hold on to. The nightmare had devastated him. Waking up in a strange bed had made it worse, none of his own familiar things around him to ground him in the present. The run through dark streets had made him feel haunted, chased by memories on every corner. Now he just felt alone.

Like she could read his mind, Gabi said, 'I'm right here. I'm not going anywhere.' He could imagine her lying on her bed too, the light of her lamp making her look candlelit, soft, beautiful.

'My phone is on my pillow too,' she said. 'It's going to be there all night.'

She was staying. Something inside him softened, even as his chest ached. Walker felt his body begin to relax, muscle by muscle, one vertebra after the other, until he sank into his mattress.

'You're not on your own. There's nothing to worry about.' Gabi's voice was quieter now. 'And if you want me, just say my name.' The same name he'd called earlier when he came. He sighed and felt his fingers relax on the sheet; he hadn't even realised how tightly he'd been gripping them. He yawned, loudly.

'Good,' whispered Gabi. 'Now, you're going to go to sleep. You're going to dream good dreams and you're going to wake up tomorrow feeling better.'

Walker closed his eyes.

'Just listen to my breathing.' Gabi's voice was close, as if she lay beside him.

He reached for the phone and moved it closer to his face on the pillow. The sound of her breathing was all he could hear. In. Out. Soft. Slow. He focused on the sound, the rhythm, and let it take him away.

# Chapter Twenty-Five

*Gabi*

Gabi awoke to the sound of Walker's contented snores. Confused for a moment, she reached a hand behind her and hit cold, empty sheets, before opening her eyes to see the phone beside her on the pillow. She blinked and rubbed her eyes, smiling at the snuffling, putting a hand over her mouth so her laugh didn't wake him. She checked the time; it was well past nine. He'd had a good eight hours after his nightmare. That should set him up for the day. She carefully lifted the phone and pressed red to end the call.

Downstairs, Amber was already home. Gabi pushed the kitchen door open to see her friend wearing the same clothes she'd had on yesterday. Her grin told Gabi everything she needed to know about how her night had gone with Alex.

'Someone's in a good mood,' Gabi teased. Amber winked, making Gabi laugh.

'You guys want coffee?' Amber asked as she turned down the music, holding up two cups.

'Just one for me,' Gabi replied, pulling out a stool and propping up her leg.

'Walker's gone already?' Amber asked, putting one cup back on the shelf. 'Got an early shift?'

'Coffee first, then I'll tell you the full story,' Gabi said. When they both had a cup in front of them, she told Amber what had happened: from the best sex of her life to the worst wake-up call ever in the middle of the night.

Amber's face fell as she cupped her coffee with both hands. 'Poor Walker,' she said. 'He must see some awful things in his job.'

Gabi went on to tell Amber about the pillow talk.

'Well, that's a different kind of late-night call,' Amber said, with a tilt of her head. 'Not one I've had before.'

Gabi sipped her coffee. 'Same here.'

'Kind of you, though,' Amber said.

Gabi shrugged. 'I was just looking forward to round two,' she said with a laugh. 'What about you and Alex?'

'I gave in to the force . . .'

'Again.' Gabi smiled.

Amber rolled her shoulders and stretched. 'What can I say? It's a strong force.'

The front door opened, and Jayden skidded in, throwing his rucksack at the hook, not caring that it hit the floor. Amber pulled him in for a cuddle, but he brushed her off.

'Was it a fun sleepover?' Amber asked and he stopped mid-mouthful, frowning, and signed something quickly to his mum. She started to respond, but Jayden was determined to finish his story. Only when he finally finished did she reach over to stroke his cheek and sign again. She held up two fingers and then a gesture that looked like the roll of a dice. He sighed in frustration but then nodded in agreement. Amber passed him her phone and he slouched at the kitchen table, watching street dance videos as he ate his second breakfast of the day.

Amber rolled her eyes and turned back to Gabi. 'He's had a falling out with his friend. Apparently, he took Jayden's phone and used up all the battery.' Gabi glanced at Jayden, but he was oblivious, focused on the screen.

'What did you say to him?'

'I just reminded him that everyone deserves second chances.' She signed it again as she spoke.

Jayden laughed out loud at something he was watching, the argument already forgotten.

The doorbell rang and Gabi couldn't help but think it might be Walker. 'I'll get it,' she said, slipping off the stool. She ran her fingers through her hair and pulled her dressing gown around her before setting off down the hall.

Alex stood on the doorstep, shy grin on his face, guitar on his back. Gabi felt her shoulders drop but managed a smile in return. It wasn't like Walker would be running round first thing in the morning, was it? He might be getting ready for work for all she knew.

'I've got something for Jayden,' Alex said, holding up a plastic bag.

'Come on in,' Gabi said. 'They're in the kitchen.' He followed her down the hall, chatting about the dinner the day before.

As he entered the kitchen behind her, she saw the look

on Amber's face, and knew she'd done the wrong thing. She stopped dead and Alex bumped into her back.

'What are you doing here?' Amber asked, eyes wide and flicking quickly from Alex to Jayden and back again. Jayden remained absorbed by his film, spooning the remnants of his cereal into his mouth. He didn't look up.

Alex smiled hopefully at Jayden before turning to Amber, but on seeing her expression, the smile disappeared. 'I brought the egg boxes ...' He held up the bag as if showing evidence. Amber frowned.

'You mentioned last night Jayden needed some for a school project ...' he trailed off and dropped the bag back down by his side. Amber moved directly in between Alex and her son. If Jayden looked up, he would only see her back and not be able to read her lips. You could cut the atmosphere with a knife.

'He does,' Amber said carefully.

Alex shifted under her gaze and a flush was creeping on his neck.

'We had loads so I thought I'd drop them in.' His voice wavered, and Gabi felt a rush of sympathy for him while simultaneously wishing she was anywhere else than in the kitchen with them. Amber took the bag and managed it without touching Alex at all. He stuffed his empty hands back into his jeans pockets and rocked on his heels.

'I wondered if you guys wanted to come to the park?' he asked. 'We're doing an afternoon set from the bandstand.'

Gabi wondered if Walker would be there. Perhaps they could all go. But any thought of that was dashed by Amber with the next sentence.

'Not happening, Alex.' She crossed her arms and shook her head. Gabi was impressed. Amber was a protective mother above everything, even if she and Alex had just spent the night together.

'It was just a thought,' Alex said, adjusting his guitar strap as if it was throttling him.

'Well, don't have any more of them.' Amber held his eye. 'This isn't anything serious. To be even more clear, when I think of you, I think fun. Not family.'

Alex slumped, looking deflated.

'I think you should go now.' Amber nodded towards the front of the house. 'We don't want to confuse the two.'

Alex nodded. 'I don't want to confuse him either, Amber. I'm sorry.' He dipped his head in deference to her decision.

'See you around,' said Amber, turning away to the kitchen sink. Her back was bristling and her head held high. He was dismissed.

'Hope so,' Alex replied quietly, just as Jayden lifted his face from his screen. Gabi watched as the little boy's face split into a grin to see Alex there, and Alex beamed back.

Alex signed something across the kitchen, putting two fingers to the base of his throat and then pointing at the boy. Jayden looked shyly surprised and then repeated the sign back, before glancing at his mum, making sure she hadn't seen.

Alex waved at Jayden, smiled sheepishly at Gabi and was gone. Gabi once again wished it had been Walker that had turned up before heading off to get dressed and get on with her day.

# Chapter Twenty-Six

*Walker*

He'd managed to avoid Gabi all week, but eventually Walker ran into her at the gym. Literally. He turned the corner to get to the free weights section and rushed smack bang into her, knocking her flying and having to grab her to keep her upright. He'd forgotten how tiny she was as he steadied her in his hands. And he couldn't help but let his eyes skim that body in her gym kit.

'Hi.' She smiled up at him and he averted his gaze. 'How are you doing?'

How was he doing? What, after his mortifying nightmare and then running off into the night without any explanation?

'Are you feeling better?' she went on.

Please don't start talking about it, Walker prayed to himself. Please don't make me relive the whole embarrassing drama.

'I was worried about you.' Her eyes were soft, probing. She was obviously determined to be nice about it. Even if Gabi thought he was a loser, she was going to be pleasant and keep up appearances so that they could all spend the rest of her time in Honeybridge on good terms. Walker clenched his jaw.

'I'm fine,' he said gruffly, pushing his hair off his face.

'Good, I'm glad to hear that.' She was still smiling up at him. Last time she'd been looking up at him, she'd been in bed with him, looking up from a slightly different angle ... He shook himself. She wouldn't want to do any of that again. He'd blown his chance for sure. There was a joke in there somewhere, but he wasn't in the mood to find it.

'Haven't seen you for a few days?' Gabi left the question hanging.

Or nights, he thought, thinking back to waking up that morning to his phone on his pillow. His call log said that he'd been on a call with Gabi for over eight hours. It had ended five minutes before he woke up. Thank God for that. He wouldn't have known what to say if he'd woken and she'd still been on the other end of the line, having looked after a fully grown man all night to make sure he didn't have another bad dream. Honestly, how pathetic.

'Work's been busy ...' he said vaguely, and she nodded, waiting for more.

'Any more emergencies?' she asked.

He shook his head tiredly and she bit her lip.

'Walker, about the other night—' she started but he cut her off.

'Better get on,' he said. 'Late already.' He nodded past her towards the weights. Her eyes widened and she took a beat before nodding.

'Sure. Well, I'll see you at the Honeybridge Awards on Saturday.'

Walker nodded, feeling like the biggest idiot in the world. He should say something, he knew that, but what? He didn't know whether he should be thanking her or apologising to her. And it probably didn't matter anyway, because she was hotter than hell and he was the town coward. It wasn't like anything he said was going to change that.

'I'm looking forward to it,' Gabi continued as she started to move past him. And then with a mischievous smile over her shoulder, she added, 'Jayden's been teaching me to breakdance. I'm looking forward to trying out my moves.'

Walker watched her go, trying not to focus on her arse. Better to steer clear and not make a fool of himself all over again. He wasn't man enough for the job.

# Chapter Twenty-Seven

*Gabi*

Gabi shimmied in the mirror. Her little black dress sparkled and clung in all the right places. Her short, inky hair was extra sleek, and her big brown eyes were dark-rimmed with liner. She looked good enough for a red carpet – which was the last place she'd worn this ensemble – at the Oscars for a film. The only difference this time was instead of wearing death-defying heels, she was sporting one sequinned silver Birkenstock on her good foot, and a protective boot on the other. She'd show Walker McBride what he was missing.

First of all, he hadn't rung or texted after their night together. Not that she'd been watching her phone or anything; he wasn't her boyfriend after all. But he hadn't even dropped her a message to say he hoped he hadn't snored during their late-night call. Because he had, actually. Even if they were very little snores like a dog in front of the fire. Kind of cosy and cute. But anyway. Not only had he not messaged, but he'd pretty much blanked her at the gym. How dare he brush her off like that?

What had she done to him apart from probably give him the best sex of his life and then ring him to make sure he was okay? He literally didn't have a word to say to her when she'd run into him, and she'd stumbled off feeling like she was the last person he wanted to see. When she'd been so looking forward to it and still hoped they would be hooking up again. She believed that he'd felt the connection as much as she had, the electricity that shot through her every time he touched her. But maybe he'd enjoyed his night and that was that. What did she care anyway? She'd be out of this tiny town soon and back to real life. She had a call scheduled with her agent in the morning. Hopefully good news about the next role. She tilted her chin at her reflection, grabbed her bag and headed out to where Amber waited in the hall.

'Holy shit, Gabi,' Amber said, licking her finger and hissing when she pressed it to Gabi's arm. 'You look smoking.'

'You too.' Gabi nodded appreciatively at the low-cut, long gold dress Amber was nearly wearing. 'Let's go and have some fun.'

Jayden waved from his seat on the sofa with babysitter Millie Malone, and they were off.

The town hall was a pretty building from the outside, stone built, and ivy clad. Internally, it was all tiled floors and wood panelling. The women left their coats at the cloakroom and headed in to find a drink.

The great and the good of Honeybridge were stacked three deep at the bar wearing sequins and suits. The air was thick with aftershave and the noise levels were high with excitement. Amber spotted a gap and slotted in, quickly reappearing with a bottle of Prosecco and two flutes. Gabi meanwhile had snagged a high, round table with two stools and they settled in.

'So, you trying to get the attention of anyone in particular?' Amber asked with a wink.

'Nope. Like I said, I think that's done,' Gabi lied with a smile. 'You?'

Amber laughed. 'Well, Alex's band is playing later . . .'

Gabi pulled a face. 'Poor Alex, I almost felt sorry for him the other day. You laying down your ground rules.'

Amber's smile dropped as she sighed.

'I can't have him thinking there's any hope for a future. We might be having fun but there's no way I'm letting him near Jayden again.'

Gabi remembered the secret sign between Jayden and Alex in the kitchen and wished she could remember exactly what they'd done. They'd looked happy to see each other, but she couldn't remember the movement to show Amber.

'So how much fun *are* you two having?' Gabi asked.

'Well, my afternoon break from Tutto Mio has never been so well put to use.' Amber smacked her lips together. 'I really am *putting my feet up* for half an hour!' Gabi laughed outright, just as the gang walked across the hall towards them. For a woman who had worked on film sets her whole life, Gabi had to admit they were a beautiful bunch. Isabella looked ravishing in red on Etienne's arm. Rosie and Wren both wore white trouser suits with heels. Fox's silver quiff set off his all-black suit. And then there was Walker, wearing a kilt and looking utterly gorgeous. Even his knees were sexy. Shit. That was the last thing she needed.

Walker made his way around the group, kissing the women's cheeks and clapping the men on the back. He avoided eye contact when he reached Gabi; the kiss he pressed to her cheek was paper dry and light as a feather. The kind of kiss you might give your great-aunt, if she smelled of kippers and had a moustache. Even so, the smell of him was like a reminder of their night in her bedroom. She had to force herself to keep her hands in her lap and not grab him by the lapels. It was over in a heartbeat and then Walker quickly moved to the other side of the table, immersing himself in conversation with Fox. Gabi poured herself another drink and tried to ignore how her body reacted to him. Even when she hated him.

# Chapter Twenty-Eight

*Walker*

That dress should be illegal. Gabi's tiny, curvy body was sheathed in the skimpiest, black sparkly number he'd ever seen. And if Walker wasn't such a loser, he'd crush her to his chest and tell her just what she was doing to him. But she deserved better. And she hadn't even touched him when he kissed her, just the tiniest inclination of her head. Enough to tell him that things had changed. She obviously wasn't attracted to him now she'd seen what a mess he was.

He practised some deep breathing, trying to keep a handle on himself. The night was stressing him out already, without adding Gabi into the mix. He'd been handed a programme on entry and scanned it as he waited for the others to check their coats. His heart had started pounding at the list of award categories: Caring Hero, Young Hero, Starter Hero among others. His heart-rate accelerated further when he saw that his section, Everyday Hero, was second to last. He'd rather get it over and done with: lose gracefully, drink a beer with the guys, and go home, alone.

They moved through to the seating area, and he made sure to take a seat between Rosie and Fox. He watched Alex pull out Amber's chair and kicked himself. He should at least have done that for Gabi, especially as she was still not on two feet. A moment too late, he half stood to offer but she manoeuvred herself into the chair and turned her head away. She very obviously did not want his help.

The mayor took to the stage and made an introductory speech about how hard it had been to judge the awards, as Honeybridge seemed to set the bar very high on heroes. Rosie patted his hand on the table, and he wished she'd stop looking at him like that.

The first category was announced, and Walker was pleased to see that the nominees were only name-checked over the microphone. The most they had to do was wave from their table when the spotlight found them. It was only the winner that was invited to the stage to collect their award. Thank God for that, because his legs were already shaking under his kilt, and he wasn't sure they would carry him. Which was unusual, considering he ran into burning buildings.

The second category was all about young heroes. He recognised the winner as one of the young waiting staff from Tutto Mio; she had apparently set up a community network for checking on your neighbours. She jumped up and down on the stage with her award over her head and he heard Isabella shouting, 'That's my girl!' above the applause. He adjusted his collar, trying to let some air into his shirt. Was it really hot in there?

By the time they'd worked down to his award, his chest was banging, and his hands were clammy and clenched tight to his thighs under the table.

'Your turn!' Rosie whispered and clapped in excitement. The noise was too loud in his ear. Too many people were looking at him. Too many expectations on his shoulders.

The mayor was introducing the nominees. A nurse who worked through Covid. A police officer who rescued a dog from the river. A paramedic who saved a patient's life. All of them worthy winners. They all smiled broadly and waved excitedly from their chairs as the spotlight hit them.

'And Walker McBride,' the mayor said, 'for his efforts in the Hearts of Honeybridge Fire last autumn.'

Walker was blinded by the light. He squinted and raised a hand in what he hoped was a cheery wave, but his smile felt stretched across his face. As the spotlight swung away to the next nominee, he bumped eyes with Gabi and was surprised to see concern in her gaze. He could feel his hand shake as he stuffed it beneath the table again.

'And the winner is . . .' The mayor opened the envelope and pulled out a card. He looked delighted as he turned towards their table. 'Walker McBride!' Walker felt suffocated, even as his table erupted into cheers and the rest of the hall clapped along.

'Go on then,' Rosie laughed, pushing him with her palm. He stumbled to his feet, wanting to pause, catch his breath. But the mayor beckoned him with his hand and Walker pushed one foot in front of the other, forcing himself through the tables to the stage.

There were only three steps, but by the time he got to the top, he was breathing as though he'd run seven storeys. It was hard to catch his breath.

'From what we hear, Walker, you single-handedly evacuated

more than ten of the residents from their homes,' the mayor was saying as he pumped his hand. 'And I also heard that just last week, it was you that saved the child from the high ropes accident.'

Walker stared out at the crowd, hardly listening. He scanned the tables. Where was the nurse who'd risked everything during Covid? Or the policeman that had jumped into a flooded river to save a dog? Surely they should be up here right now? All he could see were spotlights and sparkly dresses. That made him think of Gabi. She knew the truth. She'd probably be wondering how he had the nerve to accept the award.

Walker knew then he had to get off the stage, out of the spotlight and away from this farce. Because he knew the truth. He wasn't a hero, and he never would be.

'You really sum up what we mean when we say hero,' the mayor finished, turning them both towards a camera which flashed in his face. He felt light-headed as the mayor let go of his arm, black spots floating in his vision. Stumbling down the steps, he turned away from his table, wanting only to find somewhere quiet and dark to be alone. The mayor moved on and was announcing the nominees for the final category as Walker pulled open the nearest exit and crashed out into the corridor.

# Chapter Twenty-Nine

*Gabi*

There was something going on with Walker. When the mayor had called his name as a nominee and he waved, Gabi had seen the shake in his hand. And when they'd caught eyes, she'd seen the same strange fear in them that he'd woken with in her bed. He looked haunted. And that had turned into a look of absolute panic when he was declared winner.

She watched him move almost automatically, putting one foot in front of the other, blindly making his way to the stage. She saw alarm flash across his face as he looked at the crowd. On what should have been one of the proudest nights of his life, he looked devastated. He left the stage and rushed out of the nearest door.

'Is Walker okay?' Gabi whispered to Alex, sitting next to her. 'He looked a bit overwhelmed.'

Alex considered for a moment, then nodded. 'Probably just the shock of winning. He was a bit surprised to even be nominated to be honest. I'll go check.' He pushed his chair back to stand and accidentally jogged Amber's elbow, tipping a full glass of wine straight down her front.

'OMIGOD,' Amber gasped, and Gabi remembered she always added ice cubes to her wine, liking it extra chilled.

Sure enough, Amber delved her hand deep into her cleavage and plucked out an ice cube, while Alex grabbed a napkin and started frantically patting her down.

'I'll go,' Gabi said, not wanting to leave it any longer. The panic on Walker's face was bothering her. She grabbed her crutches and set off, bumping into Fox coming out of the men's room as she rounded the corner.

'Is Walker in there?' she asked.

'Didn't see him,' Fox replied, signalling he was off for a drink.

Gabi checked the foyer, and the side room, and finally the cloakroom, but Walker was nowhere to be seen. Maybe she shouldn't be surprised, maybe it was classic Walker: to run whenever things got hard, or scary. It's what he'd done to her the other night. And now it just looked like he'd done it again. She sighed, really wanting to be angry with him. To be furious, in fact. But she couldn't shake the look on his face, and that tremor she'd noticed when he raised his hand. He wasn't just panicked. He was scared. And however big of an arsehole he was, she didn't want him to be scared and on his own.

Leaning against the wall in the foyer, Gabi pulled out her phone and rang him, not even really knowing what she was going to say. Turned out, that didn't matter, because Walker wasn't picking up. She heard it ring three times, four times, five, in the handset and then she heard something else. A phone ringing in the room next to her, in time with the ringtone in her ear. She shuffled to the glass door, the one with a notice on it that read: *The Old Library*. And beneath it: *Closed to the Public.* She ended her call. The ringing inside stopped. She counted to twenty and then rang Walker again. Immediately, she heard the phone inside again. She had him.

She checked nobody was looking, opened the door and slipped inside, letting it swing quietly shut behind her. The room was covered floor to ceiling with books, row upon row lining the walls. With a soft carpet and some small round tables for two, it looked like a cosy reading room. The lighting from the foyer only reached so far, and the rest of the room was in shadows. Following the ringtone, and using her phone as a light, she rounded the corner. There he was, slumped on one end of a window seat, head in his hands, silhouetted by the street lights outside. The award glinted, discarded on the floor beside him.

'Aren't you going to answer that?' she asked. His head snapped up and he glanced at the phone and then at her, but his face was blank. He was lost. Her stomach fell at the sheer look of horror on his face.

Walker let his head drop back into his hands and it was then that she noticed his irregular breathing, his fluttering hands. He was having a panic attack. She'd seen co-workers before on set a couple of times when stage fright turned into something much worse. Gabi hobbled towards him as fast as she could, bent to him and took his hands in hers to reach him. He wouldn't look at her.

'Breathe with me, Walker,' she said gently. 'Follow my count. In, two, three, four, hold, two, three, four, out, two, three, four . . .' She gripped his hands tighter until he began to listen, but it was only after she'd repeated her instructions three more times that he finally raised his eyes to hers. He was back.

'You should go, Gabi.' His voice was tight with emotion, his back rigid as he pulled his hands from hers. She hopped to the other end of the window seat and sat, no intention of going anywhere.

'I'm worried about you.'

Walker groaned and loosened his bow tie, letting it hang in his collar.

'Why are you even here?' he growled.

'You looked upset on the stage. I thought you might want to talk.' She lifted her boot onto the window seat, and it stretched out towards him. He moved his legs over to make space. 'And you know I'm a good listener,' she carried on. 'I've got over eight hours of practice of listening to you, even if you weren't saying much at the time.'

She smiled but he didn't return it, turning instead to look out the window, down onto the empty Honeybridge high street.

'Okay, enough with the jokes,' she said. 'You've just won an award for being a hero. I don't understand why you aren't happy? I just wanted to make sure you were okay.'

His eyes flashed dangerously at her then in the shadows. His jaw could cut glass.

'Don't call me that.'

'It's not just me that's calling you that,' Gabi said softly. 'It's official.' She held up the award as though in acceptance. It was engraved, *Walker McBride* scrawled across it. 'You even have the shiny piece of glass to prove it.'

'Not for long,' he ground out between clenched teeth. 'I'm going to give that back.'

'What on earth for?' Gabi asked, pressing it against her chest as though to keep it safe.

'Because I don't deserve it,' Walker said. 'I shouldn't even have been nominated, let alone won. I'm not a hero. I never have been.' He rubbed his hands across his eyes.

'Well, even if you wanted to, you can't give it back now,' she said decisively. Their eyes met and held. 'The mayor's gone home.'

A moment passed as he questioned her silently with his gaze. Then he sighed, defeated.

'I could keep it for you,' Gabi said. 'Then you could give it back tomorrow.' She tucked the glass trophy into her bag.

'I won't change my mind if that's what you're thinking,' he said, as if he could, in fact, read her mind. 'I can't keep it. It wouldn't be right.'

She settled her back against the window seat, facing him. Their legs lay parallel between them.

'Why do you think you don't deserve it?' Gabi asked quietly. Walker shrugged as if it was obvious.

'I'm not as good as people think I am.'

She watched a ripple cross his face. Regret? Anger? Shame?

'Well, the town thinks you are,' she said.

'They don't know me, do they? They only know the job I do.'

'Which is pretty damned heroic,' she said. 'Walking into fires to save people, Walker. You can't just dismiss that.'

It hit her for the first time, that he did that out of choice. He didn't do what he did for personal gain, like she did. He did it to help other people. If her stunt went wrong, it just ended badly for her. If his efforts went wrong, other people died. It was a brave job to do, no doubt about it. But he wasn't having it. Any of it. He closed his eyes as if to block her out.

'That's what I'm paid to do.'

'But what about all the stuff you do for free?' Gabi tried again, leaning forward and putting her hand on his knee, shaking him gently to get his attention. He lifted his eyes, but they were doubtful.

'Like the tray you made for me? To make sure I could move things around safely with my crutches . . .'

He pulled a face as if it was nothing.

'And the fact that Rosie told me you do all the smoke alarms at their house and maintain them every year.'

He shook his head to dismiss it.

'And you lent Etienne the money to bring Alex home.' Isabella had told her that the year before. He sniffed.

'That's just money.' He sighed. 'Who cares about money?'

Gabi flinched at that. Was he commenting on her? Because he was right. Everything she did was for money; the bigger the cheque, the better. Because it bought her independence and made sure she could always sort out her own problems. Fix her own roof, pay her own mortgage, look after herself. That was important to her. Always had been. But it obviously wasn't to him. She thought for a moment.

'I saw you making sure Riley had her crash helmet at the park, before she went roller skating.' He shifted in his seat, but she pressed again on his knee. 'And I know you help Reggie with his school projects every month. I've heard about your school project winning Tyrannosaurus Rex with the acrylic nails.'

'That's just helping out a friend,' he said. 'Anyone would do the same.'

He was wrong. Not everyone would do the same.

'That's not true,' she said fervently. 'Not true at all, Walker.'

He lifted his eyes and she could see that he wanted to believe her. Her hand flexed on his knee, pressing home her words.

'You help everyone at every opportunity. Whether you're getting paid for it or not.'

She saw his shoulders drop, some of the tension leave him. 'It hasn't always been that way, though.'

'Maybe not. But not even you can be perfect all of the time. You're a good man, Walker McBride.' She smiled and saw the flicker of a smile light his face. It gave her a little lift inside, to see his mood brightening. She poked him with one finger.

'Come to think of it, you even carried me home once.'

He gave her a full-on grin this time and nudged her leg with his.

'I might have had ulterior motives that time.' Eye contact at last. And the glint in his eye made her tummy flip.

'Hmmm,' she said. 'What happened to those ulterior motives then?' Their eyes were both playful now. She flicked her tongue over her lower lip and watched his gaze drop to follow it.

'Thought I'd put you off with the nightmare.' The sounds of the party next door echoed through the walls. Gabi was more aware of the beat of her pulse now as it quickened.

'Not at all,' she said. It was true. Looking at him now, all she wanted to do was clamber over him like a climbing frame. Damn this stupid boot.

'What about the panic attack?' Walker asked, a look of embarrassment crossing his face.

'What about it?' Gabi asked. 'You're human, Walker. It would be strange to meet someone who was never affected by anything that happened to them. We all have our worries, our fears.'

'Not exactly manly, though?' he said. She interlaced her fingers through his and he lifted his eyebrows in surprise.

'You're still the sexiest Scotsman I've ever seen,' she said. 'And you're absolutely rocking that kilt.'

She dropped her eyes to his bare knees and wondered fleetingly if the rumours about the Scottish not wearing anything under their kilts was true. She crossed her fingers that she might get to find out.

Walker's phone rang suddenly, breaking the silence. As the screen lit Walker's face, he looked lighter, brighter and hot as hell. He angled the screen towards her to show it was Alex and answered on speaker. Noise and laughter burst into the library. Alex was trying to make himself heard, but Gabi could hear all the others in the background: Amber was cheering, Isabella laughing.

'You okay, man? I've been looking for you.'

Gabi bit her lip. She should have let Alex know she'd found Walker.

Walker kept his eyes on Gabi. 'All good, Al. I'm fine. You?' Walker reached out with his spare hand and encircled Gabi's ankle.

'Just about to go on with the band,' Alex said. 'Going to play that new song.'

'Hope it goes down well,' Walker said.

'Me too. You coming back in?'

Walker's hand on her ankle stroked upwards now, towards her knee, and back down again. Gabi bit her lip.

'No, I'm going to head off,' Walker said, fingers lingering on the inside of her knee this time, stroking the soft skin at the back. She widened her eyes. He was only touching her knee, for God's sake, an area which she'd never before thought of as an erogenous zone but would now firmly be adding to the list. She felt like some kind of swooning Victorian, half reclined on a window seat in the library, having her leg felt.

'Amber wants to know if you've seen Gabi?'

'Yes, she's here,' Walker said, his eyes burning into her. The intensity between them now like an electric charge. 'And she's coming home with me.'

# Chapter Thirty

*Walker*

A light rain was falling outside, and the pavements were slick and shiny. Walker carried Gabi home, not because she couldn't walk – as she asserted several times – but because she couldn't walk on her crutches fast enough for his liking. He needed to get her home and naked. Now. So, she carried her crutches, and he carried her, back to his riverside house.

The stairs didn't slow him down; he took them two at a time. When he clicked on the bedroom lamp, Fatboy Jim took off like a shot from his position mid-duvet, vacating the bed for the night shift. The cat just made it through the bedroom door before Walker kicked it shut.

He lowered Gabi to her feet and gave her a moment, to make sure the next decision was hers. She didn't hesitate, her hands roaming over his chest before grasping the ends of his bow tie and pulling him down towards her. Their mouths found each other, her lips open on his. He ground her against him, kissing her more and more deeply until she gasped. He felt himself hardening at the sound.

Gabi pushed his jacket off and it fell to the floor. Her fingers pulled feverishly at Walker's shirt buttons, tugging until she was finally pressed to his bare front, breaking from his mouth to drop kisses across his stomach, trace his tattoos with her fingers, moan into his shoulder.

Walker peeled one of the straps of her dress away from her body, and then the other. The satin fell down her arms, leaving her collarbone and shoulders pale and naked. He bit the soft side of her neck, playfully, gently, but hard enough to make her head fall back. He held her away from him to roll the dress all the way down her body to her waist, uncovering her inch by inch, his eyes lingering on her bare breasts, her stomach. She watched him now, breath heaving. He continued, moving the fabric over her hips and thighs, revealing lacy pants. Her dress now lay forgotten, a puddle of fabric on the floor.

Her hands moved to his kilt, fingers fumbling trying to work out how to unfasten it. Walker wanted her hands on him, her mouth, but not yet. First of all, he wanted to pay the right amount of respect to that body. He'd never seen one like it: delicate but so strong. It made him crazy. He caught her hands and held them still. She blinked at him, and he noticed how desire made her face soft: her lips seemed fuller, her brown eyes shone like the richest chocolate.

'I need these out of the way for a while,' Walker said, motioning towards her captured hands which he held in one of his own. He pulled at one end of his bow tie and it slid around his shirt collar, falling off in one long, black strip. He let go of

Gabi's hands and snapped his tie straight, raising an eyebrow questioningly at her.

She tilted her chin and the tiniest smile flitted across her face. She held her palms out towards him. Fuck, the things he wanted to do to her right now.

'Are you sure?' Walker asked.

'Yes.' Gabi pressed her wrists together, ready to be tied. He bound her and her breathing deepened as he pulled the knot tight. Walker nudged her backwards until she was leaning against the bedroom wall, before lifting her hands above her head.

'Keep them there,' he ordered. She nodded, eyes burning into him as he touched his hand to her throat and trailed it down to her clavicle. Then she closed her eyes and her lips parted as she drew in a deep breath. Without her distracting hands, Walker could move slowly as he touched her, brushing her shoulders, tracing the front of her chest until he dipped his head, holding her breasts in both hands and moving from one to the other, catching her nipples between his lips, nipping them with his teeth, flicking them with his tongue. She gasped and pressed into him, the urge to touch him almost overwhelming, her hands moving towards him.

'Don't move,' he ordered as though he could sense her intention and she raised them again to the wall above her head.

He knelt.

Putting his thumbs in either side of her underwear, he inched them down over her hips. They skimmed her thighs and got caught on her boot, before he freed them and pushed them to the floor.

His face was inches away from her sex. He held her in his hands, and the waiting made him harder. His hands spread across her taut stomach, moved around the curve of her hips, caressed her body until his fingers were drawn closer. Walker traced his thumb downwards until he separated her folds and felt the slick heat of her. Using his fingers, he explored her, rubbing the wetness of her.

'Walker,' she said above his head and he couldn't wait any more. He stood and lifted her in his arms in one movement and laid her on the bed.

'I want my hands back . . .' she whispered urgently, straining against the knot, and he pulled the tie undone. Freed, she wound her arms around his neck to return his force with her mouth. He was so hard for her. He pulled back to strip off his shirt and let his kilt drop to the carpet before standing in front of her, watching a small smile of satisfaction flick over her face when she got the answer to her question. Scotsmen wear nothing beneath their kilts. She put her hand out to him, urging him to the bed. He didn't need asking twice.

His hands claimed her body as it strained against him. Lying beside her on the bed, he turned her onto her side, taking the weight away from her boot. He moved behind her and encircled her with his arms, pressing his chest to her back, kissing the nape of her neck where her short dark hair ended. His hands reached around her to fondle her breasts, her nipples. His dick pressed against her buttocks, and she pushed back against him.

He reached around her hip and found her clitoris. He slipped his knee between hers and held her open as he made sure she was ready for him.

'Please,' she said, letting her head roll back onto his shoulder. 'Please.' Her begging set him on fire. He pushed two fingers into her and she arched in return. She was ready.

He lifted her legs wider with his knee and his cock nudged against her. He eased into her slowly, stretching his way, a centimetre at a time, until she moaned out loud.

'Enough?' Walker asked, grinding his jaw, trying to keep himself under control.

'No,' she whispered. 'More.' It was all he needed. He thrust into her, right to the hilt.

'Yes,' she groaned.

He withdrew, right to the tip, and thrust again, and again, and again. Their bodies rocked with each movement, his front to her back, their breath noisy, their bodies slick with sweat. His hand found her clit again and thumbed her in time to his fucking. She arched and made small, animalistic noises that made him hold her tighter, fuck her harder.

'Walker, I'm close,' she said and he lost what was left of his control. He plunged into her, again and again, as he felt the tension build and build, until he heard her cry out, and then he let himself fall into the abyss.

# Chapter Thirty-One

*Gabi*

Later, much later, when her breath had calmed down and her heart had stopped pounding, Gabi noticed the steady patter of rain on the windowpane. It sounded heavier than before. She shifted against Walker, cocooned against his chest.

'I should go,' she said into his shoulder, reluctantly.

'Really? I'll walk you then,' he murmured without moving. They lay there together and then a second later he whispered, 'Or you could stay?'

She paused momentarily. Not wanting to leave, but unsure of the protocol or the ground rules for a holiday hook-up. The room was suddenly bright as lightning flashed outside the window and a second later thunder rolled ominously. Her decision was made easy. She snuggled in.

'I'll drop you back in the morning,' he said. 'In case the pavements are slippery.'

Gabi laughed quietly. 'I'm sure I can manage a wet pavement,

Walker.' He didn't reply but she could bet he was going to drop her off anyway.

'What's this?' he asked then, tracing a silvery scar about an inch long on the back of her arm. She reached round to feel it.

'Fell off my roller skates,' she said. 'Gave myself concussion too. Didn't have someone like you strapping my helmet on like Riley.'

He dropped his chin to the spot, his stubble scratching lightly at the scar, almost a kiss but not quite.

'Ah, no. I hope your mum kissed it better?'

'Mum wasn't there. She'd left by then.' She forced a laugh.

'Where did your mum go?'

'Paris, first. With her next husband.'

'Is she still there?'

'She's now in Brazil with husband number four.'

'Wow.' She felt the shake of Walker's head on the pillow.

'That's one word for it.'

Rain was drumming now on the window and she watched it run in rivulets down the pane. She shivered, feeling suddenly bare.

'Do you see her much?' Walker asked, pulling the duvet over her and enfolding her in it.

Gabi shook her head. 'Not really. She's not what you'd call maternal. In fact, she should probably never have had children. She sends a postcard every now and then. It's so occasional, it surprises me when it arrives.'

'What about your dad?'

'Oh, *Dad* you can really rely on. He messages me religiously on the first of every month.' She laughed again. 'In fact, I think he might have it as a reminder in his diary. Because it's always the first of the month. And it's always the same thing. Are you okay and do you need anything? And I always reply with a yes, I'm fine, and no, I don't.'

'That's it?' Walker sounded incredulous.

'He didn't know what to do with me when Mamma left. I was a preteen girl, and he was a single dad who had no idea what he was doing. So, I went to Isabella's to stay and then I went to boarding school. I haven't lived with my dad since I was twelve. It made me grow up pretty quick.'

Another flash of lightning. They both waited for the thunder. Within seconds, it crashed overhead.

'But he's still there. Still asking. Still wanting you to reply,' Walker said.

'I guess so,' she said doubtfully. 'But only out of duty.'

'No wonder you're so stubborn, so independent,' Walker said.

'Well, I know I can rely on myself.'

Walker seemed to consider that.

'I get that, but it sounds like a tough gig,' he said. 'My parents were so supportive when I was growing up, I always knew they were there for me. I wish you'd been able to feel some of that too.'

He stroked her shoulder with his fingers, trailing them slowly down her back as she leaned against him.

'Even at my lowest points, I knew I could rely on them. They'd move heaven and earth to make sure I was happy. I'm sorry your parents didn't make you feel the same.'

Gabi could tell he meant it, could hear the empathy in his voice. Unexpected emotion tightened her chest and she swallowed, hard. Lightning forked across the window again.

'Can you turn the light off, so we can watch?' she said, changing the subject. Walker eased to the edge of the bed and reached out, and she saw the totality of the tattoos on his back for the first time, having only caught glimpses earlier. They were huge, spanning his shoulders and spreading over his lats, covering the entirety of his upper back.

'Wait,' she instructed, putting a hand on them, fascinated by their intricacy. He flinched at her touch, stiffened.

'These are beautiful,' she said, tracing the angel wing on each shoulder blade, the feathering on his ribs. He put his hand on the lamp to turn it off, but she stopped him.

'What's this?' She traced the words between the wings.

*Never Enough.*

'When did you get these done?' Walker looked at her over his shoulder. His sandy hair fell across his forehead.

'It's a work in progress,' he said.

'And the words?' she asked, tracing the black ink with her finger. 'What do they mean?'

He stood swiftly and snapped out the light, moving to stand in front of the window. He leaned one hand on the window frame, illuminated by the next lightning strike. The bed suddenly felt cold.

'Walker?'

Gabi wasn't quite sure what she was asking for – reassurance that he was okay, or for him to come back to bed.

'The words mean exactly what they say.' His voice was flat. 'I will never be enough.' The mood had darkened again and Gabi felt unsure as to how to bring him back.

Lightning streaked again and thunder clapped directly

overhead. His body was like marble in the blue-white light, his head tilted skywards. She hobbled over to him, feeling his vulnerability there in the storm. She wrapped her arms around his waist and leaned her forehead against his back.

'Like I said earlier, everyone I've met in Honeybridge thinks you are a good man.' She squeezed and tried to lighten the atmosphere. 'And you just proved yourself more than enough for me . . .'

The thunder rolled continuously now and the lightning lit the sky like static on a screen, flashing intermittently. They were right in the eye of the storm.

'Someone died, Gabi. Because of me. So, whatever I do will never be enough. Because I didn't save them.'

# Chapter Thirty-Two

## *Walker*

He thought he heard Gabi gasp, but if she did, it was swallowed by the thunder. He wrapped his own arms around his front, covering hers, so that he would feel if she pulled away.

Walker had never said the words out loud before. Having the tattoo done had been the recognition of the fact that whatever he did in the future and whoever he saved, it would never change the past. Someone had died because of him.

'Was it at work?' she asked and he shook his head, surprised to feel her arms tighten around him.

'You can tell me, Walker,' she said softly. 'Seeing as we seem to be in the mood for sharing tonight. Beds, bondage, my childhood . . .' She squeezed him again as she trailed off.

Maybe it was because she was holding him, maybe it was because he couldn't see her face. Maybe it was because she was slightly outside his close group of friends. Perhaps it was the sheer force of the storm outside, that mirrored everything going on inside him. But suddenly, he wanted to talk. He had to let it out. He licked his lips and began.

'I was twelve,' he said quietly. 'We still lived in Scotland.'

As he stared out the window, the river looked dark and fast at the end of the lawn. He fixed his eyes on the swirling water and continued.

'Our house was on the edge of Loch Leven, overlooking St Serf's Island. My sister and I grew up fishing and hiking and sailing. The loch was like our back garden.'

Gabi was silent. He could sense her waiting.

'My best friend Murray lived about a mile around the water. We'd cycle to each other most days after school. One winter, it got so cold the loch froze over.' He shivered at the memory. The vast whiteness of the frozen lake, the impossible smoothness of it, like a giant ice skating rink. How Murray had skidded his bike to a stop and ran to the edge to throw sticks and watched them slide across the top of the ice. Their cheeks were almost as red as Murray's woollen bobble hat. Their shouts echoed across the vast expanse of space.

'I dared us to walk out on the ice,' Walker said. The words didn't convey the fear and excitement of it. The way they had edged out, little by little, away from the shore. They had egged each other on, sliding their boots across the surface, testing for a creak or a crack before they put any weight on the foot. He remembered how the loch felt so different that day, the woods so silent and still with the cold, the trees black and skeletal and glinting with frost. He blinked away tears. He could still see every detail, still smell the air that stung his nose with the cold.

'We got quite a long way out, had some crazy idea about making it all the way across the gap to St Serf's Island.'

They'd stopped checking back to shore. Emboldened by the thrill, high on the freedom. The crack, when it happened, was louder than he'd ever imagined. It echoed across the white. There was a split second when he and Murray locked eyes. A single moment in time when they both were paralysed with fear. Then the ice under Murray's feet gave way and he disappeared into the black water beneath. It was so quick. Walker had thrown himself to the ice, lying as flat as he could and stretching his hands and legs out wide to support his weight.

'The ice broke and Murray went under,' Walker said quietly. 'And I lay on the ice and didn't try to help him.'

It had been Walker that broke the silence. His screams plumed into white vapour in front of him; he screamed until his throat was raw. His fingertips burned where they held on to the ice. Eventually a passing hiker heard him and raised the rescue alarm. And by the time they'd got to him and dragged him back to safety, Murray was long gone.

'They think the shock of the water probably made him take a breath. Or he got confused underwater and came up under the ice. Whatever happened, he drowned, right there beneath me.'

'Oh my God, Walker, that is devastating,' Gabi murmured against his skin. 'I'm so, so sorry.'

He pressed his hands together, remembering the ice burn he'd suffered on his fingertips. He could still see Murray's bike lying on its side on the shore. He wondered who had moved it eventually. Whether Murray's parents had to come and wheel it away. He shuddered. Gabi rubbed his skin, as if trying to warm him up. He'd said it. The secret was out. His biggest failing.

'We couldn't live there any more. People were always talking about it. I felt guilty for not helping Murray. And guilty that I hadn't died with him. We moved south and ended up in Honeybridge. I met Rosie at school and the rest is history.' Lightning flickered, losing its power. The thunder rumbled, now sounding further away.

'But your parents aren't here any more?'

'They moved back when I was eighteen, said they missed the mountains. But we still see each other when I have leave. And we talk all the time.'

'They must be very proud of you,' Gabi said.

'They are,' he said. 'It's just me that's not.'

Gabi moved around his body, slipping under his arm and pressing against his front.

'It was a terrible accident, Walker. I'm so sorry that it happened to you.'

'I will never forgive myself,' he said simply.

'But you were only a child,' Gabi said. 'Nobody would want it to shape your whole life. Things that happened to us as kids shouldn't hold us back when we're adults.'

He sighed and pulled her closer. The thunder echoed, distant now, and the sky was dark. An owl hooted somewhere nearby, safe after the passing of the storm.

'I mean it,' Gabi said. 'I'm sure Murray would be the first one to tell you to let it go. He would want you to live.'

'But I can't forget him.' Walker's voice was flat. He was exhausted. Mentally. Physically. Emotionally. Always so exhausted.

'Then try to find a positive way to remember him.' She tugged him lightly by the arm, led him back to the bed. 'You're freezing,' she said. 'Let me warm you up.'

The mattress was cold, and he shivered as he lay down. She climbed in behind him, tucking in tight. Her arms wrapped around him, spooning his back, rubbing warmth and comfort into him with her hands. 'I'm here,' she said. 'I'm right here.'

He tried to relax against her. Wanting sleep above all else. But he still lay there, wide-eyed until he heard her breath soften and felt her arm grow heavy. Could he let it go? Was she right? Because something inside him was growing weary with carrying it all around. The owl called again and he closed his eyes. Finally, he felt himself drifting.

When he awoke, Gabi was gone.

# Chapter Thirty-Three

## Gabi

Gabi got some funny looks hobbling home at seven o'clock in the morning, wearing a sparkly black dress and a single sequinned sandal. But she had to get home quick for the Zoom interview. The one that she'd happily scheduled for eight a.m., not thinking she would have been up half the night sharing a bed and childhood stories with Walker McBride. She pushed herself along the high street from Walker's riverside house and made her way home to Amber's, only just having time to clean her teeth, change out of her party wear and make herself comfortable in the armchair in the sitting room before her meeting started.

The casting director beamed at her.

'Greetings, Gabriella!' the woman said, flashing an amazingly white set of teeth. 'Nice to finally meet you!'

Gabi turned on her own smile and mentally shook herself to focus on the task at hand. She had one chance, and one chance only, to show the panel why she was the best woman for the job. Gabi studied each attendee as they joined the Zoom and were introduced by the casting director. She'd done her homework and knew that she had the great and the good of the film industry seated in front of her. The studio had pulled in the big guns – the best directors, actors and writers – so they obviously expected the film to be box office magic.

'So, Gabriella,' the film director said.

'Please, call me Gabi.' Gabi smiled to set the tone: professional, friendly, easy to work with. 'Everyone does.'

'So, Gabi,' he started again with a nod. 'Your CV is certainly impressive. Tell us a bit more about yourself.'

Gabi straightened in her seat and began.

'I've been in the industry for more than a decade now and enjoy the challenge that comes with every new film, every new stunt, every new scene,' she said. 'I'm always growing my skill set to make sure that I can rise to any occasion.' The man nodded.

'And what's the latest skill you've added to your repertoire?' he asked, pen poised.

Gabi froze. For some reason all she could think of was Jayden teaching her a few breakdance moves. She cleared her throat to buy herself a second, before saying hurriedly, 'Archery. I learned last year for a role in an advert.'

'That's quite a skill to master.' The casting director rejoined the conversation. 'We don't have any archery in this film, but we would need you to stunt double for the female lead in a number of "near death" scenes. Shall we describe them?'

Gabi nodded. The woman nodded at her assistant who picked up a list.

'A gunshot, first of all.'

'I was "shot" numerous times in The Gangs of Greenwich,' Gabi assured them, 'most notably while standing on the edge of a cliff, resulting in a high fall afterwards.'

'Being thrown through a window?' the assistant said.

'Again, I'm used to the various throws and know how to fall correctly.'

'An explosion will throw you through the air.'

'I will need to know the speed to manage my landing, but absolutely fine.' Gabi was quick with her assurances.

'And finally, we have some high diving scenes,' the assistant said.

'I dived from the waterfall in Gardens of God,' Gabi said. 'I have no fear of heights and can dive from ten metres or jump from twenty. Normally CGI does the rest.' She was comfortable with everything he was saying. It was nothing out of the ordinary in her life.

Relieved nods all round, followed by a sales pitch from the film director about the film itself, the location, the offer and the money. An eye-watering amount. It was all she could do to stop her mouth falling open. Gabi tried to keep a poker face, knowing that this was the pinnacle of her career to date. That it would surpass all of her lifelong ambitions. To work with big names, in Hollywood, for money that meant she might never have to work again. She took another sip of water and asked the next question she should ask.

'Are you considering other stuntwomen?'

'We are, of course.' The casting director stepped in to reply. 'But only as back-up if you can't take the role for any reason.

We did wonder if you'd already been approached for the new Spielberg that's shooting in South Africa.' Gabi smiled, but didn't confirm or deny. The woman paused and then continued, 'Which is why we've put such an attractive offer together. We want you to come and do ours.'

The discussions were all very promising. The film director understood that Gabi was currently incapacitated and was prepared to pay for a month of world-class physio in America before shooting began to ensure she was fully back in shape. An apartment of her own would be part of the deal. A full gym membership was of course included in the package to maintain fitness. At the end of the meeting, she hung up, a buzz of excitement building in her stomach. But also a slight sense of anxiety. She'd never felt so nervous about a job before. Maybe it was because she was so out of the game at the moment.

She could hear the radio playing and went to find Amber in the kitchen to tell her the latest, but that was forgotten when she found Amber glaring at her own phone as Gabi opened the door.

'You okay?' Gabi asked but Amber groaned aloud and slammed the phone face down next to her coffee cup.

'Who's bothering *you*?' Gabi asked, indicating the abandoned phone.

'Everyone,' Amber said, exhaling loudly. Her phone beeped and she turned it over momentarily before rolling her eyes and hiding it under the tea cosy.

'Alex?' Gabi asked. 'I thought you two were getting on really well last night.'

'Everyone but Alex, actually,' Amber said. 'But it's all his fault in the first place.'

Jayden ran in, dressed for his rowing club, River Rats, and Amber stopped mid-sentence. He grabbed a juice carton, oblivious that he was interrupting anything, waved at Gabi and then disappeared out the door. Amber waited until it clicked shut before continuing.

'Alex played a new song with the band,' she said, scowling. 'They made a big fuss about it, introduced it as new material, written by Alex, first ever public play, etc., etc.' Amber shook her head. 'He took lead vocals too.'

'Was it not good?' Gabi asked, not seeing any problem so far.

'Oh, it was better than good.' Amber pulled a face. 'It was beautiful. Everyone loved it.'

Gabi shook her head, bemused.

'It had this chorus, and the words were along the lines of: "*You might not hear these words, but you know what I'm saying . . . You're deep in my heart and that's where you're staying . . .*"'

'I don't get it, Amber? What's wrong with that?'

'It's the fact that when Alex introduced it, he said it was written for someone special.' She threw her hands up in disgust and then, noticing Gabi's confused face, pointed her thumbs at her chest and said, '*Me.* Obviously.'

Gabi laughed. 'That's romance right there,' she said. 'Most women would kill to have a song written about them. Me, I've never even had someone write me as much as a to-do list.'

Amber sighed.

'The problem is, now all the gang are involved.' She unearthed her phone from under the tea cosy and waved it in Gabi's direction. 'First it was Isabella; she was quick off the mark, probably because she's all loved up herself. Then it was Etienne, the original love 'em and leave 'em, telling me relationships are worth it, and then Fox even took time out from being Hot Single Dad of Honeybridge to add his two cents. All of them suggesting maybe I give Alex another chance.' She dropped her head to the table and banged it lightly. Gabi reached out to stroke her friend's hair.

'Is it such a bad idea?' Gabi risked. 'You two do really seem to have something.'

Amber lifted her head to look at Gabi in disbelief.

'Okay. I admit it. The connection is definitely there. He's attractive, intelligent, funny as fuck and hotter than hell. And now, I find out the arsehole can sing as well. So, yes, if I was a single woman with no commitments, I'd probably risk my heart and jump at another chance for a relationship with Alex Martin. But I'm not a single woman with no commitments, and I can't do it. Because Jayden's heart is way more precious than mine.'

Gabi took Amber's hand in her own and squeezed it gently. 'You're a brilliant mum,' she said.

Amber exhaled slowly, her eyes brimming with tears. 'And he's the best kid in the world.'

Gabi nodded, feeling tearful herself all of a sudden. Must be the late night. The midnight dramas.

Amber shook herself to change the mood.

'Enough of that,' she said and checked her watch. 'I have to get Jayden to River Rats soon. Although probably the whole gang will be there to keep up the pressure.'

'I could take him if you like?' Gabi asked.

'Would you?' Amber put her hands together in thanks. 'I don't think I can face any more.' She flicked the kettle on. 'Anyway, why are you home so early?'

'Call with my agent.' Gabi updated her quickly and Amber pretended to faint at the salary.

'What did Walker think?' she said.

'I left him asleep,' Gabi said, sinking into the kitchen chair. 'In fact, I think I woke up in some kind of parallel universe. I had this sexy, sensitive man spooning me. The sun was streaming in the window. We'd spent all night having sex and talking and watching thunderstorms. There was even a goddamned cat curled up and purring on the bed. I woke up in a full-blown relationship when I'd gone to bed a single woman.'

It was Amber's turn to laugh.

'Sounds terrible,' she sympathised. 'You poor thing.'

'I don't know how it happened,' she said. 'The sex was so good it hypnotised me into telling him all my secrets.' Amber put up a hand to halt the conversation.

'Just to clarify, the sex was good?'

Gabi exhaled a long, slow breath.

'The best. That man knows how to use his hose.' Amber snorted. The kettle blew steam into the air in a long whistle, and she rose to pour them both a cup of tea.

'So why are you back here and not in that warm bed waiting for Walker to wake up? You could have taken the call there?'

'I don't know.' Gabi shrugged helplessly, peering into her cup of tea for answers.

'I do,' Amber said, leaning forward to make her point. 'You freaked out.'

Gabi's heart sank. She knew Amber was partially right.

'It all just felt too much.' She cupped her hot mug in both

hands as she remembered how safe she'd felt talking to him about her childhood, his breath on her back.

'Too nice,' Amber added.

'Too intense.' Gabi remembered the explosion of her orgasm and even just the memory echoed through her as pleasure.

'Too soon?' Amber asked.

Gabi agreed. She sighed. 'I feel like I told him things I don't need to share.'

'Aha. Too intimate.'

'Definitely.'

The two women watched each other over their tea.

'Sounds like the start of a great relationship if you ask me.'

'That's the problem. I'm not here for a boyfriend.' Gabi sighed. 'I'm here for a broken leg.'

# Chapter Thirty-Four

*Walker*

Walker put himself to work. It was the only thing he could do to distract himself from the turmoil inside. After the night he and Gabi had shared, the last thing he'd expected to wake up to was an empty bed. Even Fatboy Jim had gone, leaving just a small dent in the duvet. He'd sat up, stunned, and it took a moment for it to sink in. She'd left. After everything he'd said and shared. She'd gone. All his fears had been proven true. He'd bared his soul and it wasn't enough. And he never would be.

He heaved at a fallen bough and set about clearing the debris left by the storm on the riverbank at the rowing club. The River Rats would be turning up soon for their lessons and he didn't want the kids tripping up and falling in. He dragged the bigger branches to one side and checked the jetty for damage. When he was done, he moved to the boat house to inspect the rowing boats and life jackets. By the time the kids started to arrive, he was satisfied everything was safe but felt no calmer on the inside. His guts were churning with anxiety.

He could kick himself. Why had he said any of that last night? What an idiot.

Rosie and Wren were early, their daughter Riley streaking ahead to throw herself at his legs. He caught her and swung her in the air. Rosie was rosy-cheeked; Wren was white as a ghost and carrying a water bottle.

'There he is, our resident hero,' Rosie said, reaching up to kiss his cheek.

'Shut your face,' he said with a half-smile and a shake of the head. He leaned over to kiss Wren, but she put one hand on his chest to stop him, and the other over her mouth.

'Don't,' she muttered, turning a shade of green. 'Not feeling the best today . . .'

Wren stumbled away to a nearby bench and Rosie watched until she sat.

'Anyway, Walker McBride.' She faced him again. 'Good night?' She raised a single eyebrow. Everyone knew he'd gone home with Gabi. His heart sank.

'Definitely memorable,' Walker said, resisting the urge to tell her everything. He couldn't even get it straight in his head, so had no idea how to put it into words. He'd thought things were finally on the up, but they seemed to have come crashing down again while he was still sleeping.

'Here they come,' Rosie said, watching a small procession of kids and parents arrive along the riverside path. 'Time to get this show on the road.'

Fox, Reggie and George all wore River Rats caps, although Fox wore his backwards. Etienne followed just behind, carrying the register and the money tin. Jayden cartwheeled along the bank and Walker looked for Amber. His heart sank when he instead spotted Gabi hobbling along the path. Fuck. He wasn't ready for that. And she looked good too.

'Gabi!' Rosie waved. 'Come join!' Gabi looked over, caught his eye and had the grace to blush.

Walker ignored her, turned and began bringing the starter rafts out. Ten minutes later, the younger age group, including Riley, Reggie and George, wore life jackets and were heading out on the water with their instructors. Rosie passed him a coffee and went to watch from the jetty, while Wren gagged from the smell and moved away, leaving him next to Gabi. His stomach clenched.

'Hi, you.' Her voice was low and quiet. It took him back to his pillow and the darkness in the room as she told him about her childhood. She'd been so open about things that were so painful. Was she going to act now like everything was normal? Like last night hadn't happened at all?

'Gabi,' Etienne said, striding towards them. He put his hands out pleadingly. 'I need your help. You've got to talk to Isabella about the wedding. I don't want to wait any more but she's digging her heels in.'

Walker saw Gabi's eyes flick towards him, but he moved away, wanting to escape from her and from talk of marriages. He was simmering inside with hurt. He thought they'd shared something – not just the sex, although that had been fucking amazing; more of a connection. He'd told her his secrets. He'd told her what fuelled his bad dreams and what he was most afraid of in life. Why he would never be good enough. And after laying himself bare, she obviously agreed with him. Because she'd got up in the night and snuck off, unable to even look at him in the cold light of day.

He passed Wren, who was now sitting with her head between her knees, and stormed inside to get out the rowing boats for the older age group. Jayden appeared beside him to help carry one to the water. Walker threw him a life jacket and got a thumbs up in return. If only everything was so easily sorted.

He found himself in a group again on the bank with Fox, Etienne and Gabi as they watched the older children row away. She was chatting and joining in, but he felt like he had a stone stuck in his throat. He forced a laugh when necessary, but avoided Gabi's dark brown eyes at all costs. Not allowing himself to look down into her face as she stood next to him. Conscious of how small she was and remembering how his body had covered hers in the night. He shook his head.

Suddenly the others were gone. Etienne giving Wren a lift home after she vomited behind a tree. Fox to sort out the boys as they disembarked their raft. There was no escape as Gabi put a hand on his arm. He flinched.

'Walks,' she said.

*Walks*? What was that? A pet name for him to let him down gently? He frowned.

'We should probably talk about last night?' She glanced behind her to make sure there were no little ears around. He straightened and saw the flick of her eyes to his chest as he braced himself.

'Figured there wasn't much to talk about since you were up and out so early this morning.' It sounded harsher than he'd meant it to. She blinked and he noticed the creep of colour on her neck.

'I'm not normally one for sleepovers,' she said quietly. 'And I had an interview for a film in America first thing this morning.'

He raised an eyebrow. 'You could have left at any time last night.'

She tried a smile and dared a joke. 'Not strictly true, my hands were tied.' The image of her with hands bound flashed through his mind. He kept his face impassive. He would not be drawn into banter.

'What do you want, Gabi?' He felt tired suddenly. The night had taken its toll. The anxiety of the awards, the intensity of the sex, the lows of the storm and the weight of the shared conversation. He was shattered. Gabi pressed her mouth together. He watched her and wondered how she'd phrase it. Would she just come out with it and call him a coward? Would she tell him he was a loser that watched his best friend drown? That she really didn't think they should see each other again?

'I'm only here for about another month,' she said eventually.

Aha, so she was going down that route.

'So it's probably best if we don't get into anything heavy. Maybe it's better if we keep it . . .'

She paused and he waited for the word 'friends'.

'Casual?'

He frowned.

'Casual?' he repeated. 'What does that mean?'

'It means . . .' she said. 'It means no strings attached.'

He shook his head, not sure he'd heard right. 'You'd better clarify that,' he said.

'You know, great sex but maybe not sleepovers.'

He felt like she'd just slapped him in the face. It was just as he feared. She liked his body, but not *him*. He felt frozen in time and place. Worse than he'd ever felt. He let himself look down into her chocolate-brown eyes and wanted to hurt her.

'Gabi, I don't want that.'

She blinked up at him and he watched the confusion cross her face. He lowered his voice and dipped his head towards her.

'I told you all my deepest truths last night,' he said. She blanched. 'And you couldn't get away fast enough this morning.'

She shook her head sharply and opened her mouth to speak but he couldn't let her.

'So, do I want to have sex with you again?' He faced her squarely. 'No.'

She inhaled quickly as if he'd wounded her.

'Walker,' she said, 'wait.'

'I might not be looking for someone to *commit* when I have sex, Gabi' – he fixed her with his eyes and wouldn't let her look away – 'but I'm at least looking for someone who can *connect*.'

She put a hand on his arm, but the touch ignited his fury.

'Don't worry, you're always so fucking independent, I'm sure you can sort yourself out.' He shook her off and walked away.

# Chapter Thirty-Five

## Gabi

Jayden was tired by the time they got home, and so was Gabi. She'd had to wait on the riverbank on her own for an hour for Jayden to finish his rowing class, with Walker studiously ignoring her from across the yard. Her good leg ached from standing on it for so long and her eyes burned with tears she would not let fall. She couldn't believe that Walker would say those things to her. To think she'd been worried about it all being a bit too much, too soon, and he was just wanting to finish it all together. What an arsehole. And all that bullshit about a connection? What the hell? She could connect with people. She had to, for her job.

Jayden threw his rucksack at the peg and it hit the floor as he ran to hug Amber. Gabi picked it up and hung it for him before dragging herself into the kitchen. Gabi was dismayed to see Isabella was also there at the table, red-eyed and nursing a glass of wine. Gabi checked the kitchen clock and Isabella saw it.

'It's twelve o'clock somewhere,' Isabella said. 'Don't judge me.'

'No judgement here,' Gabi said, reaching for the bottle and pouring herself a small glass. She'd earned it. Amber sighed and joined in and the three women clinked.

'What's up? You okay?' Gabi asked Isabella, as she made room for Jayden to sit at the table and open his iPad to play.

'I don't see the problem personally,' Amber cut in, rolling her eyes. 'Unless you think it's a bad thing that your boyfriend who you are crazy about wants to marry you . . .'

Isabella huffed in frustration. 'When you put it like that, it sounds daft,' she said. 'But I said I wanted a year when he asked me the first time. A year of "everything but marriage". And now he's trying to move the goalposts.'

'But only to marry you sooner!' Amber said. 'If you ask me, it's a nice problem to have.'

'Well, I've told him that unless he stops asking, I'm not marrying him at all. I want him to respect my decisions. Otherwise, it doesn't bode well for our future. You forget, I've been here before. Done this before. So, for now, the wedding is off.' Gabi reached over and squeezed her shoulder. Whatever Isabella's decision, she would support it. Isabella blew her a kiss.

'How was Walker?' Amber said, changing tack.

'Don't ask,' Gabi said, shaking her head in frustration.

'That bad?'

'Worse. He practically dumped me and we're not even boyfriend and girlfriend,' Gabi glanced down at Jayden who was intent on his game. 'Told me he doesn't want to hook up with women who can't connect.'

'Ouch.' Isabella sat back in her chair.

'Wow.' Amber blew out her cheeks.

'Honestly, I now can't wait to get home.'

Home. It gleamed in her brain like a shiny pin. Everything would be exactly where she'd left it, there would be quiet and calm. Which was the opposite to Amber's multi-coloured house where chaos ruled, and clutter was the norm. Teabags lived in the same cupboard as colouring pens. Drawers bulged with plastic bags and school lunchboxes. She was always flicking Jayden's shoes out of the way with her crutch, and Amber's bra often hung from the banister where she'd thrown it after getting home from work.

'Maybe he really likes you,' Isabella said, leaning in.

'How do you figure that?'

'Well, he's never made me a tray before,' Amber said as if that proved everything.

'You haven't got a broken leg,' Gabi shot back.

Amber screwed her face up. 'Good point, well made.'

'He just sees me as someone who needs help. So, he's doing what he always does – coming to the rescue.'

Isabella's face softened. 'Well, that's nice in itself—' she started but Gabi cut in.

'He had to catch me when he thought I was falling. He has to make me a tray when he thinks I can't carry a cup. He has to swoop in. It's probably in his nature. That's why he's good at his job. He loves to be the hero.' Gabi sighed. 'But he's got me wrong. I don't need help. I'm perfectly all right on my own.'

'Seriously, though, don't you think he's hot?' Amber persisted. 'I honestly thought you'd make a beautiful couple.'

Gabi sipped her wine, remembering the feel of his body on hers. The light in those hazel eyes. The way he said her name.

'Okaaaaay,' she nodded. 'He's hot.'

'That we can agree on,' Amber said, raising her glass, and everyone cheersed.

'But if he wants something more serious than Gabi does, it's not going to work, is it?' Isabella said.

'Exactly!' Gabi agreed. 'It was never meant to be anything more than a holiday fling. I'm out of here in a month and I'll have nice uncomplicated sex with someone on set called Aaron or Scott. And they'll not care if I don't sleep over. They'll be happy to not have to make it more than it is.'

'If that's the way you want it, you go ahead, girl,' Amber said.

'You've always done your own thing,' Isabella agreed.

Gabi nodded decisively. 'Right. And I have more important things to be focused on right now. Like getting this leg back to full strength.' She raised her glass again and took a sip.

'What about Alex?' she asked Amber. 'Any updates?'

'He rang a thousand times to say he was sorry if the song had upset me. That he'd like to meet and talk about it.'

'Maybe you should?' Gabi said but Amber put a hand in the air.

'Nope. Been there, done that.'

'You could just hear him out?' Isabella said but Amber's face said it all.

'We're better off without them,' Amber said, putting her glass up in the middle.

'Better off without them,' Isabella and Gabi agreed, smashing their glasses together and finishing their drinks.

Gabi noticed Jayden lip-reading and caught a glimpse of something on his face as he watched his mum, and then he put the iPad down on the table and left the room.

# Chapter Thirty-Six

*Walker*

Walker couldn't settle on his own. Alex was out at band practice, and he was rattling round the house. He couldn't even find Fatboy Jim for a cuddle. He presumed Etienne would be with Isabella in a love bubble somewhere, so he messaged Fox and headed round in the early evening light before he went stir crazy.

Ever since he'd watched Gabi walk away on the riverbank at the weekend, his emotions had been up and down like a yoyo. One minute he hurt afresh, remembering the fact he'd spilled his guts to her and she'd walked away. The next minute kicking himself he had turned down no-strings-attached, undoubtedly incredibly hot sex with Gabi. He tried throwing himself into work, but nothing was making him feel any better. Now he was hoping a tikka masala and onion bhaji with one of his best mates might do the trick.

He could hear that Reggie and George were still awake as Fox opened the front door, his silver quiff stuck up at all angles.

'Got the curry?' Fox asked and Walker held up two bags of takeaway, hot and fragrant, that he'd picked up from the local Indian restaurant.

Fox took one of the bags from him, and offered him a fist bump before Walker followed him in the front door. As they passed the front room, Walker waved through to the boys who were making a den on the floor with cushions. Fox might have won the battle of getting them into rocket-covered pyjamas, but he'd lost the war of wrestling them into bed.

'Ten-minute reprieve!' Fox shouted in defeat and both boys cheered. Fox swung open the kitchen door and Walker saw Etienne also there, looking like his love bubble had most definitely burst.

'That smells good,' Etienne said. 'Is there enough for me?'

'Yep,' Walker said, unloading silver trays to the wooden table. Fox handed out plates, Etienne cracked open some more beers and Dingbat the dog took up position under the table, hoping for spills.

'Bros and beers is exactly what I need tonight,' Etienne commented as everyone served themselves in silence and started to eat.

'Me too,' agreed Walker. 'Tell us good news, Fox. Cheer us up. What's happening with the game launch?'

Fox piled chicken jalfrezi on his rice. 'Launches Saturday,' he said with an incredulous shake of his head.

'Can you believe it? Your game going global,' Walker said, proud of his friend. He offered his beer across the table and the boys all clinked their bottles against it. It was an important moment and they all knew it. Fox had worked hard for it.

'I'm throwing the launch party at The Bolthole,' he said. 'Banking on you guys being there. There'll be play stations, virtual reality arenas – so many different zones, from the Wild West with a bucking bronco to a space zone with laser quest. Should be a laugh. All the big content reviewers are coming. Some gamers from America.'

'Sounds like fun. Count me in. I need all the fun I can get,' Etienne moaned.

'So, things are really going well for you!' Walker said.

'Brilliantly,' said Fox with a sigh. 'But I need to find a nanny. I think it's the only answer. The games company is already talking about a sequel. I feel guilty about the boys, I'm always half concentrating on something else. I think if I got a full day's work done, then after work I could give them my complete attention.'

Walker nodded. 'And you can afford it now, Big Daddy Warbucks.' They clinked beers again.

'I've asked Rosie and Wren if they know anyone. They're going to ask around for me.'

As if they knew they were being discussed, the boys strolled barefoot into the kitchen and Fox stopped talking. George nudged Reggie and Reggie nudged him back. George pushed his brother in the back and Reggie adopted an offhand expression and slung his arm over his dad's shoulder. George muffled a giggle and hung back by the door, watching his big brother expectantly. All three men looked at Reggie who smiled coolly.

'Can I have a beer, Dad?' Reggie asked casually.

'Sure,' said Fox, equally casually. Reggie started to smile and then stopped as Fox finished, 'In about eleven years' time.'

Reggie pulled a face and George sighed. They left together with heavier feet.

'Those boys are going to be trouble,' Etienne said.

'They already are!' Fox replied.

'Alex had good news too this week,' Walker said. 'The local radio station has been in touch. Someone was at the Honeybridge Awards last week and heard them play. They want them to go in and perform his song for them and they're going to record it and give them some airtime.'

'Woah, that's seriously cool,' Fox said.

'He could do with some good luck,' Walker said. 'Amber's called it off with him again.'

'Women,' said Etienne with feeling, snapping a poppadom. 'Can't live with them, can't live without them.'

'You okay?' Fox asked.

All eyes turned to Etienne.

'Depends which way you look at it. I had good news too this week. The planning application for the restaurant extension has been approved. But the bad news is my wedding has been called off.'

'What?' Fox paused with his fork halfway to his mouth in shock.

'What's happened to the wedding, bro?' Walker asked.

'I have absolutely no fucking idea,' Etienne said. 'Apparently, I shouldn't be asking the love of my life when we might set a date to get married. According to Isabella, it shows lack of respect for her decisions. I'm at a loss, mate. I really am.' He dropped his head into his hands.

'Good news on the restaurant, though, man,' Walker said into the silence.

'Doesn't mean anything unless Isabella is there to share it,' Etienne replied.

'You'll work it out, Et,' Walker said, hoping it to be true. He'd never seen Etienne happier than he had been the past six months or so with Isabella. Etienne pulled a face and then nodded back at Walker.

'So, what's going on with you? You don't seem too happy yourself...'

Understatement of the year. Walker drank a long mouthful of beer, anxiety bubbling away in his gut as he considered what exactly he should tell them. There was so much that had happened in his life that he hadn't told them. That he'd never told anyone until Gabi. It wasn't that he hadn't wanted to. It was that he never wanted them to look at him differently. He wanted them to think of him as someone they could rely on. Their friend.

So instead, he swallowed his secret fears again and told them the easier bit.

'Slept with Gabi but won't be repeating.'

'Why?' Etienne asked. 'Was it that bad?'

Walker shook his head.

Both friends were staring at him now, curry going cold on their plates. Walker struggled to find the words that were right.

'But she doesn't seem to like the rest of me. She said we should just have casual sex rather than conversation – or words to that effect.'

'Fucking hell, and they say men aren't in touch with their emotions.' Fox shook his head.

'So, I said no thanks. That woman doesn't want the hassle of anybody in her life. She's completely independent and always will be. I think I'm looking for a bit more connection in my life.'

'She's more footloose and fancy free.'

More F words to describe her, Walker thought, adding them to his list. Feisty, feminine, funny. And the latest one, fuckable.

'Back to the sex, though,' Etienne said, leaning in. 'How was it?'

Another F word, Walker thought. 'Fierce,' he said and finally managed a smile.

All the boys clinked beers and were suddenly aware of two small pyjamaed boys standing in the doorway.

'We're watching *Married at First Sight*,' Reggie announced.

'Righto, boys.' Fox rolled his eyes. 'Definitely time for bed.' He pushed his chair back.

'Why aren't any of you married?' George said, big round eyes taking in each of the men at the table, who all slugged back a mouthful of beer.

'Yeah, you're all old,' Reggie said.

Walker spluttered a laugh as the youngest of the group. 'Cheeky monkeys,' he said. 'I'm only thirty-six.'

'That's ancient.'

'Maybe we haven't found the right women yet,' Fox said.

'Or we have, and they don't know if they want to marry us yet,' Etienne said.

'What about you two?' Walker challenged. 'Why aren't you married yet?'

Reggie pulled a face and George laughed.

'Girls are disgusting.'

'Yeah, girls suck.'

'Don't say it,' Fox muttered to his friends as they all laughed into their beers. He pushed his chair under the table.

'First one in bed gets first choice of TV tomorrow.' The boys ran whooping towards the stairs and Fox followed them out of the room. Etienne's phone rang and he pulled it from his pocket, his face lighting up when he saw the name on the screen.

'Bella, baby,' he said. 'I'm sorry.'

Etienne let himself out the bifold doors and Walker watched his expression soften and smile as he talked to Isabella. A minute later, he was leaning back in his patio chair and laughing softly into the phone. From all appearances, the wedding was back on.

Walker pushed his plate to the side and sighed quietly. He was happy for his friend, who had found his match and wanted to be with her for the rest of his life. Happy for Fox, moving on and finding global success. Happy for Alex with his big music break. But to be honest, he was drained. He was constantly tired and now his feelings were hurt as well. The nightmares were getting more frequent. He felt like he was carrying a heavy weight, and he didn't know how to put it down.

And there was nobody to help share the load.

# Chapter Thirty-Seven

## Gabi

**Papà**: How are you, Gabriella? Do you need anything?

For some reason, this morning's monthly message was even more annoying than normal. She glared at it and formed a response in her mind.

*Actually, Pops, I'm worried about my scan next week. I'm worried my broken bone is not going to have healed and I'll never work again.*

She pulled a face.

Or, *To be honest, Dad, my feelings have been hurt by a hunky hero who seems to hate the fact that I like to rely on myself.*

She rolled her eyes.

Finally, she typed,

**Gabi**: I'm fine, thanks. And no, nothing at all.

Why did he keep bothering when it was obviously just a duty message every time? She recalled his messages when she was younger, every week the same questions. How hopeful she felt when his name appeared on her screen, and how her heart dropped with disappointment with every message that didn't include a plan to meet up, or an invitation home for the summer. He never asked her more than the bare minimum to know that she was alive, so what was the point? You'd think he'd get bored of it, his questions, her reply. Nothing changing for better or worse. The same frozen state of relationship for more years than she could remember. She stared helplessly at her own words, then pressed send and threw the phone on the bed.

Looking at herself in the mirror, she had a sense of déjà vu. Another party at The Bolthole. Another night trying to prove to Walker McBride that she didn't care what he did or said. And this time, she wouldn't give in to him even if he begged her.

He couldn't just go around making out she was somehow emotionally detached just because she didn't want to throw herself into a full-blown *relationship* with him. She wasn't going to be here long enough for more than a few casual hook-ups so what was his problem? Well, it was his loss.

She checked her outfit. The warmer weather gave her the chance to wear less. Her black short shorts almost met her bralette, and her belly button ring shone through the gap. She dusted some highlighter on her shoulders and cleavage. She mussed her hair and drew on eyeliner, smudging it purposefully to give herself a slightly doe-eyed, sultry look. She added heavy mascara and was done. Take that, Walker. See what you could have taken home tonight. She grabbed her crutches and swung herself out to show him exactly what he was missing. Fuck Walker. Fuck her dad. She didn't need any of them.

*

Fox met them at the door. Silver quiff styled to messy perfection. Stubble grizzled across his chin. He wore his signature checked shirt and jeans and greeted Gabi and Amber with kisses and hugs.

'The boys are here,' he said, looking mock sternly at first Gabi and then Amber. 'So, play nicely.'

Gabi bristled. So, Walker had been talking too. Nice. She shrugged off her coat and left Fox to check it into the cloakroom. Amber held hers out too and stood smoking hot in a blue dress that matched the ocean of her eyes, her brown curls spread high on her head in a halo. Gabi recognised the amount of effort her friend had made to look like she didn't give a fuck either. Gabi gave her an appreciative wink and they headed on in.

The Bolthole was transformed to celebrate Fox's game. Each room was a different level in the game. Play areas had been set up where people already lounged, wearing headphones, absorbed in the challenge.

The first room was a spaceship. Waiting staff wore short silver suits and bubble helmets, handing out cocktails with names like Moon Magma or Jupiter Juice. Amber took one of each as Gabi didn't have a hand free and they moved through to the back room where they usually sang karaoke. It had been turned into a Wild West bar, complete with sawdust on the floor and dancers on podiums cracking whips, which was exactly what Gabi would like to do right now. There was even a bucking bronco machine in the middle of the dance floor.

'This is more my type of party,' Gabi said to Amber, before knocking back her drink. They perched at a free table and halted a passing waiter who was bare-chested, wearing a Stetson and cowboy chaps over his jeans. He held a tray out towards them with pink shots one side and blue shots the other. Gabi passed her eyes over his muscly chest and couldn't help but find it lacking.

'Cowboy's Passion' – he nodded at the blue – 'or Cowgirl's Revenge?' He indicated the pink.

'Cowgirl's Revenge,' she and Amber both said together, taking a glass. They knocked them together and drank.

Rosie appeared a few minutes later, plaits wrapped around her head, milkmaid style. She carried a blue cocktail with her but assured them she was just having the one.

'Riley has a vomiting bug, again.' She rolled her eyes. 'They seem to go round nursery every few weeks. And I can't cope with that if I'm hungover. Wren has stayed home to look after her tonight, and I'll do tomorrow.'

Amber squeezed Rosie's shoulder and Gabi felt a pang at that sisterly bond. That empathy between one mother and another. She couldn't help but wonder if her mother had ever had that feeling. She wondered if she'd ever have that feeling herself. She swigged her drink. Doubtful. But where did that leave her? Always on the outside?

Rosie's phone beeped and she tapped a quick response.

'Just Toby checking to see how she's doing.' She sipped her drink. 'He says he'll do tomorrow night if we need him.'

She pocketed her phone again and smiled.

'He texts her every day or calls,' Rosie said. 'We really struck the baby daddy jackpot with him.'

Gabi swigged again. What had she got in the daddy tombola? The booby prize?

'Let's hope he texts more than once a month when she's grown up,' she said and sipped her drink, surprised to find it finished already. Rosie glanced her way, frowning.

'Of course he will,' she said.

'Or maybe not.' Gabi sniffed. 'Just because you think he should, doesn't mean he will. Dads aren't all perfect, you know.'

Rosie should know that sometimes things didn't end up like you thought they might. That the dad she'd picked for Riley might not live up to her expectations. Rosie threw a look towards Amber, and Gabi saw Amber do a little shake of her head. Aha, so it was like that, was it? All the locals sticking together. Gabi, as usual, not part of the gang.

Isabella and Etienne arrived, draped all over each other. It wasn't until they sat down that Gabi noticed Walker and Alex behind them in the doorway. Walker's T-shirt fit him like a charm and his sandy hair was pushed back from his face. He looked better than any of the half-naked waiters in the room, even with his clothes on. Gabi sank her Cowgirl's Revenge in one gulp.

'Tell Rosie what's happening with work, Gabi?' Amber changed the subject.

Gabi told them about the potential job in America and the interview she'd had.

'So exciting!' Amber said. 'Can you imagine?' She turned to Rosie. 'Travelling to America for work rather than walking to the high street or square?'

'Are you looking forward to it?' Rosie asked, a lingering look of annoyance on her face.

'Can't wait,' Gabi said. 'Back to my old life.' Gabi looked about for a waiter. Instead, she saw Walker and Alex move towards the bar, talking to a couple of women, one of whom was resting her hand on Walker's bicep to get his attention. Gabi's own fingers curled under the table. She needed another drink. She half stood to scan the floor.

'What do you need?' Amber motioned for her to stay sitting and stood herself. 'Another Cowgirl's Revenge?'

'See if he's got one called "Fuck Off Fireman".' Gabi laughed, but it tailed off when the girls didn't join in. She saw Rosie glance at her and then away. Just because she thought she was criticising her precious firefighting friend. 'Anything will do as long as it's alcoholic,' she said to Amber, irritation coursing through her.

Amber flagged down a passing waiter and lifted two drinks from his tray. Gabi watched as the girl at the bar laughed wildly at something Walker said. It can't have been *that* funny, surely? The woman held on to his arm and laughed harder.

'You feeling okay, Gabs?' Isabella appeared beside her. 'You don't seem very happy.'

'Just fed up with being stuck in this pokey pothole of a town,' she said and felt a sharp pang of regret as Isabella's eyes widened. 'Sorry, Issy,' she said immediately. 'I'm just frustrated by my leg. I want to get back to real life.'

'Not long now, although I'll miss not having you just down the road,' Isabella said, throwing her arm around her cousin. 'It will be months before I get to see you again.' Gabi's chest hurt. What the hell was the matter with her? Why was everything feeling so weird?

'In fact, do you think you might be able to get back at

Christmas?' Isabella pulled up a chair. 'Mamma and Papà are finally coming home from travelling. They'll be here for the holidays.'

Gabi had a sudden longing for her zio and zia. She hadn't seen them since the opening of Tutto Mio last year.

'Maybe,' she said. 'Depends if the film wraps on time.'

'Hopefully it will,' Isabella insisted. 'Then you can come and spend Christmas with us.'

Gabi threw back her drink, watching as Walker and the girl at the bar pulled up stools to talk.

'Who's that girl?' Gabi asked, nodding in their direction. Isabella craned her head.

'Not sure,' she said. 'But I think she's a firefighter.'

'Wonder if she's sprinkled his hose?' Gabi sniffed. Isabella hugged her again but said nothing. 'Honestly, Issy, I don't know what's wrong with me.' She watched Rosie head over to Walker and he got up to give her his stool. Pretending to be a gentleman but probably just using the opportunity to stand closer to the other woman. Sure enough, he leaned on the back of the girl's chair as the three of them talked. Gabi had an urge to launch her crutch at him.

'I just need to feel like me again, Issy,' Gabi said. 'The old me.'

Isabella passed her a shot.

'Maybe this will help?' They downed them. Gabi shuddered. Isabella pulled a face.

'Much better,' Gabi agreed. Etienne put his arms around Isabella from behind and she turned away to face him.

Gabi sighed. On her own again. She stood, awkwardly alone for a minute that felt like an hour, before noticing a circle form around the rodeo ride. She hobbled over to watch. The first rider, a young man wearing sunglasses inside, put on his preferred cowboy hat and jumped into the saddle. Gabi overheard his friends taking bets on how long he'd last; it didn't sound like they had much faith in him. The bull started turning, slowly at first and then twisting and bucking faster and faster. Gabi smiled to herself as the guy went from showing off with a hand in the air to hanging on for dear life within twenty seconds flat. And then he slid slowly out of the saddle and down the side to the padded floor, his friends jeering. The subsequent one jumped on and lasted even less.

Gabi recognised the next rider as Walker's girl, who strode laughing up to the bull and took the hat. Walker leaned against a table nearby, clapping her on, much to Gabi's annoyance. The girl leapt athletically onto the bull's back and held her hat in the air, looking like she meant business. She started off well and Walker whooped with encouragement. Gabi clenched her teeth and counted the seconds, secretly happy when the girl was thrown quite dramatically to the ground just before she hit a minute. Despite the fall, the girl got up laughing, did a curtsey and the crowd cheered. Dammit. Cute as well as adventurous. But now, she was the one to beat.

Gabi swung forward and dropped her crutches to the mat, mounting the bull by swinging her boot over its back in one easy move. The crowd whooped. Someone threw her the cowboy hat and she caught it in one hand, waving it in the air above her head. The machine jolted into life. The first turn was slow and jerky. She clamped the sides of the saddle with her inner thighs. The second turn included a little backwards buck and she rode it with ease. The faster the machine got, the more the club lights spun. Gabi hollered and laughed and heard the crowd yelling. Then the lights were streaming and she still held her hat in the air, bumping and rolling in the saddle, unable to keep track of where she was, or predict a next move, until she was being thrown physically side to side, back to front, still grasping the rein with one hand. The movement knocked the breath out of her lungs and she could only hold on, silently, desperately. Suddenly Gabi was off the bull and being dragged away. But she wasn't falling. She was being yanked off physically and carried forcefully from the ride – by Walker. At the edge of the crash mat, he threw her unceremoniously over his shoulder in a very stereotypical fireman's lift and marched her through the crowd with her bum in the air. She could hear hoots of laughter and wolf-whistles.

She slammed her hands against his back, shouting at him, but he didn't put her down again until they were outside The Bolthole and the crisp night air hit her like a truck. He threw her crutches beside her and they clattered to the floor.

'What the actual fuck are you doing?' Gabi stormed, mortified to be bundled out like a sack of spuds.

'My question entirely,' Walker fumed back. 'What about your leg?'

She banged his chest with her palms, and he stepped away.

'My leg is fine. I was fine. I do this for a living, you know?' Gabi shouted, exasperated beyond belief.

'You won't do if you break your still-broken leg again.'

She groaned in frustration and staggered to gather her crutches, suddenly feeling dizzy as she bent down. Maybe the motion of the bull had not quite worn off.

'You should apologise to Rosie too before you leave,' Walker said. 'You really hurt her feelings with all that shit you were spouting about fathers.'

She gasped. The nerve of him.

'You should start making your own proper relationships before you criticise other people's,' he added.

'I got my monthly message today actually so I'm up to date with my oh-so-meaningful relationship with my dad.'

'It's not just his message to you, though, is it? You reply the same shit every time. You're an adult too, you know. Apparently.'

Gabi glared at him. How dare he? She pulled herself up to her full height and tucked her crutches under her arms.

'You just have to swoop in, don't you? Be the big hero? When at night you're still a scared little boy. Well, why don't you just fuck off, Walker? Fuck off and sort yourself out.'

She saw the impact of her words hit his face. Shock turned to hurt, and then he closed himself completely, his face blank. A stab of guilt at what she'd said only made her angrier and suddenly she couldn't look at him any longer. She turned and limped away.

# Chapter Thirty-Eight

*Walker*

The sky was black and spotted with stars outside Walker's bedroom window. He watched through tired, scratched eyes as dawn lightened it to a deep navy, then a cold purplish haze. He hadn't slept a wink.

He could still feel the fury in the slam of Gabi's hands against his chest, see the look of outrage on her face as he told her what he thought of her behaviour. He'd seen the anger change, flash through hurt and end on spite as she told him exactly what she thought of him in return. Turned out he'd been right all along. He turned in the bed and pounded his pillow into a different shape.

He'd been having a good night until Gabi got up to her tricks on that ridiculous rodeo bull. Betsy from the fire station had been keeping him company. She was on good form, telling him funny stories about her boyfriend who was trying, and failing, to be a stand-up comedian. More of a lie-down comedian, as Betsy called him. He'd had a couple of beers with Alex, who was trying to keep his mind off Amber, and they'd been waiting for Fox to finish with the corporate schmooze to come and have a drink. All was going well, until he saw Gabi, wearing hot pants and waving a cowboy hat on the back of a bucking bronco. His first thought had been how hot she looked, head thrown back, arm in the air, riding that thing like her life depended on it. His second thought had been astonishment that she'd be so stupid, and then his feet had been walking towards her before his head got a chance to stop him.

Fatboy Jim sprang neatly onto the pillow and butted him softly, head-to-head. Walker closed his eyes and listened to Jim's purr, thinking maybe that would calm him, soothe him to sleep. He was so very, very tired. He felt himself slipping, sliding softly into the dark. Then he jolted awake as he remembered the fury and contempt on Gabi's face outside The Bolthole.

He turned his pillow over to get a cold side. Saw the lights of the first plane of the day cross the sky in the dawn. Wondered briefly where it was heading, and whether he'd be able to sleep if he went there.

The truth hit him like a dumper truck and he shot up in bed. Gabi was right. He wouldn't be able to sleep wherever he was, because he turned into a scared little boy at night. And it had got so bad that he was too terrified to close his eyes.

He threw the covers back, knocking over a glass of water on the bedside table. Fatboy Jim shot off the bed in disgust as Walker pulled on clothes.

The fact was, Walker was scared of so many things. Messing things up. Letting people down. Doing the wrong thing. Not making the right decision. People getting hurt or dying on his watch.

He caught a glimpse of himself in the mirror as he pulled a hoodie over his head. His eyes were dark and blank. His teeth were gritted so tight his jaw hurt. He looked haunted. He ran his hands through his hair. He couldn't live like this any more.

He picked up his car keys and ran out of the house. He knew he was driving too fast as he pushed the accelerator to the floor, but he couldn't stop. Anything was better than living like this.

# Chapter Thirty-Nine

*Gabi*

The smell of the apple crumble, freshly baked and still warm, packaged in her bag was making Gabi's mouth water as she swung her way along the pavement to Rosie's house the next day. But she figured, if she was going to eat humble pie, it might as well be a tasty one.

She'd woken that morning with Walker's face imprinted on her eyelids and a very bad hangover. This was precisely why she didn't normally drink very much. She'd been up a full five minutes swearing about him to Amber in the kitchen before she conceded that riding a rodeo with an injured leg was probably not her smartest move of all time. But that did not – *did not* – give him the right to tell her she couldn't form relationships – again. She must be able to, because she felt a twinge of guilt every time she thought of what she'd said to Rosie and knew he was right – *goddammit* – she'd have to apologise. She'd begged Amber for a recipe, an easy one as she didn't normally bake, swallowed some painkillers and got to work.

She didn't really cook at all. Usually it was fully catered on set, and she'd order takeaways if she was at home. There wasn't much point in cooking for one; it always felt a bit sad. She'd felt a prick of pride when she pulled the crumble from the oven and Jayden gave her a thumbs up.

Wren answered the door, looking mildly green and massively pissed off when she saw who it was on the step. Great, so Rosie had really taken her words to heart and shared them with Wren.

After a stiff greeting, Wren walked her through the house to the kitchen at the back, where Rosie was sitting at the island reading a book, oversized glasses propped right on the end of her nose. She peered at Gabi before carefully marking her place with a bookmark and closing her book.

'Rosie, I'm so sorry for what I said about Toby.' Gabi held out the cake tin and came straight on out with it. No point hanging about. 'I was a dick.' Rosie considered her for a moment and then nodded.

'I have no experience of dicks,' she said with a smile, 'but that smells a whole lot like pie.'

Gabi was taken aback when Rosie stood up, wrapped her arms around her and pulled her close for a hug. Just like that, she was forgiven. She breathed Rosie in and some of her tension fell away.

'Where's Riley?' Gabi asked as Rosie cut slices of crumble and pulled out cream from the fridge. 'Is she any better?'

'At her dad's,' Rosie replied. 'He took the day off work and came and collected her this morning. He said he could have a sofa day with her.'

Gabi dropped her head, embarrassed.

'I really am sorry,' she said. 'Toby sounds like a great dad.'

'He is.' Rosie grinned.

'You're very lucky,' Gabi said and was surprised to feel tears suddenly fill her eyes, and then roll down her cheeks, and for the second time in two minutes she was enfolded in Rosie's home-knitted cardigan.

'I'm so sorry I took everything out on you,' she stammered. 'I was just upset because my dad texted me yesterday.' She slumped on the sofa, thinking that yes, that was partly what was upsetting her.

Rosie looked confused. 'Wouldn't you be upset when he doesn't text you, rather than when he does?'

'It's because every month, it's the same,' Gabi sniffed. She held out her phone and scrolled through the chat history. The same questions and answers on repeat. Always on the first of every month. Rosie scrolled in amazement. In a matter of seconds, she'd covered the past few years.

'You never tell him anything?' Rosie asked, looking up from the screen. 'About your life?'

'He never asks me anything!' Gabi threw back.

'But he asks every month . . .' Rosie said, pointing at her dad's words each time.

'He doesn't really want to know, though,' Gabi said. 'We haven't really had a relationship since my mum left.'

'He's doing a good job of hanging in there.' Rosie shrugged and handed the phone back. Gabi looked at it in confusion and then back at Rosie, as if they were looking at two entirely different things. Rosie continued, 'You know, Gabs, just because you haven't had a relationship since you were a child doesn't mean you can't have one as an adult.'

Gabi sighed and sat back. Walker had said something very similar.

'Up to you, of course.' Rosie stood to pass out the pie, and make them coffee. She put her hand on Gabi's shoulder as she passed. 'It's your relationship.'

Gabi stared at the chat history again, seeing it through Rosie's eyes. And Walker's. Scrolling back through months and then years, decades even. Seeing how many times her dad had actually asked how she was, and she had cut him dead with her reply.

# Chapter Forty

## Walker

**Alex**: Hey, man, you home for dinner? Making chilli tonight.
**Alex**: I'll leave it in the fridge if you get in later.
**Etienne**: Bro. Rowing club this afternoon?
**Etienne**: You missed a good sesh. Next time.
**Fox**: Reggie wanted to know if you can make his assembly next week. He's a squirrel.
**Fox**: Walker? I was at least expecting a joke about how it might drive you nuts, but you wouldn't miss it?
**Rosie**: Whatever you said to Gabi worked . . . she came round with apology pie. Thanks, Walks. Cuppa in the week? XX
**Rosie**: Walks? Everything okay?
**Alex**: Hey, where are you, man? Not wanting to be a nagging wife, but you didn't come home last night?
**Alex**: Can you message me when you get this? I'm worried.
**Fox**: You okay, Walker? Still haven't heard from you.
**Etienne**: Everything okay, bro?
**Rosie**: Walker, where are you?

# Chapter Forty-One

*Gabi*

Gabi was just on her way home from physio at the gym the next day when she spotted Etienne, Fox and Alex going into the local coffee shop. She couldn't help but check behind them for Walker, but maybe he was on shift. She hadn't seen him, or heard from him, since the game launch at The Bolthole. That was probably for the best, seeing as he thought he could tell her how to live her life. So, why was she still looking for him? She decided to pop in and say hello to the guys.

The men were seated in a corner booth nursing coffees by the time she got to the counter and placed her order. Etienne exclaimed and pointed at her, which was a bit odd, saying, 'Hi, Gabi! We've been meaning to come and talk to you.' Fox looked up from the message he was writing and slipped his phone in his pocket. Alex collected her coffee for her and carried it to their table. They all scooted around to make room for her, propping her crutches against the wall.

'Looking for me?' she said, feeling strangely pleased, but then she noticed their furrowed brows and frowns, and the way Fox ran his hands distractedly through his hair, rather than showering her with his usual flirty banter. 'What's up?'

'Have you heard from Walker?' Etienne asked abruptly.

'Not since he carried me and my crutches out of The Bolthole,' she said, trying to make a joke of it, but they didn't laugh. 'Why?'

They exchanged sombre glances and Alex sighed. 'Because he's not been seen since.'

Etienne showed her his phone. 'He's not responding to any messages. From anyone.'

Fox shook his head. 'Walker's just . . . disappeared.'

Gabi's stomach sank. A bad feeling crept in.

'So, have you heard from him?' Etienne asked again.

'We're not exactly talking right now . . .' Gabi said. Etienne's fingers drummed the table.

'After he carried you out, he didn't come back into the party. We presumed that you guys may have gone home together,' Alex said.

'Believe me, he didn't want me anywhere near him.' Gabi blew on her coffee, remembering the set of Walker's clenched jaw, the look on his face as she left him on the pavement.

'When I went in his room the morning after The Bolthole to see if he was home, the duvet was on the floor, and there was a glass knocked over on the carpet,' Alex said. 'That, in itself, doesn't sound like much, but Walker likes a tidy room. He makes his bed every time he gets out of it, so that it's nice to get back in after a late-night shift. It's one of his things.' Gabi remembered the quiet order of the bedroom, the sense of calm she had felt there. 'And since then, he hasn't been home. It's been more than twenty-four hours.'

Gabi glanced from one to the other of the men and saw her concern mirrored in their eyes. Her chest tightened and she knew deep inside that something wasn't right.

'I messaged his sister and she's not heard from him,' Fox said.

'And Rosie has tried him several times too and he's not even replied to her,' Etienne said. 'And they're best friends.'

'What happened with you two after you left?' Fox asked.

'Because it looks like you were the last person to see him,' Alex added.

'You're making it sound like a crime scene,' Gabi said, not wanting to tell them. Feeling suddenly ashamed of the things she'd said, the way she'd acted. All three men leaned their elbows on the table. There was nothing else for it: she had to confess.

'We had a fight,' Gabi said with a grimace. 'I was pissed off that he'd carried me out in front of everyone and told him so. In return, he told me what he thought of me.' She dropped her eyes under their scrutiny, but when she glanced up again, they were all still staring at her.

'What exactly was said?' Fox asked gently. She bit her lip until it hurt before replying.

'I called him a frightened little boy and told him to fuck off,' she whispered. 'Fuck off and sort himself out, rather than keep trying to save everyone else.' She saw a ripple of shock pass over Fox's face and started to gabble. 'It sounds awful now. I just said it in the heat of the moment to hurt him.' She could feel the heat of a flush on her neck, her cheeks, and she put her hands to her face in shame. A silence settled across the booth as the men exchanged glances. Eventually, Etienne spoke.

'Unfortunately, I think he's taken you at your word and fucked off,' he said. 'It's not like him at all.'

The anxiety between them was rising. Alex turned to Gabi again.

'What did you mean – when you called Walker a frightened little boy and told him to sort himself out?'

Gabi paused, seeing the total confusion on his face. She wasn't sure how much they knew about what Walker had been through.

'Just because I think he's caught up in the past . . .' she said, measuring her words. Not wanting to discuss Walker's secret without him there.

Fox shook his head, confused. Alex and Etienne looked at each other blankly. They didn't know. Not about his past, or how deeply he hated himself. Walker had only told her, and she had thrown it back in his face.

'It doesn't make sense . . .' Fox said. 'He's normally so reliable.'

'Something's definitely not right,' Alex agreed.

'Call us – or tell Isabella – if you hear from him?' Etienne asked and Gabi collected her crutches and stumbled out, assuring them she'd call them immediately with any updates.

She hobbled home, hating herself with every step. She had a bad feeling about this. What if Walker had done something stupid? Would it be her fault? She'd basically taunted him into it.

She'd known how haunted Walker still was by his friend's death. She'd felt it after she'd seen him wake after that first nightmare, and then he'd laid his heart bare in his bedroom when he told her the full story. She should have taken him more seriously, spent more time checking he was okay. But no, she'd just been terrified about what *she'd* told *him*: the secrets about her childhood, the loneliness of her past. All she'd cared about was hightailing it out of there first thing in the morning, before he even woke up, because she was a bit freaked out, feeling she'd shared too much. *She'd* shared too much. The irony was not lost on her any more. She couldn't bear to consider how he might have felt waking to an empty bed after that. No wonder he wanted nothing to do with her. He'd told her his worst fears and she'd swept them aside. She was the worst kind of person there was.

It made it worse when she realised that none of the guys knew about Murray. The weight that came with knowing Walker had chosen her to share something that important sat heavily on her chest.

If she could be in one of the films she'd starred in where they travelled through time, she'd go back to that moment when he was standing by the window. She'd encourage him to talk more. She'd lead him back to bed and, most importantly, she'd be there when he woke up. She'd talk more in the morning. They could look at counsellors together. She would plan a road trip with him to Scotland to visit the grave if that would help. Anything, *anything* would be better than what she had actually done in real life. Run away, like she always did. Put herself first – because nobody else ever did.

Wait. She stopped, key in the front door at Amber's, tracing her own thoughts back a step. *Plan a road trip to Scotland if it would help.* And just like that, she knew where he was, with a certainty inside her that took her breath away.

'Scotland,' she said out loud. 'Of course.'

She wracked her brains for something more specific and heard Walker's broken, tired voice telling her the secrets of his nightmares.

*Our house was on the edge of Loch Leven, overlooking St Serf's Island.*

She looked at her boot on the doorstep and then glanced at Amber's car in the driveway. She sighed in frustration and weighed up her options. She couldn't drive. But she could call a taxi. She started to dial as she picked up her overnight bag.

# Chapter Forty-Two

*Walker*

Walker fixed his eyes on the small strip of beach in front of him. Sun shone on the water beyond, for as far as he could see. In the middle of the loch, St Serf's Island was spotted with sheep set out there to graze for the summer. Nobody lived there, but he could still see the tumbledown white stone remains of a monastery. It was colder in Scotland, but it was not just the temperature difference that made him shudder. He hadn't been back to this spot since the day Murray died.

When he left Honeybridge the day before, he knew where he was heading but he was scared to arrive. He had to revisit the scene to do what he was going to do. He had to be where he had failed, in order to make amends.

Seven hours' non-stop driving had got him to Scotland.

He'd sped along motorways with his foot to the floor, eventually turning off when he hit the border and cruising the smaller roads, crossing the Firth of Forth on the old bridge. He had thought he might go to stay at his parents' but shunned the idea as he got closer. How could he turn up in this state? They'd be worried out of their minds to see him like this. The anxiety in his stomach grew with every passing mile. The closer he got to home, the less he wanted to reach his destination. Finally, he arrived late afternoon.

He drove around the surrounding villages, past his old school and the public pool where he learned to swim. He hiked to the top of a nearby hill and from there he could see the loch in its entirety. He sat on a rock, his breathing ragged, overwhelmed with memories.

He and Murray had cycled round the loch once on Murray's birthday. Walker remembered the day – they'd biked the perimeter, thirteen miles to match his thirteenth birthday. It had only been a matter of weeks before Murray died. He remembered watching Murray riding ahead on the wooded paths, without his hands on the handlebars. More than twenty years ago and yet he could remember it so well. All that energy Murray had, the infectious laugh that made his eyes water. And Walker had taken the rest of his life away from him.

He couldn't bear the view any more and ran down the hillside, stumbling over rocks and tripping on tussocks of grass. He drove straight to a pub in a nearby village and drank for the rest of the day. He hadn't eaten, or slept the night before, and the drink soaked into him like blotting paper. He drank himself through sorrow to shame and slept in the car outside when the landlord rang last orders. He woke late the next morning with a sour taste in his mouth and a crick in his neck, to one abiding thought echoing through his mind. He was still alive – and Murray wasn't.

He'd walked for hours, his mind and vision a blur. He lost track of time, and day, his memories overtaking him with every well-known view or building that he saw. His anchor to the here and now felt loose. He swayed between the past and the present, unable to see any future.

Now, finally, whatever day it was, he was there, hungover and exhausted but determined to see things through.

The beach marked the halfway point between his old home, a grey-stone cottage, and Murray's smart, red-brick house. He slammed the car door behind him and forced his feet to walk out onto the sand, towards the water. He couldn't put it off any longer but his skin crawled as he felt the sand shift under his feet. He was close. He was so close.

The rowing boats were still where they used to be, beached on the shore. Nobody was there, so he lugged one himself to the water's edge and pushed the boat out far enough until it started to float. The shock of the freezing water stole his breath as it hit his ankles and shins, soaking his jeans and leather boots. It seemed to draw him on, and he welcomed the numbness it brought. Was that what he was looking for? Escape? A cold black nothing?

Walker climbed in, lifting the oars and beginning to row, keeping his eyes fixed on the shore. How far out had he and Murray gone? He remembered the fizz of excitement as they walked off the shore on the ice. The feeling of solidity under their feet surprising them, delighting them. It was safe to go on. It had to be, when the ice felt like that.

He pulled another stroke, and the boat cut through the water towards St Serf's. He'd rowed the loch before, with his parents, his sister, with Murray. They'd dipped their skinny white bodies in the water at every opportunity, sometimes staying in until their fingers and toes went blue. He shook his head. The image was too much, but it was too late.

He was suddenly imagining the water under the ice. Would it be light enough to see through that white ceiling? Or would it feel like being under a capsized boat, dark and enclosed? Would the temperature have stopped Murray's heart before he swallowed any water? Walker sobbed at the thought of it, the terror hitting him full force. Usually, these images only surfaced when he was asleep. These were the thoughts that haunted him in the dark, but now there was no escaping them. He gritted his teeth and rowed again. Glancing over his shoulder at St Serf's, he realised he was halfway in between land and the island. This must be close to where it happened. The boat drifted in the current, turning in a slow semi-circle, and Walker became aware of how loud his breathing sounded in the still air. He was there.

He stared at the water around him until it faded away, replaced by ice. This was what he saw in his dreams: Murray ahead of him, his red hat bobbing as he slipped and skated away from him.

This was it. He could feel it in the panic rising in his chest. This was as far as he had got. And it was as far as he could ever go. He was stuck here and had been for more than twenty years. The only way out of it was into it. He levered himself to standing and the boat rocked sharply in the water.

# Chapter Forty-Three

*Gabi*

The taxi driver probably reckoned it was his lucky day, Gabi thought. Who normally calls and requests an immediate cab to Scotland – six or seven hours' drive – in the middle of the morning? He whistled along cheerfully to the radio from the driver's seat, no doubt thinking about the big fat fare at the end of the day.

Gabi drummed her fingers against the armrest in the back, watching the countryside flash by, not caring about the money at all – she could easily afford it – but wishing they could go faster, get there sooner. But to be fair, if she had been driving herself, she would have been stopped for speeding already.

If her suspicions were right and she found Walker at the loch, the first thing she was going to do was apologise. For all the things she'd said and the way she'd treated him. Every time she closed her eyes she relived the wounded shock in his eyes, the physical impact her words had had on him. Guilt stabbed like a thousand tiny pins in her chest.

It was an unusual and uncomfortable feeling, and she had plenty of time to examine it as they headed north. She'd rarely felt guilt in her life, but maybe that was because she was normally on her own. Gabi didn't have to consider other people's feelings or reactions when she did her job – excellently of course. She had no one to answer to at home. She didn't let anyone down because she didn't have anyone around who relied on her. And yet she'd felt guilty twice in the last few days in Honeybridge. First, with Rosie – and that had been easily solved with an apple crumble – and now, with Walker. This time, she feared it might not be as easily resolved.

He had not deserved what she'd said to him. Gabi could see now that everything Walker had done for her was the good, decent thing. Isabella had said it was how he showed people he cared about them. He'd caught her, carried her, cared for her and she'd thrown it back at him in anger.

The driver offered her a sherbet lemon as they crossed the border, but the taste in her mouth was bitter enough already. She knew she wouldn't be able to stomach anything until she'd found Walker.

She watched the motorway turn to mountain roads and forced herself to focus on doing the right thing when she got there. First, she should apologise to Walker – for everything. Second, they should talk more about how he felt. Third, she would bring him home. The more she thought about it, she realised that the only thing she wanted to do was put her arms around Walker and hold him tight.

Her phone rang and made her jump, but it was just an

excited voicemail message from her agent, following up on her interview.

'You obviously did a great job on the interview. The film people are very keen to proceed. They are checking references and will be back in contact as soon as possible.'

Gabi sighed. However exciting that sounded, it was not the person she was waiting to hear from.

# Chapter Forty-Four

## *Walker*

*Walker rubbed his hands together, a bad feeling in the pit of his stomach as he paused on the ice. Why had he dared them to do it? It had started off as fun, but now his feet wouldn't move any more. He checked back at the shore. He was too far out. He bit his lip as he watched Murray sliding ahead and then he shouted, 'Murray, this is a bad idea, let's go back.'*

*Walker's young voice echoed strangely off the ice and into the blank sky. The loch had never scared him before, but it was scaring him now. Murray laughed and carried on.*

*Walker shouted again. 'Murray!'*

*'You go back if you want!' Murray shouted over his shoulder. 'I want to see if I can get to the island.'*

*Walker was torn. Desperate to get off the ice but not wanting to leave his friend, not wanting to go back to land on his own and look afraid. Not wanting to go forward and be with Murray just because he was being a daredevil. But Murray was always taking risks: always riding his bike without touching the handlebars, or jumping off the swing when he'd reached the highest point. He always went higher or further or faster than Walker. Always. Walker didn't normally mind, but this time it was dangerous. He watched Murray edging towards the island and knew it was a wrong move.*

*'Murray!' he shouted, one last time. 'It's not safe. Let's go in.'*

*Murray turned and grinned at him. His cheeks were red with the cold.*

*'It's solid!' he shouted back and, to demonstrate, he jumped on the spot, his two feet landing soundly on the ice with a thump. 'See?' He gave Walker a thumbs up, but Walker shook his head, already decided he was heading for shore. He didn't care if Murray called him a chicken. He had a bad feeling about this.*

*He heard Murray as he walked away, whistling tunelessly, a sure sign of bravado. Walker knew that he was loving the thrill of it. The crack stopped the whistling dead. There was a microsecond of silence and then a half-shout of shock from Murray, and they both turned instantly to look at each other, their eyes locking as the ice split beneath Murray's feet and he plunged through. Walker threw himself horizontal on the ice, spreading his weight, staring at the place where Murray had been. There was no splashing, or thrashing. Walker shouted his name, expecting him to burst from the water, shaking icy droplets from his hair. 'Just joking!' he'd shout. 'Just kidding with you!' But there was nothing. Walker shouted again, and again, his voice pluming in the chill of the air, until there was nothing but the sound of his hoarse crying and a shout from a passing hiker.*

Walker was jolted from his memories by a line of geese honking as they flew overhead, in perfect formation. He realised at that exact second what had been missing from all his dreams and his nightmares. The only noise he ever recalled was the sound of the ice cracking. The shock of that one sound rang terrifyingly through his dreams, whenever he closed his eyes.

There had been details he'd forgotten, or blocked out: the whisper of the wind through the trees on shore; Murray's whistling; his own words of warning.

The realisation rocked his memory of the day. He'd tried to warn Murray. He'd done his best to get him to come back.

His mind had been so focused on the horror of what had happened, it had lost some of the details. Pieces that slotted together to show a different side, paint a slightly different picture of what happened to those two boys on the ice. He might not have physically saved Murray, but he had tried to stop anything bad happening to him in the first place.

He hadn't let him die. He had tried to make sure he lived.

This awareness changed everything. Walker felt the swell of grief in his chest, the prick of tears in his eyes. Murray, his childhood friend, had died because he was a daredevil. It was one of the reasons that Walker had loved him, had loved being his friend. For the fun, the thrill, the adventures they shared; the rope swings, the bike jumps, the ghost stories after dark. And it was that character trait that had led to his death, not Walker. He felt the tears running down his cheeks, and finally felt ready to leave the past behind. He leaned over the edge of the boat and trailed his hand into the water where he'd lost his friend, finally saying goodbye to him. It was all so long ago.

He was pulled from his thoughts again, this time by a shout from the bank. A voice he recognised yelling his name, followed by a long, piercing whistle. He lifted his head to see the last person he ever expected: Gabriella Tucci, her crutches abandoned on the floor as she waved both arms above her head.

'Walker!' she yelled. 'Come back! Please!'

She waved again frantically. It only took him a few seconds to organise his oars and then he turned away from the past and rowed towards the bank.

Things got even more surprising when he climbed out of the boat and she threw her arms around his neck, holding him so that there wasn't a breath between them.

'Are you okay?' she whispered. 'Please tell me you're okay.'

'I'm better than I've been in a long, long time,' Walker said, pulling her tightly to his chest.

# Chapter Forty-Five

*Gabi*

An hour later, at the local bar – The Loch, Stock and Two Smoking Barrels – Walker was looking better. Gabi had let everyone know that he was fine and promised to fill them all in later. He had colour back in his cheeks and seemed to be starving hungry. She'd found them a seat in a corner and in between sips of Irn-Bru and bites of pie, he told her everything. How coming back and facing his own fear had helped to unlock it.

'I can see it all so clearly now,' he said. 'My guilt had skewed the truth of how it happened. I had it all twisted.'

He looked like a load had been lifted from his shoulders. By the time the meal was finished, he had talked it out, and she could see that he had begun to let the past go.

'It was my idea in the first place, but then I changed my mind,' he said. 'And I tried, really tried, to keep Murray safe.'

'I'm sure you did, Walker,' she said. 'Because that's what you always do.'

'But I always thought that was a reaction to what happened to Murray,' Walker confessed, but Gabi shook her head.

'I think that it's you,' Gabi said. 'You are the most caring person I've ever met, and I think you were probably like that before Murray's accident, not just afterwards.'

Walker blinked as he took that in, but looked doubtful.

'I honestly think it's the way you're made,' Gabi continued. 'You want to make everything okay, to help everyone, to make life easier if you can. And that's really special.'

Walker stared at her and she could feel the heat in her face. But she meant every word. And she wanted him to believe in himself and see himself as she did. Because he was amazing.

'I'm sorry about your friend.' Gabi reached across the table to squeeze his hand, suddenly wanting more contact. 'I really am.'

He squeezed her hand in return and she knew it was time to say what she needed to say.

She swallowed, glancing down at the old, dented wooden table between them before forcing herself to meet his gaze. 'And I owe you a proper apology too. I'm sorry about the things I said to you.' Walker considered her for a moment.

'That's okay,' he said. 'I said some pretty harsh things too.'

She felt the relief in her shoulders and broke into a smile. 'Friends?' she said, and he nodded.

'I really am glad you're okay,' she said, suddenly leaning forwards to hug him again. Her arms wrapped his shoulders and she pressed her face into his neck, happy when she felt his arms encircle her too and squeeze.

'I can't believe you got a taxi.' He laughed as they separated.

'Best fare of his life, he said.' Gabi laughed too.

'I'll drive us back,' Walker said, stretching. She could see the toll of the last few days on his face and was glad when he added, 'But maybe not today.' He rolled his shoulders. 'If that's okay with you?'

Gabi pretended to think about it. 'Well, with my extremely hectic schedule in Honeybridge, I might just be able to manage a day or two away.' She sipped her drink. 'And I've never been to Scotland before.'

Walker's eyes lit up.

'You're joking?' She shook her head and he beamed. 'Then we should definitely stay. I can show you around while we're here.'

'Sounds like fun,' Gabi said, trying to ignore the immediate dirty thoughts that sprang to mind.

'Let me get some proper drinks,' Walker said, 'and we can make a plan.'

He returned a moment later with a beer, a glass of wine and a questioning expression.

'They have a room here that we can have for the next couple of days . . .' He raised an eyebrow. 'But it's only got a double bed.'

Gabi sipped her wine coolly, unable to believe her luck.

'Well, we are friends . . .' she said, twiddling the wine glass languidly between her fingers and letting her eyes toy with his. 'So, I suppose we could add the benefits?'

Walker stood immediately, a grin lighting his face. He picked Gabi up in one arm, and her bags in the other, leaving their drinks virtually untouched and her crutches forgotten in the corner as he headed up the stairs.

Upstairs, the room was freezing. Gabi hadn't realised how much colder it would be in Scotland, compared to spring in the southeast of England, and was poorly dressed in a thin top and jeans. She shivered as Walker opened the door to the wide attic room. An iron-framed bed covered in thick blankets stood in the middle of the room, while a tartan rug covered the majority of the floorboards, but the breeze still whistled through the gaps.

Walker helped her with her bag and then sat her on the bed while he lit the fire. The well-dried kindling burst into life, and he fed it from the stack of logs to keep it burning.

'No need to worry, miss,' Walker said in an authoritative voice, 'I'm a firefighter, you know.'

'I've never had a real fireplace in a bedroom before,' Gabi said, reaching her hands out towards it and watching the flames dance. It cast a gorgeous light in the early evening dusk. 'It's so romantic.'

'Then we should make the most of it,' Walker said, his voice lower suddenly, his eyes probing hers.

'What did you have in mind?' she asked, biting her lip in anticipation.

He crossed the space between them in two strides and a small exclamation escaped her mouth as he lifted her in his arms and carried her to the rug in front of the fireplace. He laid her down gently and knelt beside her. She reached for him and her mouth found his. She felt his smile even as he kissed her more deeply. Her arms twined around his neck and they ground against each other. She groaned.

'Warmer now?' he asked and she could only moan a reply.

Walker took her top off in one smooth upward movement, uncovering a lacy white bra. Her nipples were already hard as his thumbs skated across them. He ripped the lace out of the way and lifted her breasts free. She threw her head back and offered herself up to him. He dropped his mouth, kissing and teasing her until she gasped.

Her hands found his cock and she freed him from his jeans. He throbbed in her hands as she stroked the length of him. He tore off his own T-shirt and she crushed their torsos together, her skin rubbing against his, feeling the warmth of his chest against hers.

She watched the concentration on his face as he peeled her jeans down her legs, until he realised the boot was in the way.

'I'm lying down already,' she whispered. 'I can take it off.'

His eyes were intense as he carefully undid the strapping and eased the boot gently from her foot and tossed it aside. The firelight flickered against her pale skin as he held her leg in the air and let his fingers trail down it.

She lay in her underwear, bra askew and his eyes moved over her, top to toe. She shivered but not from the cold.

Walker knelt between her legs and ran his hands over her. His fringe fell against his forehead and his tongue wet his bottom lip. Gabi could hardly breathe with wanting.

'You sure?' he asked.

'Very,' she said. He pulled her towards him and lifted her good leg up to his chest. He rested the ankle on his shoulder and looked down at her.

He ran his fingers down the strip of material, all that was keeping them apart. She was wet already, soaking. Gabi arched on the rug as he moved the scrap of fabric to one side, and she threw her head back as he put one finger, then two, inside her. He ran his fingers to her clit, making her rock against his hands. He put his fingers inside her again, and she knew she was more than ready.

'I want you inside me,' she whispered, feeling his cock hard against her leg.

He held the glistening head against her clit and she watched her own trembling as he brushed it back and forth. Gabi bucked against him, wanting more. He thrust up and down the length of her clitoris, not losing connection at any time, and she reached up a hand for him, blindly, only wanting to anchor herself. He crouched over her, still keeping contact with her core, nipping at her breast, biting hard enough to leave a mark, then flicking at the nipple with his tongue.

'Walker,' she moaned. 'Please.' She couldn't wait any longer.

He straightened, steadied himself and plunged inside her in one swift move, burying himself to the hilt. He was like hot iron inside her and she couldn't get enough. He withdrew, until he was completely outside of her again and she called for him. She wanted more. Her control was gone. She wrapped her arms around his neck and he held on to her hips and their bodies found perfect synchronicity, giving what the other needed, taking what they wanted. He thrust again and again, and when they were both close, he put his thumb on her clit between them and took her over the edge.

Later, when their breathing had calmed, Walker propped the welcome bottle of red wine on the hearth to warm, dragged some blankets from the bed and covered them in front of the fire. He wrapped one around her shoulders and smoothed it down her back. Gabi fitted snugly against him and breathed in the peppery spice smell of his skin. As the fire crackled, shadows danced across the ceiling while the sounds of the pub below came and went.

'Well, I certainly like Scotland so far,' Gabi murmured into his chest. He snorted.

'There's lots more to do yet,' he replied and she could hear his smile.

'Excellent,' she said, letting her head rest on his shoulder. He adjusted his position slightly.

'Tell me more about you. I feel like you know so much about the twelve-year-old me. All I really know is that you had a difficult childhood. Do you have any fond memories at all?' Walker asked and she felt his breath on her shoulder. She thought for a moment.

'Bike rides,' she said simply. 'I always felt so independent, so free. As soon as I learned to ride, it meant I could take myself wherever I wanted to go, as fast as I could, feeling the wind against my skin. I didn't need anyone else to enjoy it. It was the start of my love of speed and stunts, what turned me into an adrenaline junkie.'

'You started young then,' he said. 'With your career.' She nodded and her agent's email sitting in her inbox, the thought of her next job, flashed through her mind. She shook her head to clear it. She didn't need to think about that now.

'Tell me about growing up here,' Gabi prompted, wanting to imagine Walker in this place. She settled against him as he told her about the small local school and of his adventures with Murray: hiking and biking around the loch, fishing and swimming and sailing. How they would fashion their own rope swings and lose whole afternoons playing hide-and-seek. And he talked about Murray's laugh, how he'd laugh so hard that tears used to leak from the corners of his eyes. Now that he'd come back, Walker could see clearly: it wasn't just that Murray had died at the loch, he had lived there too.

'Now I can remember the whole story. Not just the ending,' Walker said, squeezing Gabi against him. 'That's down to you, Gabi. You made me face my fears.'

Gabi noticed that night had fallen outside. It must be late. But she had no desire to sleep.

'Oh, I'm sure you would have found the courage to face them yourself,' she said.

'What, me?' he teased. 'The scared little boy?'

She felt herself blush.

'Ouch,' she said. 'It's official. I'm horrible.'

He chuckled.

'I don't think you're horrible. You were hurt because of the things I said to you.'

Gabi took a deep breath. 'The thing is, you were right.'

He'd been pretty generous with the home truths he dealt her. Telling her she'd upset Rosie and was shit at relationships. But maybe she'd needed to hear it.

'Are you going to do something about it then?' he asked quietly into her hair.

She couldn't help but smile. Proud of herself. 'Already have.' She remembered the way Rosie had forgiven her immediately and pulled her in for a hug.

'Wow. Speedy work, Ms Tucci.' Gabi heard the surprise in Walker's voice.

'Thank you, Mr McBride.'

'What did you do?'

'Apologised to Rosie and took her humble crumble, because I can't make pie.'

He grinned. 'And the bit about relationships?'

'I'm working on it,' Gabi said. 'But that's all I'll say.' He held her eye and then nodded. He wasn't going to push her.

'I hope it works out for you,' he said. 'Really, I do. Because now that I've faced my fears, I feel good about myself. I feel more like a man.'

Gabi tilted her face up to his. The glow of the fire lit the orange specks in his hazel eyes.

'That sounds promising.' She held his gaze a beat too long, deliberately. The air between them sparked.

'You think?' he asked, shifting against her, letting his hands start to move over her body again.

'Maybe I should test it out for myself?' she suggested, eyes playing with his. 'If you feel like a . . . big . . . man . . . ?'

She saw the lift of his mouth in a smile just before she pressed her lips to his.

# Chapter Forty-Six

## Walker

'There's one last place I want to take you,' Walker said a couple of days later as he navigated narrow country lanes bordered with heather. 'Before we go back to Honeybridge.'

Gabi clapped her hands in delight in the passenger seat and he laughed. She was the perfect tourist and Walker had enjoyed showing her around. They'd been on a boat trip around the loch where the wind was so bitter he'd wrapped his scarf around her neck. He'd driven them to the coast, and they ate mussels with freshly baked bread. He found a viewpoint where he put his coat on the bench for her, and then pointed out eagles as they soared overhead. He'd been careful to make sure she could manage each location in her boot in the daytime and he'd had the reward of taking it off at night, along with the rest of her clothes.

He pulled up outside an ivy-clad, grey-stone house with big leaded windows and turned off the engine.

'Here we are!' he said, opening her car door and helping her out.

'Nice place,' Gabi said, admiring the stone wall outside, the heavy front door. 'Who lives here?'

Walker opened his mouth to reply at the same time as a golden retriever tore round the side of the house, bounded over the wall and hit him at full speed. He staggered under the impact but then the dog was standing on his back legs and licking at his face, and he couldn't help but laugh.

'Hello, Bonnie,' he said, reaching to scruff behind her ears.

'Walker!' He heard the surprise in one of his favourite voices in the world and turned to see his mum walking round from the garden. She clapped her hands to her face and then hurried over, pulling off her gardening gloves as she came. He wrapped her in a bear hug, lifting her feet clear off the ground, and she banged at his chest.

'Put me down!' she said. 'And introduce me properly!'

He kept his arm around her shoulder and turned to Gabi, who was stroking Bonnie and looking mildly confused.

'Gabi, this is my mum,' he said, 'and Mum, this is my friend Gabi.'

'Pleased to meet you, Mrs McBride,' Gabi said.

'Lovely to meet you too but do call me Bridget!' his mum said and then, tugging his arm, 'Come on in. Your dad's inside. What a lovely surprise!'

Hours later, after a barbecue outside and much later than he'd intended to stay, his mum brought out the family albums.

'This is the oldest album, with lots of lovely pictures of Walker as a boy,' she said, handing Gabi a faded book where the photos were displayed under sheets of clear film. 'When we used to live by the loch.'

Soon she was telling Gabi the story behind every picture as she worked her way through the book. The fire was lit, and they'd found an old embroidered pouffe for Gabi's foot. Gabi's face was rosy in the heat of the fire, and she was giving the photographs her full attention. Walker relaxed in an armchair beside his dad and the dog settled on the floor between them.

Walker's sister had popped in for an hour earlier – so as not to miss him apparently, but he thought it was probably more to do with the fact his mum had texted her to say he'd brought a woman home with him. On arrival, Helen had immediately sat next to Gabi at the garden table, and he'd heard the two women talking about everything from jobs to holidays to skincare over their plates of grilled sausages and salad. When it was time for her to leave, she exchanged numbers with Gabi and only just found time for a squeeze with him as she pulled her coat on in the hall.

'I like her,' she whispered in his ear, and Walker laughed.

'We're friends,' he whispered back, and she raised one eyebrow before yelling a general goodbye on her way out.

'How's work?' his dad asked from his adjacent chair and Walker told him about the promotion opportunity. His dad reached over and clapped his thigh.

'You deserve it, son,' he said gruffly. 'Well done.'

'What about you, Dad? How's things?' Walker asked to change the subject, and his dad started his usual updates, the ones that Walker often got on the phone but now could enjoy in person. His hours volunteering at mountain rescue. His best dog walks with Bonnie. The extortionate vet fees when she trod on a nail and cut her paw. Walker listened to his dad until he saw Gabi point to a picture and laugh out loud.

'Please tell me I have clothes on in whatever picture you're showing her?' Walker said to his mum, whose eyes twinkled.

'Don't worry, you're decent,' she said.

Gabi turned the book to him, showing him a picture of him in a kilt. He was about twelve and just starting to shoot up. He beamed and held a trophy above his head.

'The local curling team – player of the season!' he said, recognising it immediately.

'You look tiny!' Gabi said, turning it to study again, and then raising her eyes over the book. 'Did you tell your mum about the other award you won recently? Hero of Honeybridge?' She could obviously tell by the look on his face that he hadn't, as she proceeded to tell them about the night, the other nominations and how he'd been the obvious winner.

Listening to her, he suddenly realised he wasn't experiencing the normal wave of anxiety. Responsibility wasn't weighing on him like it usually did. In fact, he felt a swelling in his chest which was extremely unusual. Pride. He might not have felt it properly, in fact, since holding that curling trophy. He couldn't help but smile when his mum blew him a kiss in congratulations.

'Will you stay tonight, you two?' she asked, looking between them. 'It's too late to be thinking about that long drive.'

He glanced at the window and saw the fading light, before looking to Gabi, who shrugged and nodded with a smile. 'I'd like that,' she said. 'But I don't even have a toothbrush!'

'I have some spares . . .' his mum said, a hopeful expression on her face.

'Then I'd love to,' said Gabi.

'Great, I'll make some cocoa.' His mum stood, and he followed her out to help. As the milk heated and he stirred it with a wooden spoon like he had done for years, his mum came up behind him and whispered, 'Gabi's lovely,' in his ear, then, 'I'll make up the spare room for you both. I take it you're sharing?' He nodded. She kissed his cheek and walked off without another word.

Later, in his parents' spare bedroom, Walker climbed into bed and pulled Gabi to his chest. The duvet was heavy and warm over them. They listened to the sounds of the house as it settled for the night. He waited for the sound of the door closing across the hall and then heard the low rumble of his parents' voices as they talked for a few minutes before getting into bed. The curtains were drawn. A floorboard creaked. And then there was silence.

'Your family is amazing,' Gabi said quietly. 'I've had a great day.'

'So have I,' he said, and she nestled in more closely. He felt the curve of her breast against his chest. The length of her thigh against his own.

'They're so warm and welcoming,' Gabi said. 'But then I guess they must be used to meeting girls that you bring home for a visit . . .' She was digging for information and he knew it. He chuckled. He could play along for the joke and tell her he'd introduced scores of women to his mum in the past. But he took a deep breath and decided to tell her the truth.

'No, actually,' he said quietly into her hair. 'You're the first.'

She glanced up at him from her position in his arms.

'Really?' she asked.

'Really,' he confirmed. 'I've never had a serious relationship so have never brought anyone home.' Her eyebrows shot up and he immediately reassured her. 'Not saying that this is a serious relationship of course...'

She grinned. 'I've never been in a serious relationship either. Never really seen the attraction,' Gabi said. They fell silent, and he felt her fingers splay and begin to play on his chest.

'Suppose sex is out of the question?' she said, and he laughed softly before replying.

'Not if we're really, really quiet ... My mum reads in bed until the early hours,' he replied, his cock already lifting at the thought of all the things he'd like to do to Gabi. His hands moved over her, feeling her react just as quickly to him. The bud of her nipples. The heat between her legs. And then the only sound was their breathing, soft at first and building, growing heavier and slower, until they both came in a shuddering, gasping togetherness.

# Chapter Forty-Seven

*Gabi*

Gabi felt like she'd not seen Isabella for ages as she opened the door to Tutto Mio. In fact, it was only a few days, but with everything that had happened in Scotland, it felt longer. Nonna greeted her with a hug, a pinch of the cheek and a plate of biscuits and pointed her in the direction of their usual corner table, where Isabella was already sat with a coffee pot.

'Missed you!' Isabella said as they hugged, and it suddenly hit her as Gabi said it back. In a few weeks, she'd be gone, and she'd have to get used to not seeing Isabella for months on end again. Well, she'd worry about it when she needed to. In the meantime, she was enjoying her holiday in Honeybridge, maybe even more so now than before.

'So, Walker told the boys you worked out where he'd be and turned up on a white horse.'

'Haha. Very funny. Black taxi actually.'

'Truly, though, Gabi, that's incredible,' Isabella said, pouring coffee. 'We were so worried about him.'

'I know, me too.' Gabi remembered the sick feeling she'd had on the way to Scotland. 'But he's so much happier now that he's faced his past.' Isabella raised her eyebrows.

'It's no secret, and he won't mind me telling you,' Gabi said. 'But he's blamed himself so long for a friend's death that it was starting to affect the way he lived his life.'

She told her cousin about Murray's tragic accident, knowing Isabella would understand.

'How awful!' Isabella gasped. 'But hopefully facing his fears will have helped him to move on.'

'He says he feels like a new man,' Gabi said.

'How come you stayed for a few extra days?' Isabella asked.

'What can I say? I had a good tour guide . . .' Gabi grinned. Isabella studied her face and then realisation dawned. 'He took me places I've never been before.'

'You and Walker – again?' she said excitedly. 'And?'

'Five-star review.' Gabi laughed and bit into a biscuit, rolling her eyes in pleasure, but more at the memory than the taste in her mouth.

'Are you a thing now then?' Isabella's eyes were literally shining, and she crossed her fingers.

'We can't be. It's just a holiday fling,' Gabi said, shaking her head. 'But I intend to enjoy it while it lasts.'

Isabella kissed her own fingers and nodded her agreement.

Gabi spotted Walker immediately as she opened the doors to the gym and felt her tummy flip. He noticed her and nodded; no hands free to wave back as he was halfway through a lift. She took the opportunity to admire his form and the breadth of his shoulders. She'd not seen him since the long drive south when he dropped her off at Amber's front door. They'd waved kind of awkwardly at each other as he drove away. It felt strange after the intimacy they'd shared over the past few days. Now, she felt a rush of pleasure at seeing him again.

She let him get on with his session while she worked through her physio exercises. They navigated the gym around each other, until he stood, hot and pumped in front of her at the water fountain. She had the desire to run her fingers down his biceps and feel his hands on her hips.

'How are you doing?' he asked, and his accent took her back to the bedroom at his parents' house where they'd whispered under the duvet for hours and he'd put his hand over her mouth to quiet her laughter.

'I'm good!' Gabi replied, acknowledging how happy she actually felt. 'Is it nice to be home?' she asked.

'Truthfully, I feel like a new man,' he said. 'Walker 2.0.' He filled his water bottle and they moved outside to the sitting area, choosing a couple of chairs on the patio in the warmth of the June sunshine. 'I've slept through the night since Scotland without the hint of a nightmare. And I feel a new excitement for life, rather than an anxiety about it.' She knocked her water bottle against his in congratulations. 'How was your physio? How long until the boot comes off?' he asked.

'Just one more week,' Gabi said, lifting her leg in the air between them. He caught it and rested her foot in his lap. It felt strangely intimate, even with all their clothes on. Gabi shifted in her seat, but found she didn't feel the urge to pull away. Rather, she wanted him to run his fingers up her leg and hold her closer. She let her foot sink into him and asked, 'What about you – and the promotion?'

Walker smiled and his hair fell onto his forehead. 'I accepted today,' he said. 'I'll take up the role in about two weeks.'

'Same time I leave for America – if I get the gig,' Gabi said, wondering why she felt weird as the words left her mouth. She'd been looking forward to getting out of this boot and out of this town for weeks, and now it was on the horizon, it was starting to go by too fast.

'Not much time left,' Walker said and she felt something pull at her insides. Where was this conversation going? Did he mean with her? Now that they were friends, would he actually miss her? He'd been such a big part of her time here in Honeybridge. 'And then you'll be gone.' She pressed her lips closed, unsure of what to say. Because she suddenly realised how much she would miss him. And that she really liked Walker. Even if it was a holiday fling – it had meant something.

Walker tapped her boot and asked, 'Do you think you'll meet up with him before you leave?'

'What?' Gabi asked, wondering if she'd zoned out, thinking she'd missed something. 'Who?'

'Your dad,' Walker said, half laughing.

She shook her head in confusion, and he continued. 'You said you were doing something about the things I said in our argument. So, have you messaged him? I bet he was so pleased to hear from you.'

'What are you talking about?' Gabi said. 'I didn't say anything about Papà.'

Walker paused and she watched the confusion flick over his face.

'In Scotland, you said that I was right,' he said slowly. 'And that you were "working on it".' Gabi realised his mistake and a bolt of anger shot through her. 'I thought you meant your dad.'

'I meant I was trying to improve my relationship with you, by apologising,' she said emphatically. She drew herself upright and removed her leg from his lap. 'How and when I communicate with my dad is nobody's business but mine.'

They stared at each other.

'So, you ignored my comments about the fact that you can't have a proper relationship with anyone until you sort your relationship with your dad first?'

The words still hurt the second time around. Gabi flinched and felt her face redden.

'Looks like it,' she said.

She saw the expression on his face change from confusion to disappointment. When he spoke, his voice was quiet, but it had the impact of a bomb detonating.

'So, maybe I've faced my fear, Gabi, but you definitely haven't.'

Gabi stood suddenly and grabbed her crutches before she blew a gasket.

'That's so easy for you to say – with your lovely twinkly mum and your intelligent dad and your friendly sister. You've even got a fucking golden retriever.'

He baulked at her tone.

'You're so perfect, aren't you, Walker McBride?'

'I didn't mean it like that.' Walker stood quickly, reaching a hand towards her, which she wanted to hit away. 'I just meant that you should let people in. You don't need to do everything on your own. People would like to be part of your life. Just try it some time. Let *someone* in. If it's not your dad, start small and build up. But face your fears.'

Gabi was boiling with rage. Just when she thought they were on the same page, that they liked each other. He was trying to tell her how she could be better.

'You're saying I'm scared?' She pulled herself to her full height of five foot three. 'I'm not scared. You can't feel fear in my job or you're done for.'

Walker considered her for a moment but then smiled as if she'd missed a point.

'You might risk your body, but you certainly don't risk your heart,' Walker said. They faced each other. Her chest was heaving. 'I'm just trying to help, Gabi.'

'Help?' she fumed. 'By telling me how to live my life?' Gabi would have stamped her foot if she had one spare. 'I know what I'm doing. I'm perfectly happy as I am.'

'Maybe that's why you like working away so much, running away from any kind of attachments. You can't get close to people if you're on a different continent.'

She hit his ankle with her crutch and had a glint of satisfaction in his shock.

'Sorry, Gabi,' Walker said, putting both hands in the air. 'I really was only trying to help.'

She'd had enough. What the hell was it with this town? Everyone in each other's business all the time. She couldn't wait to get out of there and leave it behind. A name on a map. Just the place her cousin lived.

'No hard feelings, Gabi?' Walker said softly as she moved past him, resting his hand on her shoulder lightly. She let it fall as she swung by and headed for the exit.

'No, Walker,' she corrected. 'No feelings at all.'

# Chapter Forty-Eight

*Walker*

Later, Walker and Alex lounged on the sofa. Walker on his end, Alex on the other, footstool between them to share. Walker had been mulling over what he'd said to Gabi since she stormed home from the gym. Half of him had been kicking himself for saying too much. The other half wondered how they always seemed to end up rowing, which he didn't want to do. He wondered whether he should call her and apologise. He sighed. And became immediately aware of an answering sigh from Alex. He muted the TV to find out what was the matter. Because for a man whose song was now being played daily on the local radio, Alex didn't seem that peppy.

'You all right, mate?' Walker asked. Alex considered that for a moment.

'Yep, just thinking about what's next for me.'

Walker shifted to get a better look at him.

'How d'you mean?'

'Well, look at you, Walks. Career going well, promotion incoming. Nice house on the river.' He gestured about himself as he spoke and Walker saw the cosy snug of the small front room, the fireplace, the oversized sofa. 'You've even got a cat.'

On cue, Fatboy Jim sauntered into the room and sprang onto the sofa, landing surprisingly lightly for the biggest ginger cat in the world. Immediately his pneumatic purr rang out as he settled between them. Walker put a hand tentatively on his head and scratched behind his ears. Fatboy Jim spun onto his back and grabbed him with all four paws.

'What, this arsehole?' Walker joked but Alex dismissed that with a flick of his hand.

'Look at Et – The Bistro is booming; he's found the love of his life . . .'

Walker opened his mouth, but Alex held his hand up.

'And Fox – winning at fatherhood, now a global games designer about to be a millionaire.

'Then look at me,' Alex said. 'I live in my mate's spare room, I play in a not-famous band and do some part-time music lessons for kids. And the woman I love hates me.'

'You're getting yourself together, though, Al. Let's face it, you've had a tough few years.'

'I know that. I know I used to gamble to escape things – my parents' deaths, for example. But I haven't played poker or even a fruit machine for more than five years now. And still I feel like I'm not getting anywhere. Maybe I should just take a chance on the unknown and move on.'

Walker watched his friend, one of the nicest, kindest men he knew. He wished he could help him.

'What do you want, Alex?' Walker asked. 'If you could design your ultimate life.'

'I want Amber, and Jayden,' Alex said simply. 'And that's not on the cards. So maybe a fresh start would be the next best thing.'

'How are things with Amber then?'

'She should know I would never, ever do anything to hurt Jayden.' Alex's expression was fierce. 'The only reason I left last time was because I didn't want to put him in danger and it killed me. Literally one day he told me he loved me and the next day I saw one of the Dougall family – the ones who were after me – in the town where Amber and I were working, and I panicked. I thought I had to run. I packed up and left within an hour, leaving no trace, no link that might lead them to Amber or Jayden. I really believed I had to disappear to keep them safe.'

Walker blew out softly. 'Have you ever told her that's why you left?'

'She's never given me the chance. Every time I try to bring it up, she says she's not interested.'

'That's tough, man.'

'Yep.' Alex closed his eyes. 'Anyway. What about you? You and Gabi seem to be back on . . .'

Walker rolled his eyes, unsure where to start.

'Think we're off again after today,' he said. 'Literally, it's the best sex of my entire life, but with the most infuriating person ever. That woman gets under my skin in a way I've never known. I'm drawn to her like a magnet, but it feels like there's always something that holds us apart.'

'Sounds like love to me,' Alex said with a nudge. Walker snorted.

'Gabi wouldn't let anyone love her. She's too determined to live alone.'

'And that bothers you why?' Alex said, serious all of a sudden. Walker met his gaze, found himself frowning. He examined the thought that was underneath everything. The thing that kept him coming back for more of Gabi every time.

'Because, actually, if she could let someone in, I think we'd be perfect together.'

The words sat between them, along with Fatboy Jim who was licking himself with the dexterity of a much more athletic cat.

'You like her,' Alex said. 'Thought so.'

'Turns out I do,' said Walker with a wry smile. 'Not that it counts for anything. Yet again, Gabriella Tucci hates me.'

Credits started to roll on the television programme. Both men sighed.

'Looks like you and I will have to stay married,' Walker said, standing up.

'For now,' Alex agreed.

'I'll sort the kitchen,' Walker said.

'I'll do the bins.' Alex stuffed his feet into his trainers.

'Thanks, darling.'

'Any time, babe.'

# Chapter Forty-Nine

## Gabi

'For someone who seems the favourite choice for a top job and gets their boot off for good in a week, you don't seem happy about it,' Isabella said to Gabi later that afternoon.

She and Gabi lay at either end of the sofa, in Isabella's apartment over the restaurant, top to toe as they painted each other's toenails. Gabi, tongue poking from the corner of her mouth, didn't answer until she finished painting Isabella's big toe in turquoise.

'Aren't you looking forward to it?' Isabella pressed and Gabi lifted her eyes from her task.

'The leg, yes,' she said. 'I can't wait to get this thing off.'

'And the job?'

She pulled a face and then frowned at Isabella, nail varnish brush in one hand, pot in the other. Gabi took a deep breath as she prepared to ask her cousin one of the many questions that had been bothering her lately.

'Do you think I use my job to run away from people?'

'Woah, deep and meaningful conversation coming up,' Isabella said. 'Lids on for this kind of talk.' Both screwed their bottles shut, one foot painted each. 'Now, where did that come from?'

'Walker.'

Isabella considered that, nodding.

'I couldn't say for sure, Gabs. But your jobs have taken you all around the world since you were old enough to fly solo. Maybe you have been running from something.'

Gabi's mouth opened in amazement. She'd always presumed she was running towards something – like success, and money, and independence, for example – and had never seen anything wrong with that. But maybe there was a kernel of truth in what Isabella, and Walker, said. After all, she chose to spend all of her time with the one person she thought she could rely on: herself. Was she running away because she didn't trust other people enough to stick around? The niggle of doubt made her ask the next question that was on her mind.

'And do you think I find it hard to form relationships?'

Isabella looked her right in the eye and Gabi braced herself.

'Have you ever had one?' Isabella asked.

Gabi gasped at that one. Her cousin wasn't holding her punches tonight.

'Not a long one, no . . .' Gabi said defensively.

'How long is not long?' Isabella probed. 'Because I've never met one of them.' Gabi grimaced.

'I've never made it past date five,' Gabi confessed and Isabella raised an eyebrow.

'Why not?' she demanded.

Gabi squirmed and put a cushion over her face.

'It was when he started talking about planning a weekend away together,' she said from behind it. 'I couldn't bear the thought of listening to him mouth breathe for more than a few hours at a time. I would have smothered him in his sleep.'

'Mmm-hmmm. There's your answer, Gabs.' Isabella paused, then frowned. 'When did Walker say all this to you exactly?' Isabella asked, pulling Gabi's cushion away, leaving Gabi feeling pink in the face, exposed. She wished she'd never started this. But she couldn't keep running for ever.

Gabi sighed and told her everything. Isabella listened wide-eyed and open-mouthed, only remembering to shut it when Gabi wrapped up, 'And then I stormed off home. Tell me honestly, Issy. How would you describe me?' The two women faced each other, and Gabi knew that Isabella would tell her the truth. She trusted her with her life. Always had.

'You're fabulous, Gabi, you're fun, feisty and full of life.'

'But?' Gabi braced herself. She could tell by the way that her cousin was looking at her there was more to come.

'I *can* see what Walker means when he says you find it hard to let people in. It probably comes from your childhood. You are independent to the point of getting the bus to your hospital appointment with a broken leg rather than asking someone for a lift...'

'But I don't want to trouble anyone – and I *can* do it.' Conflicting emotions suddenly left Gabi's eyes filled with tears.

'On your own, yes, I know.' Isabella tweaked Gabi's big toe, taking the sting out of her words. 'All I'm saying is, don't be *too* independent if you don't want to end up alone.'

Gabi blinked, swallowed, nodded. It was good advice. She just didn't know how to follow it.

'Do you think I can't form relationships?' Gabi asked. She might as well get the full story. Isabella laughed and rolled her eyes.

'That's difficult for me to answer because you're the best cousin in the world.'

Gabi accepted that one with a nod.

'And Amber says you're the best housemate she's ever had.'

Gabi accepted that one too. Living with Amber had been fun, and it would be a wrench to leave. No more early morning coffees in their PJs when they communicated in grunts and nods. No more late-night glasses of wine on the sofa when they laughed until their stomachs ached.

'And the gang love you. They always say nights out are more fun with you there. Bucking broncos, firemen's poles . . .'

Gabi felt some of the tension leave her. Maybe she wasn't such a failure after all.

'So, I'd say you're pretty good at making friendships. In fact, great at it.' Gabi felt a swell of happiness. She'd never really had friends before. Just Isabella. Becoming part of the gang at Honeybridge, that had made her feel good.

Etienne wandered in, barefoot, coffee in hand, and opened his mouth to speak but was cut off by Isabella, who suddenly drew a sharp intake of breath and grabbed Gabi's foot, hard, to get her attention.

'The question might actually be, what kind of relationship, *exactly*, is Walker saying you're not good at?'

The two women stared at each other. Etienne stood between them, listening.

'Why is he so keen for you to let someone in?' Isabella whispered. 'Sounds to me like Walker wants more than whatever friends with benefits situation you've had going on.'

Gabi's stomach lurched, and she dropped her eyes to look at the foot that Isabella held in her hand. She remembered the casually intimate way that Walker had pulled it into his lap earlier. How good it had felt to rest it there, on his thigh, cupped in his hands. She'd wanted to stay there all day. Maybe it wasn't just him wanting more.

'Do you think?' Gabi asked tentatively, unsure what she wanted the answer to be. Isabella's blue eyes held hers, but it was Etienne that spoke.

'I'd put money on it,' he said, with a nod.

'You don't gamble,' Gabi challenged but Etienne disregarded that with a shrug.

'I think this is what Alex would call a sure thing.'

Gabi's heart pounded in her chest even as she started to deny it. Walker might want her body, but he didn't really want her – the whole package, as she was – did he? Wasn't it just that he had such a hero complex on he wanted to save her in some way?

'I don't think so somehow.' She shook her head decisively at Etienne, and picked up the nail varnish again to finish Isabella's feet. 'Walker McBride hates me.'

# Chapter Fifty

*Walker*

Walker had been keeping busy for a whole week. He knew he was just trying to distract himself. Since that afternoon at the gym, he'd discovered he was unable to work out without thinking of Gabi. And erections in jogging pants were not a good look on the bench press.

But he also couldn't pick up his phone without wondering if he should text her to apologise. He couldn't drive through town without attempting to spot her on her way to physio or swinging along on her crutches to Tutto Mio. It was getting ridiculous. He couldn't go anywhere in his own town without thinking about her. The sooner she left for that new job, the better. But that thought gave him no comfort either. Then he'd never even stand a chance of bumping into her.

So, in the spirit of throwing himself into things that didn't involve Gabi Tucci, he'd agreed to marshal the River Rats regatta that weekend. It might stop him worrying that he'd really hurt her feelings. Had he said too much? He remembered the sadness she'd tried to hide when talking about her family. Who was he to push her?

He'd already safety checked the boats and the life jackets. He'd walked the course early in the morning to make sure there were no blockages in the river, but it was flowing free and fast. Everything was in full bloom, the trees were at their fullest, the sun was out. Walker stopped for a moment, surprising himself by thinking it looked quite romantic. 'What the fuck?' he asked himself out loud, before shaking his head and marching back to the club house.

Walker scanned the crowd, not honestly sure if he was looking for Gabi or checking she wasn't there. But it didn't really matter which it was, because she was nowhere to be seen. Rosie and Wren were there with Riley, who was as springy as a spaniel, chasing after Jayden on the riverbank. Next, he spotted Amber carrying coffees to the other women from the kiosk. He headed over and arrived at the same time as Etienne and Isabella sidled into the group, rosy-cheeked and smiling.

'We came by yours to give you a lift,' Amber said to them.

'Oh, did you?' Etienne said vaguely, avoiding her eye.

'We fancied a walk ...' Isabella said, entwining her hand with Etienne's.

'A *walk*, was it, that you fancied?' Amber said, picking a couple of leaves out of Isabella's hair and waving them in her face.

'Mmmm-hmmm,' replied Isabella with a wink. 'And what a walk it was.'

'Where's Fox?' Alex asked. 'He said he was bringing the boys.'

'And Gabi?' Isabella turned to Amber. 'She told me she'd be here.'

On that note, it was time to make his exit. 'Just going to check the boats,' Walker said and he turned away.

He spotted Fox's car pulling into the car park alongside the boat shed as he approached. Fox unfolded himself from the driver's seat and circled the car, opening the back doors for the boys and watching them clamber from their booster seats, before sprinting towards their mates. Walker put up a hand to Fox, but he was busy opening the front passenger door and helping out ... Gabi.

Walker stopped, shielded his eyes against the sun, and watched in disbelief as Gabi took Fox's hand and he helped her up to her feet. Walker noticed reluctantly that she looked incredible. Her tan had come out over the last week or so, and it only made those doe eyes shine brighter – the same eyes that were gazing into Fox's face. She laughed and balanced a hand against his chest as he tucked one crutch under each arm. She beamed at him the whole time before leaning in to kiss Fox's cheek. Fox clicked the car door shut and followed her towards the gang.

What the *fuck*? Walker asked himself for the second time that day, his surprise turning to dismay.

# Chapter Fifty-One

## Gabi

Gabi looked all over for Walker as she waited for her breakfast sandwich at the kiosk and sighed in disappointment when she couldn't spot his broad shoulders rising above the crowd. Even with all the trouble between them, she enjoyed fighting, or flirting, with Walker more than anyone else in Honeybridge. Since Isabella and Etienne had suggested that maybe Walker might be interested in her as a serious, long-term thing, she hadn't been able to get him out of her mind. Not that it made any difference obviously. She didn't need a boyfriend full stop, but especially so now, when she was leaving so soon. And she wasn't a great pen pal. So, might as well forget the idea.

Anyway, she hadn't heard from him in the week since their argument. Not that she'd messaged him either. She had found herself thinking about what he'd said, though, and how Isabella had put things too. She did want to be close to people. She didn't want to be alone. But it made her nervous to think about relying on anyone else. What if they let her down? She couldn't bear to be hurt again.

She'd kept herself busy with Jayden as he trained for the regatta, and she'd upped her physical training, but the week had dragged.

Now, she tucked her bacon bun under her chin to keep her hands free and swung in a circle on her crutches. But as she turned, she swung straight into someone's chest and knew who it belonged to immediately, for the sheer scale and sexiness of it.

'Walker!' she exclaimed, resting on one leg and snatching the bap from under her chin so that she could look up at him properly, a smile already breaking through before she saw the frown on his face.

'Hi,' Walker replied. Not exactly the warmest welcome but then what was she expecting after the way they'd left it?

'How've you been?' she asked, noticing how gorgeous his hazel eyes looked in the sunshine.

'Busy,' he replied, kicking a stone with his boot. Man of few words today, clearly. He was obviously still annoyed at her. She'd been hoping he might have softened. She bit her lip and tried again.

'I'm glad I ran into you …' she said and then laughed awkwardly. 'Well, not "ran into you" exactly because, well, obviously…' She lifted her boot, and her mini-skirt rucked another inch up her thigh. She saw his gaze dart there and then away. 'But yes, I'm glad I've seen you,' she said again. When he didn't reply, she cleared her throat and poked his ankle with her stick.

'I just wanted to let you know that I'm trying to do what you said, about attempting to let people in.'

'Great,' Walker said with a stiff nod. What was with him? You'd think he'd be happy about the fact she was making an effort. She pushed on, determined to get back on a good footing.

'I know it's early days, and baby steps,' Gabi said, 'but Fox said yes when I asked and that went well, so I feel like I can go further maybe. Take some bigger chances.'

Walker's mouth dropped open. Literally. Gabi stopped mid-sentence at the look of horror on his face.

'And you honestly thought I'd be happy about this?' he asked.

'I thought it was at least a step in the right direction,' Gabi said.

'With *Fox*?' Walker said furiously.

'Just for starters,' Gabi said, embarrassed now.

'Starters?' Walker was wide-eyed in disbelief.

'Yes,' Gabi said, reaching her bacon bun hand towards him, unsure quite how the conversation had turned into this. 'I *really* don't want us to fall out, Walker. I'd love us to be friends.'

He straightened himself to his full height and braced his shoulders as if against a body blow.

'I don't think that's a good idea, Gabi. In fact, I think the best thing would be for you to stay the hell away from me.'

He stamped away and Gabi was left holding a cold bacon bap wondering what the hell had just happened. Well, fuck Walker McBride and the horse that hero rode in on. She'd had enough of trying to impress him. Twice she'd taken his advice on self-improvement now and it still wasn't enough. Maybe it never would be. So now, she was doing things her way. She brushed furious tears from her eyes – how dare he treat her like that? – and headed away from the gang. Isabella would spot her face at a million paces. The last thing she needed was someone being nice to her right now. Instead, she headed to the riverbank to watch Jayden. He was pulling his life vest on as he headed to the river, togged up and ready to row. She threw her congealed sandwich in the nearest litter bin, her appetite gone, and caught up with him on the bank. Maybe he could cheer her up and she could forget all about Walker and his impossible-to-live-up-to expectations.

Jayden was lowering the boat to the water, getting ready for the next race, rowing with a buddy from school. He was excitedly gesturing to his friend as to what to do and tapping out a rhythm on the side of the boat to demonstrate the speed that each stroke should be.

'You okay?' Gabi spoke slowly so that he could lip-read. 'Going to win?' He grinned and gave her a thumbs up, just as his crewmate doubled over on the bank and threw up his breakfast. When he stopped being sick, he promptly burst into tears.

'I can't do it,' the boy sobbed. 'My tummy hurts.'

Jayden looked stricken, kindly patting his pal on the back in encouragement.

'I can't do it,' the boy sobbed again. 'I'm going to find my mum.' He turned and ran off without a backward glance. Jayden kicked the side of the boat in disappointment.

'Oh, Jayden,' Gabi said, pulling his scrawny shoulders in for a hug. She knew how hard he'd been training for this. She'd brought him here after school every afternoon and he'd been so proud when he got the fastest time in the club that he was going to represent the River Rats in the double scull race against the other local societies as their star rower. That night on the way home he'd told her that he wanted to show that he could do it all, despite being deaf. 'My arms work, even if my ears don't,' he'd written down and laughed.

A loudspeaker told all boats to head to the starting line.

Gabi glanced at the rowing boat. It was pretty tiny, but then, so was she. She lifted Jayden's chin to get his attention, pretended to row and thumbed her chest. 'I can row,' she said. He blinked but didn't look convinced.

She repeated herself, thinking about how often she rowed in the gym, how she'd set the personal best record in her apartment gym three years in a row. Jayden still looked dubious.

'Why not?' she asked and he pointed at her leg. She laughed and played his own words back to him.

'My arms work, even if my leg doesn't!'

She threw her crutches to the ground and pointed at the boat. He got in first and held it steady by the side. She lowered herself in and picked up her oars as the loudspeaker made a final call. Jayden stuck a finger in the air and then tapped his life vest. Gabi looked down at her T-shirt and mini-skirt and shrugged.

'I'll be fine,' she said and pushed them off the bank.

# Chapter Fifty-Two

*Walker*

A stomp around the car park had done nothing to improve Walker's mood. Gabi had fucked up his day. Make that his week. His entire spring.

There was no way he was supposed to be this worked up over a woman. He was supposed to be getting on with his career and having fun. She was the most infuriating person he'd ever met. Somehow, he couldn't get enough of her physically but that didn't get him as close to her as he wanted to be. The realisation hit him like a fire truck. Fuck, he had it bad. He wanted more.

And now she was taking his advice about letting people in – with Fox – and wanting him to be happy about it. She obviously didn't feel the same way about him. In fact, it would seem she felt nothing for him at all.

He found himself back at the riverbank and Rosie waved him over. The whole gang was there, including Fox, and Walker felt a pang of jealousy. He wondered where he and Gabi had been before they arrived at the rowing club. Looked like a nice little family day out, Reggie and George in the back seats. He groaned and tried to push the image from his mind.

'You okay?' Rosie asked, nudging him. She could always read his mood.

'Fine,' he said and then, softer, 'I'll tell you later.'

'Beer, mate?' Fox asked, holding out a bottle.

'I'm working,' Walker said shortly, and he turned away to watch the river, but not before he glimpsed the flick of hurt on Fox's face. Serves him right. Now he knew how it felt. He took out his multi-tool knife and flicked it open and shut, open and shut, just for something to do.

The gun went off further upriver, and he heard Amber announce to everyone that it was Jayden's race. He kept his back to them all, not trusting himself to be nice even though he wanted to be. He felt all over the place, thinking about his best friend with the woman who was driving him crazy.

The gang moved closer to spectate and someone stood beside him, eyes on the river. He knew it was Fox without looking. He snapped the knife shut and pocketed it, keeping his own eyes on the river.

'You okay, mate?' Fox asked quietly. 'You seem a bit upset.'

Walker snorted quietly and shook his head. He didn't want to get into this right now but, then again, why not?

'When were you going to tell me about you and Gabi?'

Fox swivelled to face him.

'What about me and Gabi?' he said, surprised, looking silver-grey gorgeous in the sunlight. It was obvious what Gabi saw in him.

'I saw you in the car...' Walker ground out.

'Oh, that. I gave her a lift to her hospital appointment,' Fox said. 'She rang and asked me this morning, told me she was trying to ask for help more, let people in a bit.'

Fox had Walker's full attention now. He caught his friend's elbow to hold him still. 'She said what?' he stuttered.

'Said she was taking advice that sometimes being too independent means she might push people away,' Fox said, peering at Walker, trying to read his face. 'Walker, you didn't think... there was something between us, did you?'

'I don't know what I thought,' Walker said. 'But I certainly got it wrong.'

'You were jealous!' Fox goaded with a light punch to the shoulder. 'You thought she'd fallen for the Fox Meister.' He laughed out loud.

'No way,' Walker said, punching him in return.

'So, tell me why you were so pissed off at me?' Fox said. And then the words that Walker himself had been thinking: 'You got it bad, man.' Fox clapped him on the back, as if in congratulations, or sympathy. Walker wasn't sure which was more appropriate.

'I'm not sure what's going on, but I think I need to talk to Gabi once and for all,' he said. 'We're going round in circles.'

Fox pointed out to the water. 'Well, you'll have to wait until she's out of the boat and back on dry land.'

Walker followed Fox's finger until he saw Jayden and Gabi, rowing full pelt down the river towards them. Her leg boot was straight out in front of her, her shoulders leaning into the stroke. Jayden was shouting the rowing rhythm, and they were in perfect time.

'What the *fuck*?!' Walker exploded. His new favourite phrase of the day. What the hell was she doing now?

# Chapter Fifty-Three

## Gabi

They faced backwards up the river, knowing the finish line was only a hundred metres away and they wanted to get there first.

It might just be a kids' race, but Gabi wanted to win, for Jayden mainly, but also for herself, to prove she wasn't a complete loser that got everything wrong. The only thing on her mind was to get past the finish line before anyone else. Reach, pull.

Damn Walker McBride and his sexy shoulders. His gorgeous face and how he was never afraid to tell her what she needed to hear. Why was it so important anyway that he liked her, or approved of the things she was doing? She'd be gone soon and then she could forget all about him. Reach, pull.

They passed another contestant, narrowly missing each other's oars. The course was quite crowded with this number of boats on it at the same time.

'Watch out!' A warning shout from the bank and a scream from the water ahead, and then their boat hit something mid-stroke, full force. The jolt pushed her teeth firmly into the plump flesh of her bottom lip. She heard Jayden grunt from the force of the impact; his feet kicked her hard in the back, and she was thrown from her seat and off the side of the boat. She hit the water without having time to take a breath.

The water was freezing and murky and, for a second, she lost her bearings, bubbles rushing past her face, the shock making her disoriented. She saw the hull of the boat above her and pushed for daylight with her good foot. Where was Jayden?

She surfaced in the middle of the river, carried along by the fast current. Her boat was floating upside down and she struck out to grab the side. She felt relief course through her as she saw Jayden's smiling face, as he held on to the other side of the boat. He shook his head and gave her a laughing thumbs up and she returned it, relieved he was okay.

The boat they'd hit was also capsized, but both kids were holding on to it and swimming it towards the bank. The parents were already congregating to help and shouting from the bank side, and she scanned for the gang. Amber had both hands to her face, watching Jayden in the water, obviously worried. Gabi should get him back onto dry land as soon as possible to put Amber's mind at ease.

Using her arms only, Gabi edged round the boat towards Jayden. Her boot was heavy and cumbersome under the water. She realised she wouldn't be able to swim back like the other team had and she wasn't wearing a life vest. She'd have to get back in the boat, there was no other way.

She told Jayden what she was going to do. Help him back aboard first, and then she'd pull herself in and they'd row in together. He watched her words and nodded his understanding. 'On the count of three,' Gabi said.

Holding on with both hands, he pulled himself up as hard as he could, with Gabi helping to push him up and out of the water, quickly, before grabbing the boat again. Her leg was dragging her down and she swallowed a mouthful of river water and spluttered, coughing. The boat rocked precariously, but a second later, Jayden was sitting in his seat. She swallowed another mouthful of water and spat. They were being pushed downriver but she knew there was no bridge, or shallow area that might help them. The only way out was to the bank.

'Are you okay, Jayden?' Amber shouted from the bank and Jayden gave her a cheery sign for 'perfect', not perturbed in the slightest. Good. Gabi didn't want to worry anyone. She just wanted to get Jayden out safely. Her body was shuddering with cold now and her teeth were chattering.

'Gabi? Do you need help?' Amber shouted next and Gabi waved a hand at her, dismissing the offer.

One of Jayden's oars was still in its hold, the other was empty. He glanced around the boat and pointed. It was floating towards them in the current. Holding on to the boat, she stretched out her arm, but it was still a good foot away from her fingertips. She looked at Jayden and then back out across the water. The oar was gaining on them; it was now or never.

She struck out with her arms, away from the safety of the hull. She grabbed the oar in one hand, and the gang clapped on shore. Someone whistled, probably Wren. She turned, seeing the boat had moved ahead and there was now five feet, maybe six, between them.

Breath heaving, she saw the gang on the bank. Isabella clutched her hands under her chin, Etienne stood behind her with his hands on her shoulders. A simple sign of support for Isabella. Something that Isabella might not even notice. Gabi suddenly knew she wanted someone to do that for her. She wanted someone to look after her when she was worried. To hold her. So that she didn't have to look after herself all the damn time.

She struck out with her free arm, but didn't get anywhere. She tried again, choking on the water, but she was stuck in the same place. Gabi kicked then with her good leg and realised the problem. The reeds in the middle of the river were so long that they had twined around her boot. Now, they caught her other leg, binding her in the current, pulling her under. She blinked the water from her eyes and saw Jayden's expression. He was drifting further away, he was scared. She had to get the oar to him and then sort out these reeds. With a massive effort, she arched her shoulder backwards and launched the oar through the air. It landed with a bang on the boat, and she saw Jayden grab it. Thank God.

She watched, fighting to keep her head above water, as he fastened the oar in position. When he glanced back at her, she tilted her head back to speak.

'I'm stuck in the reeds,' she said as clearly as she could, but she was swallowing water, and she wasn't sure he understood. Could he lip-read what she was saying?

Forcing herself not to panic – the first rule of being a stuntwoman is not to feel frightened – she ducked under the water and tried to reach with her hands into the gloomy water. She felt the tendrils around her thigh, but as she pulled them with her fingers, they seemed only to tighten.

She thrust to the surface again and spat out a mouthful of river, before submerging again. There had to be a way to free herself, but this time it felt as though there were more plants clinging to her. The more she struggled, the more entwined she became. For the first time ever, she felt fear. It flashed through her and turned her mind white with panic. She ripped at the reeds; they slipped through her fingers. Her lungs were bursting, and her limbs were heavy with exhaustion. She pushed for the surface again, just managing to break through with her face, and screamed.

She screamed the only name she knew would save her. The name that had been on her mind now for months.

'Walker!'

# Chapter Fifty-Four

*Walker*

'What the ACTUAL FUCK?' Walker knew he needed to expand his vocabulary but honestly. The boat crash impact had shocked everyone on the bank, but Gabi and Jayden were now in the water, grinning and giving each other a thumbs up. Amber lowered her hands from her face as she saw Gabi heaving Jayden back onto the boat, but Isabella had the same thought as he did. Gabi was still in the water, and she didn't look fully confident.

'Is her leg back to full strength?' Isabella asked anyone who might be listening.

'She'll be fine,' Etienne said. 'She's holding on.'

And then all of a sudden, she wasn't holding on. Instead, she was swimming out into the middle of the river for the oar, which she caught, earning herself a round of applause. But something was wrong. He could feel it in the pit of his stomach. He could see it in the fright that flashed over her face. She threw the oar to Jayden, and he fixed it in place.

Why wasn't she swimming back to the boat? She looked to

be treading water, but she couldn't be, she only had one fully working leg. And that boot must be cumbersome under the water. He saw her say something to Jayden but couldn't hear from the bank. Walker stepped forward, right to the riverside, scrutinising her face. Her cropped hair was slick to her head. Her big brown eyes were wide. Suddenly, he knew there was more to this than met the eye. She ducked under the water and the band of anxiety tightened around his chest.

Jayden stuck his oar in the water and turned the boat so that he was facing the bank and then waved his hands above his head. SOS.

Amber stepped forward, signing already. What is it? Jayden signed back and Amber gasped.

'Oh my God. She's stuck in the reeds,' she said. 'She's trapped.'

'The current will pull her under,' Isabella said helplessly.

Walker watched her thrashing under the water for a split second, and then she burst free, her eyes facing his way but not seeing him. And then, she screamed his name.

The sound went through him like a knife. He dived from the riverbank before her scream had finished. He swam out as fast as he could, ignoring the shock of the water, the weight of his boots. He carved his way across to her in seconds, but she was already under the water again. He reached the spot where she'd been dragged under and didn't hesitate. He took a huge breath and dove.

The water was muddy brown and the reeds covering the riverbed were a deep velvet green. He saw her struggling, tearing at her legs, and pushed himself deeper until he hit the bottom. He caught her hands, and she struggled against him for a moment, until she saw him through her panic and stopped thrashing. His fear was that she was making matters worse, tying herself up in her terror. He pulled out his pocketknife and began to slice through the nearest vines. He slashed the entire length of her boot, knowing he couldn't hurt her, and cut her free. He manoeuvred under the water, twisting her body in his hands to reach the other leg. It was snagged at the ankle and he cut away, cringing when he felt his blade hit something more solid, but carrying on. He had to free her. Cuts would heal. Drowning would kill her. His own lungs were screaming as he slashed the last plant away, pulled her to him and pushed with her for the surface. As they burst into the sunlight and she clung limply in his arms, he realised that his whole life had been heading to this point. To this exact moment of holding this woman against him and keeping her safe. To saving Gabi. She was what he was there for.

# Chapter Fifty-Five

## Gabi

Walker swam with her to the landing jetty. Her lungs hurt with every breath as she hungrily gasped for air, but he felt solid and strong next to her, talking quietly to her as they made their way, using soothing words of encouragement, gently calling her name. She held on tightly to his shoulders, her mind trying to cope with what had just happened. Not the collision or the reeds or the terror of being trapped underwater. But the fact that he'd jumped without a second of hesitation. He'd come when she needed him. He'd saved her.

She wrapped her arms tightly around him as they got to the bank and instead of using the steps, he waded to the beach entry and carried her out in his arms. She didn't want to let go, and he adjusted his grip to hold her to him. Everyone surged forward, surrounding them; Isabella wrapped a towel around her shaking body, while Etienne threw another around Walker's shoulders.

'Are you okay?' Isabella was holding her face, peering into her eyes. Gabi coughed and cleared her throat.

'Where's Jayden?' she asked.

'He's here,' Amber said, and Isabella moved aside so that Gabi could see him, looking worried and cold. He signed 'are you okay?' and only gave a trembly smile when she used one hand to give him a thumbs up, before putting it back around Walker's neck.

'That was a dumbarse thing to do – no life vest and a medical boot.' Isabella rolled her eyes and then planted a big fat kiss on Gabi's cheek. 'I was so worried.'

Suddenly there were too many people around and she just wanted to be alone with Walker. She lifted her gaze to his and found his hazel eyes fixed on her, his hair dripping water down his face.

'Can you take me home?' she asked him.

'Emergency room first,' Walker said. 'We need to get your leg checked.'

'Then home?' she pleaded. His eyes softened and he nodded. 'Let's go.'

'Shall I come too?' Isabella asked, already moving alongside them, concern etched on her face.

Gabi glanced at Walker again and their eyes confirmed that nobody else was needed.

'Don't worry, Isabella,' he said, adjusting his grip to hold Gabi more securely against his chest. 'I've got her.'

The exhaustion finally hit her as they pulled into the driveway at Walker's house. Walker parked and jogged around the car to open the door and lift her out. She could have walked, maybe, although her limbs felt like lead, but instead she twined her arms around his neck, giving in to being carried, and not just enduring it, but loving it. He felt safe. He felt solid.

He hadn't left her side all the time they'd been at the hospital, while they waited, were assessed and, finally, were given the all clear. The boot was removed for good. Her leg was unveiled. It felt strangely naked after so many weeks of being covered.

Now, at his riverside house, he carried her up the stairs to the bathroom and only then did he lower her to stand on the bathmat. She stood, feeling the rug underneath her toes, the air around her calves, a strange sense of vulnerability at her damaged leg now being unprotected. Turning on the taps, Walker added a good glug of bubble bath that smelled of lemons and swilled it with his hand.

'We need to get you warm – and clean of river water,' he said, piling white fluffy towels on the chair. 'Can you manage to get in on your own?'

She nodded, feeling torn and suddenly tearful. She didn't want to be on her own. She wasn't used to feeling so vulnerable.

'Can you come back?' she said. 'When I'm in?'

'Of course,' he said. 'Give me ten minutes. Let me grab a shower.'

Gabi was in the bath with bubbles practically up to her ears when Walker knocked and came in with a towel hung low around his hips. Gabi's shivering had stopped; her body was relaxing, letting go of its fear into the warmth of the water. She felt recovered enough to appreciate the width of Walker's chest, those flat, defined abs. Mind you, she'd probably have to be dead before she didn't appreciate those. He sat on the chair opposite the bath and smiled ruefully.

'Damn. I put far too much bubble bath in there for you,' he said, deadpan. 'Can't see a thing.'

She laughed, delighted he felt similarly, and lifted a leg in the air. White suds slipped down her calf, her thigh and back into the bath. Walker stared and a muscle ticked in his cheek.

'Someone's feeling better,' he said quietly.

'Much, thanks to you . . .' she said. Their eyes met and held.

'Walker—' she said.

'Gabi—' he spoke at the same time. Gabi smiled. 'You go first,' he said, sinking down to sit on the floor next to the bath, his back resting against the wall. The fact he was settling to listen relaxed her even more. He wasn't going anywhere.

She took a handful of suds and watched them glistening in the light. The bubbles popped delicately, and she let them drop off her fingers into the water. Now the opportunity was here, where should she start? She knew it was time – and she wanted to do it – but this was a big thing. Opening herself up to him. She started with the obvious.

'You've driven me mad the last few months,' she said, and he laughed.

'The feeling is mutual,' he replied but she held up a finger and he raised his eyebrows, waiting for more.

'Because you're right,' she continued. 'I do push people away, hold them at arm's length. I do try to do everything myself. Because I'm scared of getting hurt.' He nodded and she exhaled slowly. It felt good to say it out loud. To admit how tightly she was coiled. 'But I realised over the last few weeks that it's not so bad to have someone to rely on. Someone to really trust. I've seen what Isabella and Etienne have and it makes me think that . . . maybe I do want someone who's there for *me*.'

He hooked his arm over the corner of the bath and let his fingers trail into the water near her feet, listening intently.

'The thing is, I've never wanted it before. I've always been too scared to dare.'

'You? Scared?' he teased.

'Terrified,' she said seriously, and he reached further under the water until he found her ankle, where he circled it with his fingers, pulling her leg closer to his side of the bath. She gasped. 'That I'd like someone that much.'

'I was scared too,' Walker said. She murmured a denial, guilty still for ever calling him that, but he squeezed her ankle gently and shook his head. 'It was true,' he continued. 'Until you came along and forced me to look back, I couldn't look forwards. I was never thinking about tomorrow with anyone. I was trapped in the past.' He tweaked her foot playfully. 'And then this morning, when I thought you were starting something with Fox—'

'*What?*'

'I realised that I kept telling you to let people in, because I meant me. Let me in.'

'Fox just took me to the hospital . . .'

'He told me that afterwards.'

Gabi snorted.

'You were jealous!'

'Very.' Walker's fingers were trailing a line to her knee under the water, and she felt every millimetre he crept upwards.

'That's why I got on the bucking bronco at The Bolthole,' she confessed.

'You looked so sexy riding that thing,' he admitted with a rueful grin.

'I was jealous of the girl you were talking to.' Gabi had never in her life admitted her feelings like this before. Not to any man. Not ever. And he was listening, and taking her seriously, and . . . it felt good. It felt as though with everything she said, every feeling she admitted to, they moved closer towards each other. Not just physically, with his hand still moving up her leg, but emotionally too. Her heart was expanding with every sentence.

Walker laughed.

'Believe me, nobody else has had a look-in since a daredevil stuntwoman arrived in town.'

'Same here, since a handsome firefighter caught me on a pole.' Oh my God, she was actually saying it out loud. That since that day, all she'd thought about was Walker: impressing him, making him laugh, touching him, kissing him.

'So.' Walker stroked her thigh beneath the bubbles but held her gaze. 'You do feel something for me?'

Gabi's heart swelled. Every cell felt on fire; her skin was hypersensitive to his touch. She stopped worrying about how the words sounded and instead just said what was inside her heart.

'I do. I can't stop thinking about you. I look for you everywhere. When I was frightened in the river, you were all I could think of.' She shook her head in disbelief at the memory. 'And you came when I called.'

'Of course,' he said simply.

Their eyes were locked on each other now. She wet her lips,

felt the heaviness of her breathing. There was no going back now. She just wanted to go forwards, with Walker, with this man who walked through fire to save people. The man who challenged her, who she craved, who saved her every time.

'What now?' she asked, her voice barely above a whisper. Walker smiled, as if it was a simple question to answer.

'I want to see you all the time,' he said.

'And I want to be with you as much as I can.' Her words came out in a rush. It was as easy as that.

He stood suddenly, water cascading from his wet arm. The towel still hanging on his hips, low under the line of his taut abs. He towered over her, eyes scanning the surface of the water, hungry for what it concealed. She pressed her thighs together, wanting him with a desperate, sudden need.

'Still scared?' he asked.

She swallowed.

'A bit,' she said, wondering if it was more excitement now than fear.

He bent at the waist and put both hands on the side of the bath. His face was close and her stomach was doing somersaults.

'Thought you told me there was a rule for stuntwomen?' It took her brain a second to recollect a rule she'd lived by for many years.

'Don't be scared of falling . . .' she said, her stomach lurching.

'Well then,' he said as he leaned in slowly and lowered his face to hers.

# Chapter Fifty-Six

*Walker*

Walker kissed her with everything he had. Holding her head in his hands, he tasted her mouth, softly at first, and then building to a ferocity that made him drop to his knees beside her on the bathroom floor. He pulled her towards him, lifting her up from the water, feeling the silk of her skin, oiled by the bubbles. Gabi wrapped her arms around his neck and kissed him back with the same urgency, her tongue finding his, her lips soft, her mouth hot. He'd never known a kiss like it. She broke first, gasping for air.

'Walker,' she said. 'I'm nervous.'

He ran his hand down the delicate front of her throat until his hand spanned her collarbones. He tipped her head backwards so that she looked at him. Her chocolate eyes were soft and dark, questioning him. 'Trust me,' he said. This felt different now. It felt like suddenly they understood each other. They knew this was something, more than just attraction. It was connection.

In response, she caught his hand in hers and brought it to her lips, kissing the palm before gently sucking on his index finger, enveloping it in the heat of her mouth, tugging at it until his cock was hard as rock under his towel.

He stood, pulling her with him until they faced each other, her still standing in the bath, him on the floor. She stood, naked, chest rising and falling with each breath and he let his gaze drop, taking his time to admire her fucking unbelievable body. Suds dripped between her breasts, over her hips and he watched them as they made their way back to the water.

He pulled his towel free and dropped it to the floor. Her eyes dropped to his cock and he saw the part of her lips, the tiniest glimpse of her tongue.

'I'm going to wash you now,' he said, and his voice was low in his throat. He had to touch that body, he wanted to get to know every inch of it, feel the softness of the skin, the contours of her bones.

Submerging a sponge in the water, he drizzled it with bubble bath and squeezed it gently, watching her anticipation grow. The tremor of her stomach, the rise of her nipples, before he'd even touched her. Walker couldn't help but smile at the power they held over each other. He lifted the sponge to her shoulders and began at the top, soaping her arms down to her fingertips and back, before circling her breasts and hearing the slightest of noises escape from her mouth.

'Does that feel good?' he asked, as he moved the sponge down over her ribs and continued over her stomach.

'Yes,' she murmured before gasping as he turned her to face the wall. He began again at the top of her back, taking his time, rubbing in small circles, soaping her shoulder blades, the narrow pinch of her waist, the swell of her hips and the perfect round of her butt.

'Good?' he asked again.

'Yes,' she whispered.

'Hands on the wall,' he said, letting his sponge tease her body up and down, up and down. He couldn't decide whether he wanted to plunge himself into her now, or if he wanted to tease her until she screamed. She moaned quietly and put both hands on the tiles, leaning onto the wall for support, and it made up his mind for him. He had to make her scream.

He followed the line of her back all the way down now, parting her legs and pushing the sponge between and right through to her core. She dropped her forehead to the tiles, giving him better access and he squeezed the soapy sponge against her, forward and back until she rocked with the same rhythm, moaning quietly.

Walker let the sponge drop and replaced it with his fingers, feeling the soft slip of her against his skin. His dick was pulsing now, desperate to be inside her. He tested her with his fingers, first one and then two, fully aware he felt bigger than ever before. She pushed back against him, arching her back, so he thrust his fingers further, stretching her out, withdrawing them only to circle her hot bud before plunging them inside her again. He found the sponge again with his free hand and sluiced her with water, rinsing the soap and watching it run in rivulets down her body.

He twisted Gabi back around to face him. Her eyes were half closed, her mouth half open. She had never looked more beautiful. He lifted her and laid her down on the bathroom mat.

She reached for him, but he held her flat with one hand as he positioned himself between her legs, dropping to his knees to taste her. She was hot and wet and soft. He found her clit with his lips and rolled it until she groaned out loud, running her fingers through his hair. He brought his fingers back to her centre and teased her until she cried out for him.

'Walker, please . . .'

He knelt between her thighs and replaced his fingers with his cock, sliding it between her lips and over her clit, playing with her, teasing that tiny nub with the steel of his dick again and again until she suddenly stilled, arched her back towards him and locked her eyes on his.

'Come with me,' she gasped and it was enough. He lined up his cock and sank in one movement, filling her entirely as she screamed.

# Chapter Fifty-Seven

*Gabi*

Gabi woke to find herself held fast against Walker's body, his arm slung over her, heavy in his sleep. Fatboy Jim was curled in front of her, head under his paw, and she didn't dare stretch for fear of disturbing one or the other. Instead, she sank back into the pillow, luxuriating in the softness of the bed, the weight of Walker's arms, the rhythmic purr of the cat. She felt a smile lift her cheeks. Did she want to run home? No. Did she regret any of the intimacy they'd shared? She waited for the pang of cringe to hit her, but it didn't. No. What she did feel was ever so comfy, ever so relaxed and ever so happy.

It could be the result of a night of the best sex of her life, but she knew it was more than that. It was the connection between them that made every touch mean something more. It felt like a new adventure and coming home all at once.

Her phone went off at exactly the same time as Walker's. He threw an arm towards the bedside table to reach it as she did the same. Fatboy Jim stretched and stood, padding off the bed with a thump.

#### Girl Gang WhatsApp group

**Isabella**: Meatballs on me at Tutto Mio today.
**Gabi**: Sounds messy.
**Isabella**: Haha. Come at 1 p.m. I've saved us a table. The guys are coming too, so Gabi, you can come with Walker.
**Gabi**: Already have.
**Isabella**: TMI!
**Amber**: You go, girl.

Walker and Gabi both read their messages and typed their responses before simultaneously dropping their phones to the bed. She turned to him and they faced each other on the pillow.

'Meatballs for lunch then?' he said. His hair was tousled, his chin already rough with stubble. He looked completely edible himself.

'As long as you're my breakfast,' she said, pulling him closer.

Isabella and Etienne were already seated in the corner, holding hands beneath the table, talking quietly with their heads close together, when Gabi and Walker arrived. The long table was beautifully laid with little ceramic vases of fresh red tulips, set with gorgeous mismatched cutlery and water glasses of different colours.

It felt very odd to be walking without crutches, Gabi noted, as she made her way across the restaurant. Her leg felt bare in the warm air, although strangely, her whole body felt naked, exposed in a way it never had before. It felt like everything was brand new.

'Come sit here,' Isabella called, pulling out the chair next to her. Gabi slid in and kissed her cousin, who whispered in her ear, 'I want to know everything.' Gabi thought about the last couple of hours with Walker and the bed they'd left, and blushed. Maybe she wouldn't be sharing quite *everything*. The things that man could do were probably covered by the official secrets act. If they weren't already, then they should be. She smiled as Walker took the seat next to her, glad he hadn't chosen to sit opposite her – that would have been too far away.

The noise levels suddenly increased as Wren, Rosie and Riley arrived with Amber and Jayden.

'Kids this end!' Rosie called and they laid claim to the end of the table, saving two seats for Reggie and George, who arrived next with Fox and Alex. But then Jayden spotted Gabi and dashed to her end of the table to put his arms around her and squeeze her tight. Gabi, her face tickled by his hair, squeezed him back in surprise and looked at Amber.

'He's been worried about you,' Amber said as she pulled out a chair.

Gabi lifted his chin with her finger so that he could lip-read as she spoke. His dark brown eyes were clouded with concern.

'I'm fine, Jayden. You know me! Always up to tricks!' He grinned in response and nodded, looking relieved, before returning to the kids' corner.

'Gabi!' Wren called. 'How are you?'

'I can't believe you almost drowned!' Rosie said.

'Good news your leg is all mended now, though,' Amber said, pouring herself a hefty glass of wine and passing the bottle over.

The table was alive with conversation, everyone talking over each other and laughing. The kids played thumb wars. Nonna popped out from the kitchen to kiss Gabi's cheeks and exclaim over the events of the day before, then kiss Walker on both cheeks and thank him for saving one of her favourite granddaughters. Eventually, the meatballs arrived and everyone tucked in. Isabella grasped the moment and leaned close to her cousin.

'So, what's going on with you two then?' Isabella asked quietly as Walker talked to Alex on his other side.

Gabi had known it was only a matter of time. But what to say? She shrugged and blushed and then laughed. Isabella raised an eyebrow inquisitively and leaned closer.

'Sex?' Isabella asked.

'Obviously,' Gabi said.

'Feelings?' Isabella prompted.

'It seems so . . .' Gabi admitted.

'Love?' Isabella whispered.

Gabi took a swallow of her wine and could feel Isabella's eyes boring into her, waiting for a response.

'How would I know?' Gabi shot back, thinking of the way she felt around him. The pull in the pit of her stomach when he touched her. The swell of her heart when he looked at her. The feeling that she was on the high board every time their eyes met. Was that it? Was that love? How would she know? She'd never experienced it before. It was probably just a severe case of holiday romance combined with the best sex of her life. Isabella took her hand on the tabletop and squeezed.

'You'll know,' she said gently. 'When you feel it.'

Gabi squeezed back.

Lunch lasted for most of the afternoon. The kids played around the table while the adults poured more wine. Nonna joined them for desserts and rum liqueurs. Toby popped in with Jesse, who was up for the weekend from London. They only meant to say hello, but ended up staying for a drink. Space was made for them, more chairs found from somewhere, and soon the table was crammed to bursting with chat and laughter. Walker put his arm around the back of her chair and pulled her closer. Full and happy, she leaned against his side, tired from the last couple of days but more content than she could ever remember feeling before.

'We should do this on the first Sunday of every month,' Isabella announced, raising her glass to the table.

'The meatball meet-up,' Amber said.

The idea went down a storm, everyone clinked glasses and the children cheered with spaghetti sauce-stained faces. Gabi's stomach tugged as she realised she would potentially not make the next one.

Gabi's phone rang and she pulled it from her bag under the table. Her heart sank as she saw the international number.

'Sorry . . .' She excused herself, pushing back from the table to take the call. Walker glanced at her with a smile before leaning his head towards Alex to talk. She accepted the call and put her other finger in her ear to hear more clearly. The call was remarkably clear. The casting director might have been standing in the next room, rather than in California. She recognised her West Coast drawl immediately as the woman managed to sound like they were already best friends. She apologised for calling on a Sunday but the company needed to get contracts signed and sealed and she was pleased to say she'd be emailing Gabriella's over that minute for her signature. Gabi's heart stopped in her chest.

Usually, a new job was like a shot of adrenaline, as though she were standing on the edge of something, waiting to jump. It wasn't the money – although the money was always good – that drew her on. It was the adventure, the drama, the challenge. New people, new places, new skills to be learned. No expectations or obligations – all she had to do was her job. It felt like a fresh start every time.

So why was this one not igniting that same excitement? Particularly given that it sounded like it had the potential to be the biggest movie she'd ever starred in.

'So, I guess the last thing we need to check, Gabi,' the director said, 'is whether you will be bringing family with you if you came to America for six months? We would just need to know so that we can start looking for your accommodation.'

And there it was. She'd be on her own again. Normally, the words didn't faze her. She was used to it, so why this sinking feeling?

Maybe she'd lost a bit of confidence with the broken leg. The vulnerability she'd felt, everything she'd been through, had certainly shaken her. But, even if she wasn't jumping for joy at the moment, she knew this was what she wanted. To get back to her old life. Honeybridge had worked its magic and she was healed – so it was time to jump back in. She mentally kicked herself and refreshed her smile.

'No,' she said. 'It would just be me.'

The woman continued, talking about having located the best physio in town for Gabi's recuperation and welcoming her to the team before she signed off and hung up. Gabi felt like she'd been hit in the stomach as she let her phone fall back to her side.

She walked back to the table feeling strangely numb, like she was outside of her own body. She was leaving Honeybridge. She was leaving Walker.

'Everything okay?' Walker asked as she slipped back into her seat. She reached for a glass of water and drank it down in one.

'What is it, Gabi?' Isabella asked. 'You look pale.'

Walker took her hand, his face creasing with concern and she made herself look at him squarely. 'Tell me,' he said quietly.

'I got the job in America,' she said. 'I leave next Sunday.'

# Chapter Fifty-Eight

*Walker*

He held Gabi's hand as they walked home from Tutto Mio, but they were both lost in thought. He couldn't believe how the day had changed. The sun was going down now, and both of their moods were dropping with it.

'Scenic route?' Walker asked, nodding towards the river. Gabi tried to muster a smile, but it was joyless.

'Sure,' she said, and they took the gravel path that led along the water to his house. The only sounds were the crunch of their footsteps and the gentle gurgling of the river. The silence between them weighed heavier with each and every minute that passed. Walker made it as far as the halfway-home bench and then couldn't keep it in any more. He had to know what she was thinking. He sank onto the seat and pulled her down to sit next to him.

'Talk to me,' he said. Gabi turned to him, her face furrowed, and he couldn't help but think how beautiful she was when she was worried. 'Tell me more about this job.'

She took a deep, deliberate breath, then began.

'It's a great opportunity,' she said. 'Predicted to be a huge blockbuster.' He nodded to encourage her on, feeling a swell of pride for her whilst simultaneously wishing that it didn't sound so amazing. 'It's a massive A-list cast, the crew are all experts in their fields.'

'Which is why they want you for the job.' He stretched to put his arm around her shoulders on the back of the bench.

'The money is incredible, the accommodation fully luxury and the film credit will put me at the top of my game.'

'Sounds terrible,' Walker deadpanned. This time she laughed and he thought how gorgeous she was when she did.

'It's my dream job. Everything I've been building up to my whole career.' He could see the flash of excitement on her face and then it disappeared as quickly as it came.

'But it means the Honeybridge holiday is over for me. It's six months, Walker,' she said, her eyes searching his face, her teeth worrying her lip.

'And?' he said, pushing her. He wanted Gabi to face up to what was in front of them; he wanted her to really let him in.

'And I felt like this morning could have been the start of something and now I feel like it has to be the end.'

He stared at the water as her words hit home. A family of ducks swam past, five little golden ducklings in a line behind their parents, before disappearing into the shadows of a weeping willow tree on the far shore. Summer was in full force. Everything in nature was full and ripe, bursting with life. By the time Gabi finished her job in America, these leaves would have dried and fallen. The trees would be bare. The ducklings grown. The sun would have lost its heat. He took a long, slow, deep breath in and asked the question that was killing him.

'Do you want this to end?' Everything inside him longed to find a way for this, whatever it was, to last a little longer. Gabi lifted her face to him again.

'No,' she said simply. 'I don't. But we always knew I wasn't going to be here for ever.' Her eyes shone with unshed tears and the sight hurt his heart.

He nodded in defeat. It was true. They had always known. Even though it had gone deep, it was only ever supposed to be a short-term thing. He'd been a fool the last few days to think it might be anything more.

'It was good while it lasted, though, eh?' he said, trying to keep the atmosphere light. He chucked her gently under the chin when all he really wanted to do was hold her tight against his chest.

'I've had the best time,' Gabi agreed and managed a smile.

'But you have to go and be the best stuntwoman in the world . . .' he said with a roll of his eyes.

'And you have to be the everyday hero of Honeybridge,' she countered with a laugh.

Although he would never ask her to turn down the job, he suddenly wished she would say she couldn't bear to leave, that he was more important to her than any role in a film. But that wasn't fair. He knew that, and what her job meant to her.

He wrapped his arms around her shoulder, squeezed hard and then tugged her to her feet. Turning on the towpath, he set off in the direction of home.

'Let's go,' he said. 'If we only have the next week before you go, then we'd better make the most of it.'

# Chapter Fifty-Nine

*Gabi*

Friday night was Walker's next night shift, and therefore Gabi's first night back at home with Amber since the weekend. When Walker had said he wanted to make the most of their last week together, he'd certainly meant it. They hadn't left each other's side for days. He'd driven her to physio, they'd had sex, they'd gone for coffee, they'd had sex, they'd watched a movie – and interrupted it with sex. He'd turned her every which way and now she was home for a rest. It felt odd to put her hand out and not find him there beside her. Instead, Amber was there, at the other end of the sofa, and Jayden was on the floor doing his homework and the radio was playing in the background.

'Bet you'll be glad to get your house back to yourselves,' Gabi said, looking round the cosy room. She noticed a new photo in the frame on the windowsill – a selfie that she and Jayden had taken at the park one afternoon after school. She was grinning, Jayden's face full of laughter, his eyes shut and mouth opened wide. The frame was nestled next to a group photograph of

Amber with Isabella, Rosie and Wren, gathered around a table sharing a bottle of wine. The bookcase was overflowing with magazines Gabi had bought to flick through. She had 'her end' of the sofa and a specific mug in the cupboard that she liked for her morning tea. This house had turned into more than just a place to stay.

'No way, I'm going to miss you.' Amber threw a cushion her way. 'It will take some getting used to, being on our own again.' Gabi nodded, having been thinking just the same thing.

'At least you won't have to put up with my singing in the shower any more,' Gabi joked.

'True. And you won't have to hang out with ten-year-olds any more . . .' Amber laughed.

Gabi glanced at Jayden where he lay on the carpet, chin resting on his hands, fixated on his workbook, and realised, with a sharp pang, how much she would miss him too. His endless energy, his cheeky smile, his sense of fashion. Plus, he'd taught her basic sign language and shared some of his breakdancing choreography with her. Skills that surely could come in handy, especially in her line of work.

'Believe me, Jayden's been the highlight of my day more times than you know!' Gabi said. 'I'm really going to miss you guys too,' she said.

'But America awaits you,' Amber said. 'Whereas here, the only thing waiting for me is the washing-up.'

Gabi threw the cushion back.

'I'll do it, it's the least I can do,' she said.

The now very familiar introduction to Alex's song started on the radio and Amber gritted her teeth and groaned out loud.

She jumped up from the sofa and stamped across the room to change the station, cutting Alex off rudely before he got halfway through the first line. Gabi laughed.

'Personally, I think it's quite catchy.' Gabi began to sing the chorus, *'You might not hear these words, but you know what I'm saying...'*

Amber put her fingers in her ears and stuck her tongue out. Gabi continued, *'You're deep in my heart and that's where you're staying.'* Amber threw the cushion at her head.

'Seriously, though.' Gabi giggled as she caught the cushion. 'Maybe you should hear Alex out. You might be lonely when I'm gone.'

Amber snorted. 'No way.'

Gabi hesitated, hugging the cushion to her chest as she thought about what Walker had told her. But that was a conversation between him and Alex. Was it her place to pass it on? Seeing now how stubborn Amber was being about Alex, Gabi realised it could be the turning point to get them back together.

'Walker told me something, Amber,' she said decisively. 'Alex only left you to keep you safe. Because the gangsters he owed money to had tracked him down, and he wanted to put distance between them and you.'

She held Amber's eye and saw the knowledge land. Amber pressed her lips together and Gabi held her breath.

'Still left me without a word, though, didn't he? And after Jayden told him he loved him. How could he leave like that?'

'He did what he did for you. And Jayden. He put your safety first.'

'Jayden deserves someone who he can rely on. And until I find that – and see it for myself – then it's a no from me,' she said firmly. 'However much I think Alex Martin could be *my* next big thing, I can't build a future with him.'

Gabi sighed. It was a shame, but it didn't look like anything would alter the situation.

'Anyway, enough about me.' Amber changed the subject. 'What's going on with you and Walker?'

'I think I'm going to miss Walker more than anyone,' she said and watched Amber's eyes widen. 'I'm sitting here tonight, and I've thought about him every minute since he went to work.'

Amber considered that for a moment.

'I'm so sorry. That's a tough one. But maybe you'll get used to being on your own again, after a while,' she said.

'That worries me too,' Gabi sighed. 'I've always been so independent, just doing my own thing without any thought for anyone. What if I slip back into bad habits?'

'So, you're scared you're going to miss him too much and you're frightened you're not going to miss him enough,' Amber said.

'That about sums it up.' Gabi gnawed at her lip. 'I feel so torn. I never expected to catch feelings.'

Amber met her gaze. 'Could you not just see how it goes? Maybe try long distance?'

Gabi wrinkled her nose. 'Our lives are just so different. Even when I'm in the UK, I'm not normally in Honeybridge . . .'

'There's always a room for you here,' Amber said, and Gabi felt a surge of love for her. She blinked back unexpected tears. God, she was all over the place.

'Thank you,' she said. 'I'll be fine when I'm gone. I always am.'

'Maybe you should follow your heart,' Amber said, her big blue eyes serious now. 'Seems such a shame...'

'Don't worry about my heart,' Gabi said, pulling herself together and squeezing Amber's hand. 'Walker was always meant to be a holiday fling, and I've still got until this weekend to make some hot memories.'

'You need to make the most of every minute,' Amber said before picking up her phone. 'Right, talking of the weekend, let's get your leaving do sorted.'

### Girl Gang WhatsApp group

**Amber**: Goodbye Gabi party at ours on Saturday afternoon. Kids welcome.
**Wren**: We'll be there!
**Isabella**: Wouldn't miss it.
**Amber**: Bring booze.
**Isabella**: And tissues. I'm going to miss you, Gabi!
**Gabi**: I'm going to miss you girls too. See you Saturday.

# Chapter Sixty

*Walker*

The night shift always went one of two ways. It was either crazy busy with callouts, or quiet as a graveyard and boring as hell. Tonight was the latter and it was giving Walker too much time to think. He wanted to speed through deserted country lanes with the sirens blaring, or walk into a house fire with an oxygen tank to rescue someone. He wanted anything apart from to be left alone with his thoughts.

Walker's team were all sleeping in their bunks. They'd done their drills, they'd checked their kits, their engine was ready and waiting if they got a call. But now, at 1.30 a.m., it was silent. And so, they took the chance to sleep as long as they could.

Walker lay on his narrow bed and tried to rest but his mind was racing. Every time he closed his eyes he saw Gabi. Her face looking up at him, wearing her mischievous smile. Her twinkling laugh. His chest swelled with a strength of feeling he'd never had before. Tired of tossing and turning, he quietly took himself outside.

Walking over to one of the fire trucks in the forecourt, he climbed up the ladder and onto the roof, where he lay back with his hands behind his head, and breathed deeply. The cloudless night sky was spangled with stars, and he felt himself wishing on them that Gabi didn't have to leave.

This was the longest he'd been away from her for a whole week, and he was already desperate to get back to her. He imagined her at Amber's, asleep in her bed, and wished she had stayed at his. Not that he would be there right now, but at least then he could have snuggled in with her in the morning when he got off shift. They only had a couple of mornings left and he wanted to make the most of every minute.

He'd heard about her goodbye party on Saturday, but even the words written on his phone made his stomach drop. How was he actually going to say them in real life to her on Sunday when she left for the airport?

He watched a satellite on its long curving mission around the world. He imagined Gabi's plane taking off on Sunday night, flying her to California to a future without him. The flight itself was just the start of it, flying her back to a life on her own. Leaving him here to do the same. His arms ached to hold her again.

He palmed his phone from his pocket and messaged the only person he knew would be up at this time of night, reading in bed while his dad snored beside her.

**Walker**: You awake, Mum?

He only had to wait a second for the response.

**Mum**: I am, love. Everything okay?

He knew he wouldn't have to elaborate. His mum would understand. So he kept it short.

**Walker**: Gabi leaves on Sunday. She's got the job in America.
**Mum**: Ah. I see. That's a shame. We all liked her.
**Walker**: I'm really going to miss her.

His chest felt tight as he wrote the words.

**Mum**: Is there no way to work around things?
**Walker**: I feel like we're from two different worlds.

It was the understatement of the year and he sighed, exhausted by everything he was feeling.

**Mum**: Hold on in there, son. Sometimes, worlds collide.

He felt the flicker of hope, like a tiny flame, somewhere deep inside him.

**Walker**: Love you, Mum.
**Mum**: Love you more.

# Chapter Sixty-One

*Gabi*

It was Saturday afternoon, and Gabi had dressed carefully in a fitted asymmetric top that almost met her jeans. Not just because she wanted to look her absolute best, but because she had to plan what to keep out of her suitcase, which was otherwise packed and standing at the end of her bed like a flashing beacon of doom. She'd mussed her own hair and checked her eyeliner was just smudged enough to give her a smoky eye and not look like she'd been crying most of the morning. Which she had. Which was ridiculous.

She could hear people arriving and heading out to the garden. She'd been banished to her room for an hour while Amber got everything ready but now, she heard the shout that she could attend her own party. The one which was meant to be fun and to say goodbye, although how those two things went together were a bit beyond her.

All the gang were there. Toby and Jesse had even popped in. All her favourite people in one place, the people that had turned from strangers to friends over the past few months. Tunes were playing on the speaker; the sun was out, and the sky was blue. And although it might be ten degrees colder than where she'd be the next day, she reckoned it was twice as beautiful.

The first person she looked for was Walker. He stood at the end of the garden talking to Fox, his T-shirt fitted across the span of his chest and shoulders, his jeans hugging his thighs. Damn, he looked good. Better than good. She headed for him, just wanting to be near him for these last, precious few hours.

'There she is!' Wren shouted, before she reached him. He turned at the words and their eyes locked, and everyone and everything else fell away.

Amber popped a bottle of champagne, and everyone cheered. Reggie and George ran onto the patio as a double act and shot party poppers around her, trailing streamers as they went. Glasses were handed out and by the time hers was filled, he was beside her, his arm around her shoulders, his breath in her ear.

'You look hot as hell,' he whispered, pulling her closer into his side. She went to reply but found her throat constricted. She coughed to clear it and squeezed him back. He smelled of peppery spice and she wanted to bury her face in his neck and breathe him in. No chance of that until later, though. Everyone encircled her, glasses poised.

'To Gabi,' Amber said, raising her glass in the air. 'My favourite flatmate ever. Sorry you ate my face mask once thinking it was yoghurt.' The guys gagged and the girls laughed.

'Easily done!' Gabi said. 'Quite tasty too.'

'To Gabi,' Isabella continued. 'My favourite cousin in the world.'

'Your only cousin in the world,' Gabi corrected.

'Not the point!' Isabella just shrugged and blew her a kiss, before pulling a handkerchief out of Etienne's pocket and blowing her nose loudly.

'To Gabi!' Wren and Rosie lifted their glasses, although they both seemed to be drinking milk for some reason. 'For teaching Riley that women can be strong and fearless.' To demonstrate the fact, Riley cartwheeled across the garden three times before bowing.

Gabi's eyes pricked with the start of fresh tears, and she blinked them away.

Jayden stepped forward and Gabi suddenly thought she might have to borrow Etienne's wet hanky too. He made direct eye contact with her and held his two hands connected in front of his chest and shook them once. She knew that one. Friends. She nodded and signed back. Always. He grinned and dashed forward to hug her. Gabi held his narrow shoulders against her and glanced at Amber over Jayden's head, and her eyes were now full of tears too.

'No more!' she half laughed, half cried. 'I can't take any more! This is meant to be fun!'

Everyone shouted cheers or good luck and clinked glasses and drank to her health, apart from the kids who threw shots of lemonade down their throats like tequila.

'I should have done a toast too,' Walker said into her ear. 'To Gabi, for sliding down my pole?' She laughed.

'Truthfully,' he said, 'I'm so happy I met you, Gabi. Of all the poles in all the places, I'm glad you chose to stupidly slide down mine.' She laughed as he pulled her closer, tilting her face up to him.

'Honestly, I'd do it all again,' she said. 'It's been so good spending time with you.'

He hesitated a moment and his expression became serious, before saying urgently, 'I don't want to just be a holiday romance. I want us to be more than that, Gabi.' His eyes burned into hers; his arms tightened around her waist. 'I wish you could stay.'

She jolted, conflicting emotions rushing through her. Hope, anticipation, regret, sadness. She dropped her eyes, unable to sustain the intensity of his gaze.

'You know that's impossible,' she said and it came out harsher than she meant it to. She glanced upwards and he blinked.

'I'm just trying to find a way for this not to be the end. We could make a real go of things if you were staying in Honeybridge.'

Gabi shook her head in disbelief.

'Or if you were in America maybe!' she exclaimed.

'You know my job is here,' he said, holding his palms to the sky.

'And mine is there,' Gabi shot back. She sighed in exasperation and they eyed each other in an uneasy stand-off. 'Why did you have to say that and spoil things? I don't want to leave on a bad note.'

'I had to say it,' he said with a shrug, letting his hands fall to his sides. 'I wanted to be honest. I'm falling for you so hard, Gabi. I can't bear to lose you.'

Gabi knew her mouth was open and snapped it shut.

'I'm sorry,' she stammered. 'I never meant to hurt you.'

Walker closed his eyes and a small nerve in his jaw ticked. She reached for his hands but they hung in hers. Guilt and tears blocked her throat. He opened his eyes and she hated herself for the hurt she saw in them.

'I know,' he said finally. 'You can't help it if your feelings aren't the same.' He forced a smile but she could feel him already backing away, protecting himself.

Someone chimed a fork against a glass for attention and Walker stepped away from her, focusing instead on Rosie on the patio, waiting for silence. Gabi felt bereft, even though Walker was only a foot away.

'Ahem,' Rosie said theatrically and everyone stilled. Toby edged towards her, and she put a hand out to him, pulling him beside her and Wren. Riley ran to them all and Toby hoisted her onto his shoulders. When everyone was settled, Rosie said, 'While we are all together, it's the perfect time to share our news. Toby, Wren, Riley and I went to the hospital yesterday and we're pleased to announce that Wren is officially pregnant!'

Wren automatically patted her stomach, which still looked pretty flat, although Gabi thought maybe she could see the hint of a curve.

'I wondered why you were drinking milk!' Isabella said.

'I have terrible heartburn and it helps.' Wren rolled her eyes.

'And I'm her sister in solidarity,' Rosie said, holding Wren's hand. 'I remember only too well what it's like being the only sober person at a party.'

'And we have our due date confirmed,' Wren said, biting her lip in excitement. 'And it's early January!

'Oh my God!' Amber shouted.

'It's so exciting!' Isabella said.

Rosie, Wren and Toby shared a look, laughing between themselves. Gabi marvelled at the love and happiness between them and felt the stab of it. It only accentuated what she didn't have.

'No, actually,' said Rosie, slipping her arm around Wren's waist. 'What's really exciting is . . .'

'We're having twins!' Wren said, which was followed by a roar of amazement from everyone as they surged in to congratulate them. Rosie and Wren laughed in delight; Riley shouted about how she was going to be a big sister. It hit Gabi like a brick. Not only were people falling in love and getting married, they were growing babies and families all around. Just not her.

Gabi stumbled forward to congratulate Toby and he grinned proudly and immediately put his hand back to steady Riley on his shoulders. Gabi stared. The tiny movement reminded Gabi of something. Something she'd long forgotten.

Papà. His hands were always there to catch her when he was teaching her to ride her bike in the park near their house. Her mamma wasn't there; Gabi remembered her being away, although Papà had been vague about where exactly. But her papà had taken her to the park and run behind her for hours, his hands on her back to guide her, his encouraging words speeding her on: 'I'm always here, Gabriella. I'm always here. For whenever you need me.'

The sun had been going down by the time she pedalled from one end of the path to the other and realised that she was cycling on her own. That night her papà was just as proud as she had been. He had told her how brave she was as he tucked her into bed. And she'd loved cycling her bike ever since that day that he supported her as she learned. But it was his words that stuck in her mind now. Tears pricked her eyes as she watched Toby slide Riley down to hold her in his arms and kiss her before setting her on the ground to play with the children now that the announcement was over.

She had an urge to see if her papà had messaged, but shook herself, knowing full well the date. His monthly text wasn't due for another week and she'd be in America by then. On her own. Again.

# Chapter Sixty-Two

*Walker*

He'd seen Gabi fighting her emotions since the start of the party. He recognised in her face what he himself felt inside. Her face changed from tearful to beaming from one minute to the next, her voice cracking when she laughed. He wanted to wrap her up in his arms and carry her home, as he had done when she had her broken leg.

The radio was turned up again and more drinks were poured. Gabi was talking to Wren and Rosie, and he could hear them telling her to come and visit when the babies were born. His stomach dropped. Christmas seemed so far away. How could he think about dark nights and log fires when the sun was this warm and the flowerpots on the patio were overflowing with cornflowers? Amber appeared beside him and deadheaded one of the small blue flowers he was looking at.

'Holding up okay?' Amber asked quietly and he sighed.

'Is it that obvious?' he replied.

'You look like someone who won the lottery and lost the ticket.'

He managed a laugh. 'Sums it up perfectly,' he said. She tidied another flowerpot with her fingers. 'Did you do those?' Walker asked and she nodded.

'I love gardening. Just don't get enough time for it,' she said. 'Although I read something the other day that said if you really want something, you have to make time for it.' She looked at him meaningfully. Subtlety never had been Amber's strong point.

'I know what you're getting at, Amber,' he replied. 'But there's really nothing I can do ... She knows how I feel ...' he trailed off as he felt someone beside him. Alex held out a beer for Walker and a glass of champagne for Amber, a tentative smile on his face.

'Hi,' Alex said, looking only at Amber. 'Can we talk?'

Walker was almost holding his own breath as the two looked at each other. The emotion was palpable between them, the pull of attraction, the push of fear. Alex lifted the glass again in Amber's direction, but she didn't reach out to take it. The suspense was broken by the sound of breaking glass splintering across the patio and then Amber turned and was gone, striding towards the noise, telling people to be careful as she went. Alex sank, dejected, into the chair beside Walker and downed the champagne in one, long mouthful. Walker sipped his beer thoughtfully.

'Mate,' he said eventually, 'I want to help.'

'Don't think there's anything you can do, man.' Alex sighed. 'I just need to talk to her about the song. That might be the one thing that changes her mind. But she just won't hear me out.'

The radio was turned up a notch again and Jayden was

breakdancing on the lawn. Walker could have predicted what would happen next and was soon proved right. Gabi put down her drink and joined him. Sidestepping and clapping in time to begin with and then the two of them broke into a routine that she had obviously learned and practised – with a broken leg – and was now perfect. They spun and top-rocked, popped and locked and ended up both in a freeze. The gang erupted and Jayden and Gabi high fived and hugged like a dance duo. This woman had the biggest zest for life of anyone he'd ever known. Her smile was like a prize. His heart was literally hurting.

The next song started, the all too familiar introduction of Alex's song.

'I love this song!' Isabella shouted and the volume went up again.

'If this song is the one thing that might change Amber's mind,' Walker said, 'then here's your opportunity. My girl might be leaving, but yours is staying right here.' He took Alex's beer from his hand and pushed him gently in the direction of the gang. 'Go get her, man.'

# Chapter Sixty-Three

*Gabi*

'Not this motherfucking song *again*!' Amber muttered under her breath when she heard the opening chords. 'Seriously, I can't take any more.'

'What are you going to do if he gets super famous and plays this at every global concert in the world – and *dedicates* it to you?' Gabi whispered back. Amber pulled a face.

Gabi shook her head. 'I still think you should talk. I think there are real feelings there.'

'I can't let there be.'

'I wasn't talking about yours; I was talking about his.' Gabi looked at her sternly, wishing above everything that she could help her friend find happiness before she left. Etienne and Isabella started to sing the words out loud beside them.

'That's it,' Amber fumed. 'I'm putting my playlist on.' She picked up her phone to change the music. Gabi found herself looking for Walker again and spotted him pushing Alex in their direction. Wren and Rosie joined in with the lyrics, arms around each other's shoulders. Gabi rested her hand on Amber's forearm to get her attention, seeing the look of determination on Alex's face as he approached them, but Amber kept scrolling. Alex was almost to them, but at the last minute, to Gabi's confusion, he cut towards Jayden standing on the patio.

'Got it!' Amber said, and Gabi nudged her, hard, to stop her changing the music when she saw what was happening.

'What?' Amber said, rubbing her side.

'Look.' Gabi pointed to where Alex stood in the middle of the lawn, facing Jayden. The song played and everyone sang along; even Toby and Jesse knew the words. Alex sang too, but it wasn't the words he was singing that had everyone's attention. It was the fact that he was signing at the same time. His hands flashed through the words, his fingers moving swiftly as though he'd been signing his entire life. He knew each and every sentence, every last word, in sign language. Amber gasped beside her.

Jayden's face was a picture. Tentative. Hopeful. Surprised. He watched Alex singing and signing to him, just him, so that he could understand the words. Looking at him, Gabi felt her own heart in her mouth. Anyone could see how Jayden felt about Alex. It was written on his face. Everyone was watching now, a circle formed around the two.

The chorus started and Amber clutched at Gabi's hand.

'*You might not hear these words, but you know what I'm saying,*' Alex sang and signed simultaneously. Suddenly the words had a different meaning. Gabi began to understand and knew Amber did too as she clapped her hand to her heart.

'*You're deep in my heart and that's where you're staying.*' Alex continued to sign, and Gabi watched Jayden's smile break through. It lit his face like a firework display.

The song finished a moment later, Alex signing to the very end. And then when it had finished, he very clearly signed three words that everyone recognised.

'That damn song wasn't even about me,' Amber said incredulously.

'Seems not,' Gabi said, feeling tears prick her eyes for the millionth time that day. Walker slid his arms around her from behind and she rested back against the strength of his chest.

'Go.' She pushed at Amber and watched as she stumbled into the middle of the circle. You could have heard a pin drop in the garden as everyone parted to let Amber through. She stopped in front of Alex, and he blinked at her, as though waking from a trance.

'You wrote it about Jayden.' It wasn't a question. Her blue eyes were wide with understanding.

'I did,' he said. 'I've always loved Jayden. Just as I've always loved you. I only needed you to believe it.'

Amber bit her lip and glanced at Jayden, whose brown eyes were bigger than Gabi had ever seen. He moved towards his mum and lifted his hand. The number two. The roll of a dice. Gabi gasped. Second chances. Everyone deserved second chances. Amber put her hand out towards Jayden and he went to her. She kissed his little hand in hers and they smiled at each other, in complete agreement. They moved together, to Alex, who opened his arms to them both.

'Oh my God! Yes!' Wren shouted, tears pouring down her face. 'It's the hormones . . .' she added, trying to swipe them away.

'I can't blame it on hormones!' Isabella said, wiping away tears of her own.

'Nor can I!' Jesse said, catching his as they dripped off his perfectly trimmed beard.

Gabi watched Alex and Amber kiss, the sweetest and most loving of expressions on their faces, before Alex conducted a long and complicated high five handshake with Jayden. She turned to look up at Walker and saw him fighting back tears too. Her tummy flipped and her heart swelled to bursting in her chest. Damn, this was so much harder than she'd expected.

Etienne clapped his hands loudly, and everyone looked his way.

'While we're on the subject of good news,' he said, pulling a beaming Isabella to his side. 'I'm happy to say that Isabella Tucci has finally agreed to marry me before the year is up and we are looking forward to a winter wedding!'

Reggie and George shot more party poppers and Riley cartwheeled across the lawn again.

'And you're all invited!' Isabella shouted and everyone roared in delight. Gabi felt a rush of love for her cousin and flew across the garden to smother her with kisses.

'Photograph!' Toby shouted, setting his phone up on the table and herding everyone with his hands towards the lawn. Everyone surrounded Amber and Alex and Jayden, arms around backs, children in the front. Walker tucked Gabi under his arm, and kissed the top of her head as he held her tightly against him. Wren turned sideways so that the photograph would catch the tiny, almost non-existent, curve of her baby bump, and both Rosie and Toby put a hand on it. Jesse sneezed as the photo was taken and it was caught for ever as everyone laughed with tears in their eyes from what had gone before.

The photo was circulated to the group chats and a moment later, Gabi was zooming in on the faces of her friends and their children, marvelling at the happiness contained in one single shot. She distanced herself from the group to the bench at the bottom of the garden, and sat with her back against the ivy-covered wall.

She looked at Amber and Alex, hands entwined, and knew she was moving out at exactly the right time. They would want to be together, night and day, having wasted so much time already. She could imagine them at the wooden kitchen table over breakfast, Alex in his pyjama bottoms, Amber in a vest top and shorts, exchanging contented, satisfied smiles over coffee. She suddenly wanted to cry.

Walker spotted her and raised his chin in a question. She tried to smile but her lip quivered, and she bit down, hard, to keep it under control. She lifted a hand instead and beckoned him over. A second later, he was there, beside her on the bench, arm around her shoulders.

'What is it, baby?' Walker asked, the hazel of his eyes clouded with worry. She knew what she wanted to say, but for a second the words blocked her throat. She clasped his hand and pulled it onto her leg.

'I'm going to miss you so, so much, Walker.'

The alarm on her phone sounded. It was time to go.

# Chapter Sixty-Four

*Walker*

The taxi arrived as Gabi had asked for; she didn't want him to drive her, saying it would be too much after everything that had happened. She was probably right, although he would have done it in a heartbeat. He carried her monogrammed suitcases to the drive and the taxi driver moaned about how heavy they were as he loaded them into the boot.

Everyone took their turn in saying their goodbyes, Isabella holding on tight for a fierce, long hug before Etienne put an arm around her shoulders and peeled her away. Everyone slowly drifted back into the garden and left the two of them alone. Amber clicked the side gate shut and the cabbie sat in the driver's seat, happy to wait now that the meter was ticking.

Gabi sniffed and smiled, and he could see she was determined to put on a brave face. His own jaw ached with the same pretence.

'All checked in for your flight?' he asked.

'Yep,' she said. 'First class to Los Angeles.'

'Go show America what it's been missing,' he said, pulling her to him. She wrapped her arms around him, and he heard her sigh deeply before she answered.

'And you look after yourself, as well as you do everyone else.'

He lifted her chin and drank her in, wanting to commit her face to memory.

'Travel safely,' he said. 'And if you ever break another bone and need to recuperate,' he said, trying to sound upbeat, 'you know where we are.'

She nodded and tears spilled down her cheeks. He thumbed them away and kissed her mouth, gently, just one last time. This was killing him. But he'd taken his shot, and it had fallen short. Now he just had to let her go.

She pushed his hair from his forehead and forced a smile, before physically pulling herself together and taking a step backwards, letting her hand trail down his chest before it fell back to her side.

'Bye, Walker,' she said. 'Thanks for everything.' He noted how tightly she was holding herself as she slid into the back seat of the taxi. He raised a hand in goodbye and the car crunched over the gravel and pulled out.

A moment later, a hand slipped into his and Rosie peered at him through oversized tortoiseshell glasses.

'You okay?' she asked quietly.

He looked back to the road as the taxi disappeared around the corner.

'No, Rosie,' he said back. 'I don't think I am.'

# Chapter Sixty-Five

*Gabi*

The airport was full of people in a rush to get somewhere far away, but Gabi could only think of what she was leaving behind.

Her luggage had been tagged and weighed and disappeared on the conveyor belt. The next time she would see it would be in America.

She went through security and the alarm beeped. A tall woman frisked her, running her hands efficiently over Gabi's body, and all Gabi could think of was that the last person to touch her had been Walker.

She'd managed to wave out the window of the taxi as they pulled out of Amber's drive but then she'd sobbed all the way to Heathrow.

For the first time in her life, she didn't want to be on her own. The people in Honeybridge had shown her that having someone to rely on was a good thing – a beautiful thing even. And now, she knew that it was actually all that she wanted. Not to have to live on her own any more. She wanted that intimacy that came with being with someone all the time. Living life together.

She made her way through crowds of strangers in the duty-free shops to the gate and found a seat facing the window where she could watch the planes landing and taking off. Normally she'd be feeling the thrill of excitement at the thought of soon getting stuck into a new project, but this time she felt she'd left her heart behind in Honeybridge.

She checked the flight board. On time, as scheduled, no delays. Her phone pinged and her stomach flipped over, but it was just an email from the film company, telling her there would be a car waiting for her at the other end.

She put her phone away, trying to understand her feelings, somehow knowing her life had been changed for ever. Walker was the most caring, loving, funny person she had ever met. He had shown her that facing your fears opened up a whole new life. Maybe it was time for her to do the same.

Was she ready for another leap? She held her breath and thought about Walker in Scotland. How he'd faced his childhood demons to move on with his life. Yes, absolutely, she was ready for a new phase. And to do that, she had to make peace with her past.

She checked the date on her phone. The next message wasn't due to arrive from Papà for another week. But it was her turn to reach out. She'd kept him on the sidelines for too long already. Her fingers trembled as she typed.

**Gabi**: Hi, Papà, are you there?

She pressed send and stared hard at the screen, wondering what he might be doing at this exact second. The second that she realised she wanted to let him in. She wanted to be part of his life and for him to be part of hers. Please, she thought, don't let it be too late. Her phone went off, and she held her breath as she opened her messages.

> **Papà**: I'm always here, Gabi. Are you okay?

Gabi felt the tears stream down her cheeks but laughed out loud. Walker had been right. Through blurry vision, she typed a reply. The first proper reply she had extended in years.

> **Gabi**: I'm fine, Papà. I'm at the airport on the way to America for a new job.
> **Papà**: Wow, Gabi. That's amazing. I'm very proud of you!

Gabi hiccupped in surprise. It was as though he'd been waiting all along.

> **Gabi**: I'll give you a call when I'm settled the other side, and we can catch up?
> **Papà**: Can't wait. xx

She typed three kisses and pressed send, before clutching the phone to her chest. She realised now just how changed she was, and why it felt so hard to leave Honeybridge. Because she now wanted to surround herself with people she cared about. And more than anyone, that meant Walker. Leaving Walker was more painful than any broken bone she'd ever had. And she finally realised that was because it was breaking her heart.

She stood quickly and approached the floor-to-ceiling windows in front of her. A plane taxied on the runway, getting ready to depart. Soon that would be her, jetting off to her old life when all she really wanted was a new life. A rising sense of panic made her put her hand to the glass, steadying herself as the plane started its engines and moved down the runway. Steadily picking up speed, it soon nosed into the air and a moment later was just a speck in the sky.

An announcement over the tannoy interrupted her thoughts. They were calling her flight. It was time to board.

Gabi gasped. She had to act. She had to talk to Walker now. Even if it was just to tell him how she felt. She could not leave him like this. Not with him thinking he was just a holiday romance when he was much, much more than that. She lifted her phone, ready to dial, when she heard a voice – a very soft, Scottish voice – gently say her name.

She spun in disbelief, and hope, and there he was. Walker.

She made a sound, unable to speak, and they crashed into each other's arms. She held on, never wanting to let go, feeling the strength in his arms, the safety of his chest.

'What are you doing here?' she asked as they broke apart.

'I realised I couldn't let you go,' he said simply. 'Not like this.'

Gabi's stomach flipped.

'What I mean is, I know you and I come from different worlds, but sometimes worlds collide. I don't want to do six months without you, but I know how much your job means to you. And I know how independent you are. And I would never stand in your way with that. It's one of the things that I love most about you.'

Gabi nodded, her breath catching at the word love, but Walker took hold of her hands between them and continued.

'But what about if we broke the six months down? Say, I come out on holiday in six weeks' time? And then we separate again for six weeks, and then I come out again?'

Gabi blinked in surprise.

'I don't want to get in your way,' Walker reassured her. 'I know it's your career, your life. But I don't want to lose you, Gabi. I want us to be together, whatever that looks like.' He held her hands against his chest, and she could feel his heart banging. 'And then, when the film is finished . . .' He cleared his throat and all she could do was hold her breath. 'I'll transfer with the fire service to London so that I can be near you all the time.'

Her lips parted and she made a small sound of shock.

Walker's eyes bored into her, searching for an answer. His jaw tightened in anticipation of her response, a tiny muscle twitching deep in his cheek. She could see what this meant to him, it played out on his gorgeous face.

But he couldn't see what it meant to her, because it was so deep inside her as she'd never felt it before. She cleared her throat.

'But when you come out on holiday, I'd be working all day.'

Walker shrugged. 'I can sightsee while you're busy. And then I can be waiting for you when you're finished.'

'And you'd move to London?'

He smiled nervously and nodded. 'I'd go wherever you are.'

It hit her then. Walker was ready for a new life too. Everything he knew, loved and lived by. He'd change it all for a life with her.

And it was right then and there that Gabi knew what she felt, just as Isabella had told her. Love. Epic, action-packed and technicolour love. Her heart filled with a surge so strong that it took her breath away. It bloomed and filled her chest. It sparked into every cell and made her fingers tingle and her eyes brim with tears. Isabella had told her she would know when she felt love and there was no denying this. She let it pour through her, overcome with emotion. Walker slumped onto the chairs beside them.

'You hate the idea,' he said. 'I'm sorry, I didn't want to look like I was taking over your life.'

She sank beside him, grasped his hand and lifted it to her lips. She pressed her mouth against his knuckles, hard, kissing each one before lowering it again. She wanted to kiss every inch of him, make him feel the depth of her love.

'I love the idea,' she said, 'Nobody, and I mean nobody, has ever put me first in that way before. Nobody has ever made so much effort and offered so much of themselves.' She put her hand to his face, smoothed his sandy hair back from his forehead. 'Nobody has ever impacted me like you. Hell, I just messaged my papà!' She saw the whites of his eyes as they widened, the tiniest lift of his lips. The flicker of hope. She took a deep breath and felt the same adrenaline rush as she felt flying through the air on a swing at fifty feet.

'I've been such a fool, Walker, because I want to be with you too.' She grinned as she said it out loud. 'I am an independent woman, you're right. But I want to share my life with you, whenever I can. And if, for the next six months, that means a week here or there, then that would be more than I ever dreamed of.'

His eyebrows rose and a laugh broke through.

She pulled her phone out of her pocket and showed him the group photo. All that happiness caught in one second.

'But when I come home from this job, I want to come home to Honeybridge, not London,' she said. 'To you, and this gorgeous gang of people. I'm going to sell my apartment and buy something in Honeybridge.' Walker punched the air and this time she laughed.

The trapeze she was on felt fantastic. It was higher than anything she'd attempted before in her life, but she knew she had a safety net. It gave her courage to keep climbing, to go higher, to try harder, to let people in.

'There are lots of shorter jobs I can do in the future,' Gabi said. 'Ones that don't take me away so far or for so long.'

'But I thought that was half the attraction,' he said.

'It used to be,' she agreed. 'But things change. Now you're the main attraction, Walker. I want to be where you are.'

He exhaled slowly and she could see the excitement in his eyes. An announcement sounded. They were calling her name. She needed to go to the gate. Her flight was about to depart. They shared a long look as they listened. This was it. But suddenly she wasn't afraid of leaving, because she knew what, and who, she was coming back to. And it was the best feeling in the world.

Walker pulled her to standing and wrapped his arms around her.

'So, I'll see you in six weeks?' she said and felt the kiss he pressed to the top of her head.

'And we'll speak every day,' he confirmed.

'And luckily I already know you're good at phone sex,' Gabi said, and he laughed out loud.

She had never felt so excited, so happy, so sure. It was the same feeling she got on the high diving board. She leaned back in his arms and got ready to take the leap from the very top platform.

His face was gentle as he looked down at her, his hair falling onto his forehead, his eyes soft.

'I love you, Walker,' she said. 'You're the biggest thrill I've ever had in my life.'

He tipped her chin with his finger and thumb, holding her face still.

'And I love you, Gabi,' he said. 'With a burning passion.'

He lowered his mouth to hers and she finally let herself freefall into the love of her life.

# Epilogue

## Gabi

Gabi heaved the one remaining box to the doors of the van where Walker waited, shoulders nicely stretching out the T-shirt he wore. She shielded her eyes against the spring sun to appreciate his body and the fact that he was all hers. Finally. Walker caught her looking.

'Stay focused there, Gabi.' He winked. 'We've got work to do.'

Gabi laughed. 'Not for long,' she said. 'This is the last one.'

They'd hired the van that morning and packed it full of her old life from her apartment in London. Walker had driven them back to Honeybridge, one hand on the wheel and one on her thigh, just the way she liked it. The miles had sped past until they pulled up at their destination, Wisteria Cottage, Honeybridge.

'I've got it,' he said, making the box look light as a feather as he lifted it and carried it away, which gave her an opportunity to check out his bum in his jeans. She scanned to ensure there was nothing left to unload and then did a neat somersault from the tailgate and onto the lawn beside the cottage.

Not just any house. Their house. And not just their house. Their home.

Gabi bit her lip, excitement coursing through her, as she let her eyes sweep over the sweet frontage that she and Walker had both fallen in love with. The delicate wisteria that twisted around the front door and up to the bedroom window. The white gables, the red brick. It was so old and so quaint and so different from her sleek London apartment – and she was pleased about that. Because it made this a complete change. A new phase of her life was just beginning.

And for Walker too, it was the same. He'd sold his riverside house after Alex moved in with Amber and Jayden, wanting a new start with Gabi. Something that would be theirs together.

Walker emerged from the front door again having deposited his box, brushing his hands. He joined her on the lawn to admire the view, slinging his arm around her shoulders and pulling her close. She didn't think he had stopped smiling since she got back from America at Christmas.

'Happy?' he asked.

'Very,' she said, lifting her face to kiss him, for the thousandth time that day.

'Good, because I love you, Gabi.'

'And I love you, Walker,' she said, never meaning anything more.

It had been a long, hard six months apart, but they'd done it. Walker's visits to the States, and her surprise trip back over for Isabella's hen weekend, had punctuated the time with pockets of happiness when they'd filled up on each other, making the most of every minute together before having to separate again. And each time they were forced to be apart only seemed to emphasise how much they were meant to be together. When her contract ended and she took that final flight home, she knew she didn't want to be separated from Walker again any time soon. The flight home from America hadn't felt like the end of something, it felt like she was on her way to a new beginning. In fact, a flight had never felt so long.

Walker had met her at the airport, holding a bunch of red roses, which he had to drop as she threw herself into his arms. She didn't doubt he would catch her and he didn't let her down. Those first ecstatic moments of holding each other, knowing there was not a ticking clock in the background as to when they would have to part, was the best feeling she'd ever had. She was exactly where she wanted to be. She was with Walker. She was home.

Since then, they'd alternated between time at his riverside house and her London apartment, working around his shifts as they negotiated next steps. Her flat sold quickly to a young couple working in the city, whose tick list included access to a gym and views of the London skyline. All the things that Gabi had looked for too when she came for a viewing and signed on the dotted line.

Now, standing in the front garden of Wisteria Cottage, she realised how much her tick list had changed. It didn't include security access or solar panels, marble islands or sunken baths. The only things she had on her list were: Walker himself, doorways wide enough to fit his shoulders and a cat flap for Fatboy Jim.

She turned them on the spot and snapped a selfie, with the cottage as the background, before whizzing it off on a message.

'Just sending it to Papà,' she said. 'He's so excited for us.'

'He'll see it for himself next weekend,' Walker said. 'Will be nice to see him again. And he'll get to meet my parents too.'

'True. We'd better get the spare beds ready,' Gabi said. Walker enfolded her against his chest and she heard a different tone in his voice.

'I'm more interested in *our* bed at this precise moment in time.' Gabi could smell the peppery spice of his aftershave as he whispered into her ear.

She laughed.

'Thought you were telling me a few moments ago we had work to do.'

'I think we've earned a lie-down,' Walker said, eyebrow raised. She couldn't resist. Not that she wanted to.

'Well, you'd better carry me over the threshold then,' Gabi said, raising an eyebrow back at him, fully expecting him to sweep her into his arms. She saw the glint in his eye too late as he lifted her bodily and threw her over his shoulder in a fireman's lift.

'Walker!' she laughed, slapping at his back.

'Gabi,' he replied striding towards the front door, giving her upturned bottom a smack for good measure. He carried her inside before gently setting her on her feet, closing the front door and hanging the key on its hook on the wall.

'Welcome home,' he said, cupping the back of her head and

kissing her deeply. The world stopped for an instant as she felt herself melting against him. He smacked her bum again and nudged her. 'Now get up those stairs!'

Fatboy Jim ran for cover as they both bolted for the bedroom.

# Acknowledgements

I'd like to thank every single brilliant woman that has helped to bring this second spicy book to life:

My editor, Kat, for your every comment and thought that made the book better.

My agent, Judith, for your constancy and belief.

My writer friends who have kept me sane along the way, Sarah Clarke, AA Chaudhuri, Emma Rae, Sinead Nolan, Shayna Wilson and Blanka Hay.

My fellow spice girl, Bella North, for the daily motivation and belly laughs.

Lucy Martin for her brilliant Devon Writer's Retreat where I cracked the back of this book (helped along by wine and cake).

I'm thankful for all of you and everything that you do. I hope your hearts are full and your beds are bouncing for many, many years to come.

# Discover more from Pippa Nixon

# *All Mine*

Isabella Tucci is not looking for love. Leaving London and her cheating ex far behind to open her dream restaurant, she's promised herself: no men, and no distractions.

Chef Etienne runs his own place, right across the square. And he'd be more than happy to show the new girl in town around. After all, he's never met a woman he couldn't charm. But he's never met anyone quite like Isabella.

Between long days of renovations and late nights with new friends, Isabella tries to steer clear of her blue-eyed, strong-jawed neighbour. But it's a small town, and the more she gets to know Etienne, the more Isabella begins to wonder if some rules were made to be broken . . .

*A perfectly sexy, spicy small-town romance perfect to curl up with on cosy nights.*

Out now in paperback, eBook and audio!

QUERCUS

## RAISING READERS
**Books Build Bright Futures**

Dear Reader,

We'd love your attention for one more page to tell you about the crisis in children's reading, and what we can all do.

Studies have shown that reading for fun is the **single biggest predictor of a child's future life chances** – more than family circumstance, parents' educational background or income. It improves academic results, mental health, wealth, communication skills, ambition and happiness.[1]

The number of children reading for fun is in rapid decline. Young people have a lot of competition for their time. In 2024, 1 in 10 children and young people in the UK aged 5 to 18 did not own a single book at home.[2]

Hachette works extensively with schools, libraries and literacy charities, but here are some ways we can all raise more readers:

- Reading to children for just 10 minutes a day makes a difference
- Don't give up if children aren't regular readers – there will be books for them!
- Visit bookshops and libraries to get recommendations
- Encourage them to listen to audiobooks
- Support school libraries
- Give books as gifts

There's a lot more information about how to encourage children to read on our website: **www.RaisingReaders.co.uk**

Thank you for reading.

---

[1] National Literacy Trust, Book Ownership in 2024, November 2024
https://nlt.cdn.ngo/media/documents/Book_ownership_in_2024

[2] OECD. 2021. 21st-century readers: developing literacy skills in a digital world. Paris, France: OECD Publishing.
https://www.oecd.org/en/publications/21st-century-readers_a83d84cb-en.html